Finally Forever

Endorsements

What a sweet story! I loved both Ben and Caroline so much. They had amazing chemistry!
—**Becky Monson**, *USA Today* Bestselling Author

Karin Beery brings a fresh voice to sweet contemporary romance in *Finally Forever*. Caroline and Ben danced their way into my heart.
—**Nan Reinhardt**, *USA Today* Bestselling Author of the River's Edge Series of Books from Tule Publishing

I couldn't put it down! *Finally Forever* is a wonderfully crafted love story from a master storyteller. Beery's characters are genuine and believable in their journey. The dejected former football player and a twice-scorned woman kept this reader on the side-lines cheering for their happily-ever-after.
—**Cindy Ervin Huff**, award-winning author

Take one hunky almost–NFL player and add a workaholic businesswoman and amazing ballroom dancer who's sworn off men. Throw them together in a charity dance-off and what do you have? A delightful romance of opposites forgetting past failures and finding love on the dance floor. If you like dance competitions, you'll love *Finally Forever*. It's the stuff Hallmark movies are made of.
—**Carol Grace Stratton**, award winning author of *Deep End of the Lake*

Karin Beery has written a classic romance in *Finally Forever*. When Ben waltzes back into Caroline's life, neither imagines all the twists and turns ahead. This is a story worthy of a Hallmark movie.
—**Diana Leagh Matthews**, author of *The Carol of the Rooms*

Beery's latest novel, *Finally Forever*, pulls the reader—as well as a would-be NFL player—into the glittering world of professional dance. This captivating romance is full of hope, friendship, family, and the courage to reach for your dreams.
—**Austin Ryan**, author of *Pirate's Treasure* and *A Winter Proposal*

What does a promising football player do when an injury demolishes his hopes of an NFL career? What does a woman do when a younger man takes an interest in her, especially after past failed romances? These are questions Ben Allen and Caroline Novak will find answers to in this entertaining and well-written romance novel. I recommend the book, not just for the romance, but for the treatment of bias when an older woman and younger man fall in love. Romance is never without conflict, and Karin Beery has brought the issue forward in a page-turning book. Well done.
—**Linda Rondeau**, author/speaker

Finally Forever

Karin Beery

A Christian Company
ElkLakePublishingInc.com

Copyright

Finally Forever

First edition. Copyright © 2024 by Karin Beery. The information contained in this book is the intellectual property of Karin Beery and is governed by United States and International copyright laws. All rights reserved. No part of this publication, either text or image, may be used for any purpose other than personal use. Therefore, reproduction, modification, storage in a retrieval system, or retransmission, in any form or by any means, electronic, mechanical, or otherwise, for reasons other than personal use, except for brief quotations for reviews or articles and promotions, is strictly prohibited without prior written permission by the publisher.

This is a work of fiction. Names, characters, businesses, places, events, locales, and incidents are either the products of the author's imagination or used in a fictitious manner. Any resemblance to actual persons, living or dead, or actual events is purely coincidental.

Cover and Interior Design:
Editor(s): Cristel Phelps, Deb Haggerty
Author Represented By: WordWise Media Services

PUBLISHED BY: Elk Lake Publishing, Inc., 35 Dogwood Drive, Plymouth, MA 02360, 2024

Library Cataloging Data

Names: Beery, Karin (Karin Beery)
Finally Forever / Karin Beery
306 p. 23cm × 15cm (9in × 6 in.)

ISBN-13: 9798891341265 (paperback) | 9798891341272 (trade paperback) | 9798891341289 (e-book)
Key Words: sports romance books; clean and wholesome romance books; Christian romance novel; Hallmark type books; small town romance; women's romance fiction; contemporary

Library of Congress Control Number: 2024930012 Fiction

Dedication

For my sisters, Camille and Michelle.

Acknowledgments

Once upon a time, Swingshift and the Stars Dance-Off for Charity raised more than a million dollars for charities in northern Michigan. I had the pleasure of covering that event for a local newspaper, but I never imagined it would inspire a novel. The dance-off no longer exists, but its impression will remain.

There are a few other people who inspired and helped me along the way:

Austin Ryan, Bethany Macmanus, and Jessie Anderson: thank you for your encouragement and feedback. You made Caroline and Ben better people.

Steve and Ruth Hutson, Deb Haggerty, and Cristel Phelps: thank you for fighting for this story and making this book a reality.

Camille Gabel and Michelle Morrison: I wouldn't understand sisterhood without you. Thanks, I guess.

Matthew Verner: thanks for everything. You're my favorite.

Most importantly and always: thanks to God for the inspiration but also for the frustration and discouragement that keep drawing me to him and strengthening my faith (Romans 5:3-5).

Chapter 1

The crisp manilla folder taunted Caroline as she stepped into her office. She flipped on the light before setting her briefcase-sized purse on the floor. The leather chair squeaked under her weight as she picked up the file.

ORIENTATION.

Not her favorite way to start the week. Opening the folder, she scanned the list of new hires as the sun warmed her through the third-story window. She recognized a few names, but one made her pause. Ben Allen. It couldn't be. She flipped through his paperwork.

Football player at Western Michigan University. Degree in business analytics with a minor in accounting. Graduate of Traverse City Central High School. All-American defensive end. No doubt about it, he was the same Ben Allen who had graduated with her younger sister Christine.

"Good morning, Caroline."

She looked up to find her boss standing in the doorway, casual as ever in khakis and a short-sleeved button-down shirt. "Morning, John. I was just looking through the file you left me."

"That's why I stopped over." He smiled, his fatherly face crinkling. When he shut the door, Caroline perked up.

John Marsh rarely needed to discuss confidential things with her. If he felt the need to close the door, she was going to give him her full attention. "I suppose you recognized Ben Allen's name."

"I did."

"Then you know he's a bit of a celebrity."

An understatement. "Division one football players usually are. I was surprised to see his name. I didn't realize he'd moved home."

John sat in one of the chairs across from her. "Not many people know. Ben and the family have been quiet about it. They weren't even sure he'd come home until his father spoke with Al."

"Al Morrison?" Owner and founder of the company? Interesting.

"A friend of the Allens. After physical therapy, they wanted Ben to come home, but he was hesitant. Al wasn't. He offered the kid a job as soon as he read Ben's résumé."

Caroline's heart cracked a little. She couldn't imagine settling for insurance work after training for the NFL. It had to be hard for a twenty-three-year-old to process. "I'll find him a good mentor. I was thinking of—"

"I want you to be his mentor."

"Excuse me?" Her heart tightened as she glanced at the folders still in her purse.

"I need someone who won't be starstruck."

"I don't mentor anymore." And she had no desire to start, even for a celebrity.

"Just this once. You'll be able to work with him objectively. Teach him the ropes without getting distracted. You'll be perfect." John tapped the desk twice before standing. His unofficial sign-off. "Ben will be here later today. Meet me in my office at one. He'll start orientation next week with everyone else."

Without another word, John disappeared. Panic swirled in Caroline's mind and throat as she imagined her free time disappearing. Needing the comfort of a familiar voice, she grabbed the phone and dialed Chris.

"Caro, what's wrong? Why are you calling?" her sister asked.

"Did you know Ben is working at Morrison?"

"You interrupted my PE class for this?"

"My boss wants me to be his mentor. I'm not sure how to keep press, stalkers, and groupies out of the office." And she doubted the mentoring stipend was adequate compensation for the hassle.

Chris laughed. "Don't be dramatic. No one will know he's there. He's been pretty quiet since the injury. Now, stop calling me at work unless it's an *actual* emergency."

The line went dead, and Caroline sighed. Chris was right. Sure, Ben was the biggest celebrity Traverse City had ever produced, but it was only Traverse City. Population fourteen thousand. She doubted there were enough professional photographers in the whole county to make up a respectable group of paparazzi. And maybe it wouldn't be that bad. If Ben wanted a quiet life, Morrison would be the perfect place. There wasn't much about the classic car insurance company that would remind him of football *or* attract a fan base.

Ben checked his reflection in the window. He'd driven past the Morrison Insurance building dozens of times in his life, but this would be his first time inside. Unfortunately, it wouldn't be his last. If he thought about it too long, he'd want to put his fist through the glass, so he pushed the temptation aside. Time to face reality.

He opened the door, and a cool blast of air washed over him. A nice-looking woman smiled at him from behind the receptionist's desk. With her chin-length gray-blonde hair, wire-frame glasses, and bright lipstick, she reminded him of his aunt.

"Good afternoon. How can I help you?" she asked.

"I'm Ben Allen. I'm here to see John Marsh."

"I'll let him know you're here." She motioned behind him. Ben walked over to the small sitting area. He'd have to fold his six-foot-three frame in half to fit in the tiny chairs. Instead, he walked to the refreshment bar and helped himself to a bottle of water.

On the other side of the tinted windows, cars cruised slowly down the street. A woman about his age pushed a stroller along the far sidewalk. No one noticed the county's greatest disappointment watching them through a plate-glass window.

"Ben."

He turned at the sound of his name. A gray-haired man in khakis and loafers walked toward him. Ben self-consciously straightened his tie. "Mr. Marsh. It's nice to finally meet you."

The older man took his hand and gave it a solid shake. "Thanks for being here. I'd show you around, but we have an appointment with Caroline Novak in my office. She's our training and event coordinator, and she's going to introduce you to our processes and help you get settled in."

Ben cringed. "I appreciate that, sir, but I don't need any special treatment."

John nodded as he led the way to a nearby elevator. "I know, and you're not getting it. All of our new employees are paired with a mentor. Caroline doesn't usually take on mentees, but you two knew each other growing up, so I thought it might be a good pairing." They stepped into the elevator, and John pressed the fourth-floor button.

Ben and Caroline sort of knew each other. He tried to remember the last time he'd spoken to her. Maybe when he and Chris graduated high school. He remembered Caroline yelling at him and Chris for eating too much cake. Was that at his open house or Chris's?

The elevator doors opened to a lobby similar to the one downstairs. More blue and tan furniture with dark brown rugs covering parts of the tiled floor. Large windows offered a view of downtown. With few buildings standing more than four stories tall, Ben could see the rooftops of most of them.

John stepped off the elevator and turned right. Ben followed a step behind him. Only a handful of offices lined the hallway, all with window walls inside and out. Each office contained the same blue-and-brown striped carpet, tan walls, and oak furniture, but pictures, plants, and memorabilia gave each room a unique flair. They walked around the corner and into a fairly plain office. Pictures of John, his wife, and two sons covered the side table.

John motioned to one of two armchairs on the near side of the desk. "Caroline should be here soon. Until then, do you have any questions for me?"

Ben resisted the urge to loosen his tie as he sat. "I can't think of anything off the top of my head."

"Sorry I'm late. I hope you haven't been waiting long."

Caroline rushed into the office, her arms full of files and a smile on her face. A black skirt hugged her slender hips and legs, and she wore a light green, button-down shirt. He couldn't see all of her dark brown hair. Just the tight knot on the back of her head like she'd always worn it.

As she sat beside him, Ben checked his watch. It wasn't quite one o'clock. "I don't think you're late."

John laughed. "If Caroline isn't fifteen minutes early, she's late."

She set the files on the corner of John's desk and her purse on the floor. She turned, focusing on Ben. "Welcome home. I didn't realize until today you were back in town."

"ESPN isn't as interested in me selling insurance as they were when I was playing football." Neither were many people from his college life.

"I can't promise life here will be as exciting as you're used to, but you might attract some attention from the other employees."

"Which is why I asked Caroline to come out of retirement, if you will, to be your mentor." John leaned back in his chair. "Knowing your families' history, I thought it might be easier for you to work together without distractions. Caroline, do you have Ben's file there? I'd like to discuss some things with you both."

She grabbed the stack of files, flipping through the tabs. "I have it here someplace."

"Are those all of the other new employees?" Ben hadn't realized how many people worked at Morrison.

"No, most of these aren't even work related. Here it is." She pulled out a single file and passed it to John. He flipped to a page, then passed it back. Her face scrunched. "We don't have a Business Analytics department."

"I know," John said."

Caroline raised an eyebrow. "Are you letting Ben name his own position or just waiting until he finds something he likes?"

"What?" Ben stiffened. "Wasn't I hired as a business analyst?"

"I don't know. I didn't have a lot of time to review this." She practically glared at Ben. "I assume they hired you for your accounting minor."

Ben turned his attention to John. His temper simmered. "I know Al and my grandpa are friends, but I don't want special treatment." Like a made-up job for a washed-up ex-football player.

John lifted a hand. "Don't be too hasty. Your hiring wasn't standard, but it also wasn't an unmerited favor. You graduated with a three-point-eight GPA in business analytics while breaking and setting football records on the field at a division one university. You'd be an asset to any company, and Al wanted to make sure you didn't get away. You didn't get this job as a favor to you or your grandfather. It was a favor to us."

Confusion and embarrassment tied up his tongue. "I didn't realize …"

Cool fingers touched his hand. He looked at Caroline as she squeezed his arm. "You were always Chris's hardest working friend. That type of work ethic would be an asset anywhere."

Ben searched her blue eyes for any hint of patronization, but only sincerity looked back at him. Unsure what to say without embarrassing himself more, he nodded.

The corners of Caroline's mouth lifted.

For the first time all day, he relaxed.

"Would you mind giving John and me a minute?"

That couldn't be good.

Chapter 2

Caroline stuffed down her judgment. Ben stood, his shoulders broad under his dark gray jacket. How could a football player look graceful in a suit? Caroline pulled her gaze away and toward John.

"I'll wait outside," Ben said.

When the door clicked behind her, she slid to the edge of her seat, her annoyance heightened. "He doesn't even have a job here, and you want me to mentor him? What do you want me to do?"

John raised his eyebrows. "I expected you to review the file *before* our meeting. I assumed you saw his position listed there."

Heat radiated through her cheeks. She resisted the urge to look at her files—the reason she hadn't read Ben's file. "I had a busy morning."

"Then here's the short version. Ben's talent will work in any department. Put him everywhere. See where he shines. I wasn't exaggerating when I said he impressed Al. You know as well as I do the company's growing. Within the next year, we'll be expanding into insuring classic boats, and the five-year plan includes luxury vehicles of all types. We're going to need people with Ben's analytical talents, and Al doesn't want to let him get away."

Caroline tried to rub the tension out of her forehead. She didn't even know what a business analyst did. "Until then?"

"Start him in claims. When he's competent there, move him over to underwriting. Take him to the call center and the accounting departments. Familiarize him with every aspect of the business. The more he knows about the company, the better employee he'll be."

Caroline tried to predict how much time Ben would need. "If I give him a week or two in each department, that's two months of training." Five weeks longer than the average new employee.

"Enough time to establish a good foundation. And you'll be compensated for the extra time."

She grabbed her things and stood. At least her checking account would be happy. "I guess I'd better get Ben settled in then."

"I appreciate you doing this."

The frustration eased from her body as she opened the door. It returned when she saw Ben leaning against the wall. He reached for her stack of folders. She turned, blocking them from his reach. "I can carry these."

"I know you." He took the folders anyway, then stepped out of her way. "Where to?"

"My office." She walked toward the elevator. When she reached the matte-gray doors, she pressed the button and willed the doors to open quickly.

"How's your sister?" Ben asked.

"Chris?"

"She texts me every few weeks. I know about her. How's Carmen?"

"In Germany, playing cello with an orchestra in Frankfurt."

"Amazing. I shouldn't be surprised, though. I remember hearing her practice. She's great."

When they finally stepped into Caroline's sun-filled office, she smiled. No matter how busy work was, her view made it bearable. Even mentoring. She took her seat, and Ben set her files on the desk.

"Where do we start?" he asked.

"The basics. You need to fill out your W-9 and other tax forms. I also need you to read and review the employee handbook." She pulled the paperwork out of his file and handed it to him. "Let me know if you have any questions."

"Thanks for doing this."

"Doing what?"

"Mentoring me. You don't seem too excited. I assume it's something you didn't want to do, but I appreciate it."

She kicked off her shoes and pulled her feet under her legs as she tucked herself into her chair. "It's not that I don't want to mentor you, I just thought I was out of the mentoring game for good."

Ben unbuttoned his jacket, then relaxed into a chair. "What's so wrong with being a mentor?"

"It's not mentoring that I don't like." Caroline glanced at the files on her desk. When she looked back at Ben, he was looking at the files too. Without asking, he leaned forward and grabbed the top two. Her pulse spiked. "You can't read those."

He tilted his head as he examined the folders. "Erica Mendel. Mary Peterson. If they aren't new employees, who are they?"

"Friends." She reached for the files.

He passed them back to her. "You keep files on your friends?"

She set them on top of the pile before pulling all of the files toward her. "It's something I do outside of work, and it's how I'd hoped to spend my free time. There's a lot of paperwork involved with mentoring."

He nodded at the folder. "Your friends won't understand?"

"It's complicated." And not something she wanted to discuss with her little sister's friend, especially when she had a grant application to worry about.

Ben filled out one page before tossing his pen on the desk. "You know how I ended up at Morrison. How did you get here? I thought you were going to be a special education teacher."

"What? Why?"

He shrugged. "You were always helping with the special ed program at school. I assumed."

"I never wanted to teach. I just liked working with the students." She reached out and touched the stack of folders, her heart warming at the thought of the women they represented. "There are a lot of nonprofit organizations that help people who can't take care of themselves. There are even a few here in Traverse City."

"Pathways."

She sat back and smiled. "You know about them?"

"Don't look so surprised. I have a life beyond football."

"I didn't realize." His smile faded, and Caroline realized how conceited she sounded. "I didn't mean it like that. Or maybe I did. I just assumed football consumed all your time. I didn't think you'd have time for anything else."

"I get it. A lot of guys live and sleep football, but my parents never allowed it."

"They didn't make you go to camp and play league games year-round?" That made Ben laugh—an echoing, rumbling sound that filled the office and tickled Caroline's spirit. "Why is that so funny?"

"I forgot you don't know my parents, but Chris could tell you stories."

"What kind of stories?" Before he could explain, her office phone rang. Caroline raised a hand to pause the conversation as she answered. "This is Caroline."

"Caroline, this is Phil from human resources. Is Ben Allen with you?"

"He is. Do you need to talk to him?"

"No, just have him stop by after he fills out his paperwork. I have his name badge and office key code. I'll be here until five."

"I'll make sure he sees you." As Caroline hung up the phone, her neck and shoulders tightened. That happened more and more often when she was at work. Maybe she needed to dance more. She hadn't danced for fun in weeks.

She'd worry about that later. Reaching across the desk, she tapped Ben's paperwork. "We should get to work. The HR department wants to see you later, but we need to finish some stuff first."

"All work and no play." Ben winked.

Caroline froze. Was he flirting? Rolling her eyes, she pointed at the handbook. "I won't insult you by going through every page with you. You've got your standard legal documents plus Morrison Insurance policy and procedures. Read through the pages and sign what needs to be signed, then let me know if you have any questions."

Ben grabbed the pen off her desk and leaned back. "If we have time later, I'll tell you about my mom's chore chart and mandatory volunteer hours when I was in college."

The muscles in Caroline's neck twitched. The last thing she needed was to get to know Ben on a more personal level. She had enough to worry about, including the files she'd taken away from him. The thought of Erica and Mary put a smile on her face. Four hours before she saw them again.

Chapter 3

Caroline knocked on the red craftsman door, but she didn't wait for an answer before letting herself in. The door squeaked on its hinges, but no one had any plans to fix it—it was the cheapest security system Pathways could afford.

She stepped into the mid-century, ranch-style home, her shoes thumping quietly on the laminate floors. She left her purse in the coat closet before heading into the open-concept living main room.

Erica stood in front of the stove stirring a pot of boiling liquid. Her face brightened when she saw Caroline. "Hi, Caro." She waddled around the island in her standard uniform—a Detroit Tigers T-shirt and jeans. Her brown eyes shone as she wrapped her arms around Caroline's waist, her head barely reaching Caroline's shoulder. "You're early."

Caroline returned the hug. "What are you making today?"

"Macaroni." As quickly as Erica had abandoned her pot, she returned to it. Behind her, the dark countertops and oak cabinets were clean and tidy, though their age and wear gave everything a dingy appearance. Caroline should paint the cabinets. Maybe in the summer if she could find the time.

The television turned on behind her. Caroline turned around as Lucy sat on the worn, brown sofa. None of the women complained about the used furniture, old carpet, or outdated appliances. They were happy to have a home of their own, but Caroline wanted more for them than a scratched-up dining room table and an ancient, boxy television. At least the mismatched furniture hid most of the carpet stains.

"Lucy, have you seen the vacuum?" Susan Miller walked into the dining room from the direction of the office. Pathway's founder smiled when she saw Caroline. "What are you doing here today? I wasn't expecting you until tomorrow."

"Weird day at work. I wanted to stop by to see everyone."

"Hi, Caroline." Lucy hopped off the couch. "Would you like something to drink?"

Caroline froze. In two years, Lucy had never offered a drink. "No, thanks. I'm fine."

Susan chuckled. "Lucy's been working on her hospitality skills."

Caroline smiled. "I'll have to invite her to my house next time I throw a party. She can work the door."

"Are you planning something soon?"

"It's a hypothetical party. Someday, I might have time to host one or maybe just have someone over for dinner."

"Until then, I need to talk to you about something. Unless you need to talk to me first. Is there a problem with the grant application?"

Not that Caroline knew, but she hadn't started it yet, so she didn't really know. Instead of admitting she was late getting started, she shook her head.

Susan relaxed. "Good, because I need to talk to you about something." She motioned to the dining room table.

"I wanted to wait until all of the details were set before I mentioned anything."

"Details about what?" A dozen possibilities popped into her head, most of them bad.

But Susan smiled. "I didn't want to say anything until it was official, but Pathways was selected as one of the five charities to compete in this year's Dance for Hope's Dance-Off for Charity."

"The dance-off?" The most successful nonprofit fundraiser in northern Michigan? The fundraiser that could put Pathways over the edge, finalizing their fundraising efforts for the new home and possibly opening another paid position within the organization? Excitement tickled Caroline's toes. "I didn't know you'd applied."

"I didn't want to say anything in case they didn't accept our application, but they did, and we're in!" Susan's eyes twinkled. "It took five years, but we finally made the cut. The board wants you to be our dance pro."

"Of course!" Finally, Caroline could use her years of ballroom training for something worthwhile! "Have you picked a star yet? When do we start rehearsing? What else do I need to know?" Her favorite dance routines tangoed through her mind—would they be too difficult for a new dancer, or could she pull it off?

"The board is working on a list of candidates. We're meeting later this week to pick our top choices. After we find someone willing to work with us, you two can plan your rehearsal schedule, but you can't say anything to anyone until the dance-off officially announces the charities and teams in two weeks."

That wouldn't be a problem. The only people Caroline talked to were family, and they wouldn't tell. How long would it take to get to know her partner, figure out his abilities, then choreograph a routine? And when would she do it? The extra time mentoring Ben wouldn't open her calendar any.

Susan swiveled in her seat. "Do you hear something?"

Caroline relaxed her jaw and stopped grinding her teeth. "Just thinking about how I'm going to squeeze in the rehearsal times, that's all."

"That's why I want you to think about this before you commit. I know how busy you are, and I don't want you to overextend yourself."

Caroline reached across the table and grabbed Susan's hand. "The only thing I *really* want to spend my time on is helping Pathways succeed. Don't worry. I'll make this dance-off my top priority."

Susan clapped her hands. "I can't tell you how excited I am about all of this. Being in the event is an honor in and of itself, but having a two-time state ballroom dance champion on our team will give us such an advantage."

Only if Caroline could figure out how and when to bring her partner up to speed. Fast.

Chapter 4

The early evening sun warmed Caroline's naked feet as a breeze carried a smoky aroma across the deck from the grill. Chris would be over soon with the salad, not that they needed it. Caroline had made enough kebobs for a dozen people. They would have leftovers for a week. As long as Chris arrived on time, dinner would be perfect.

Caroline's cell phone rang. She cringed. It had better not be Chris. She'd already canceled dinner twice. Caroline rushed inside. When she picked up the phone, she recognized Susan's number. It had been a week since they'd talked about the dance-off. Maybe she had news. "Hi, Susan. What's up?"

"I need your help."

Her shoulders tensed. "Is it the girls or the house?"

"Neither. It's the dance-off."

Dancing she could handle. "I should be able to help with that." Her body relaxed.

"I hope so. We can't find a local star to be your partner."

"Who've you asked?"

Susan rattled off news anchors, DJs, business owners, and the realtor with the biggest billboards in the county. "Between travel plans, stage fright, and injuries, we've gone through fifteen people."

Yikes. "Did you talk to the dance-off committee? What do they recommend?"

"Historically, dancers who have a connection to their charities raise more money. They can help us find someone, but ..."

Pathways needed as much money as they could get. "Give me a few days."

"Thanks. If we find anyone before you do, I'll let you know."

Caroline snatched a soda from the fridge before plopping onto her couch. She could ask Tony. His family owned the dance studio, so a lot of people knew him, but she doubted the organization would let her compete with her former dance partner, even if it was for charity.

"I'm here!" The front door opened, and Chris clomped in wearing tennis shoes, black yoga pants, and a Traverse City High School tank top.

Caroline rolled her eyes. "Did you come straight from school?"

"I had a late meeting." Her sister's blonde braid swung over her shoulder as she helped herself to a soda before joining Caroline on the couch.

"Where's the salad?"

"Ben's bringing it."

Her mentee? Caroline stifled a groan. "Why'd you invite him?"

"I called him after you told me he was in town. He's staying with his parents, so I thought he might want to get out of the house." Chris's eyebrows rose. "You don't mind, do you?"

"I guess not." She'd hung out with other coworkers outside of work. At least he was bringing the salad.

A breeze stirred through the apartment again, swirling something stale and damp through the air. Leaning toward

Chris, Caroline sucked in a deep breath. "Why do you stink?"

"End of the school year. I don't have any clean clothes left in my office."

"Gross. Take a shower, and you can borrow something of mine."

Chris's hazel eyes—the same as their mother's eyes—widened. "Can I wear your green sundress with the holes on the bottom?"

"They aren't holes, it's lace, and it's in my closet."

Chris hopped up and disappeared into the bedroom.

The shower turned on at the same time someone knocked on the front door. Caroline opened it to Ben. Unsure what to say, she went with, "Did you bring the salad?" He held up a large bowl full of brightly colored fruits and vegetables. "Wow."

"Were you expecting something else?"

"Well, yeah. Chris usually brings a salad in a bag and I have to put it together."

He laughed. "Sounds like Chris."

She stepped aside to let him in. An earthy, un-salady scent came with him. "You can leave it on the counter. I need to check the grill." Grabbing a platter off the table, she stepped back onto the deck, her mouth watering as the rich, buttery scent of kebobs welcomed her. After she filled her stomach, she'd be able to focus on the dance-off. She just needed to survive dinner with Ben and Chris. Maybe Ben had matured more than Chris had, or it would be a long night.

She opened the door, and Ben took the platter from her. "I thought Chris was supposed to be here."

"She's in the shower." As if Chris had a sixth sense, the shower stopped, so Caroline walked to the bathroom door and knocked. "Ben's here."

"Out in a sec!"

When Caroline returned to the kitchen, Ben was setting the table. "Oh. Thanks. You don't need to."

"Remind me to introduce you to my parents."

"Something smells awesome." Chris stepped into the dining room, her bare feet smacking against the tile. Wet hair stuck to her shoulders, and a green sundress hung snuggly against her muscular frame. Bruises colored her collarbone and knees.

Ben looked at her and laughed.

Chris crossed her arms. "Rude."

"Sorry," Ben said, smacking her shoulder, "but it reminds me of the first time I saw you in a dress. You had scrapes all over your arms."

"You probably gave them to me." She punched his shoulder as she walked past him. "Dinner smells great."

As they sat around the table, Caroline's phone dinged. "Let me check this message. You go ahead and eat." As she expected, Susan's name appeared.

Here's the list of men we've contacted.

Caroline scrolled through the names and sighed. Several were people she would have called too, including John Marsh and Al Morrison. Finding a partner might be harder than she'd expected. Turning down her phone's volume, she set it on the counter and returned to the table. "What did I miss?"

"Nothing important," Chris said. "What's up with you? You look ... like Mom."

Caroline cringed. "Mom on Christmas morning or Mom trying to cook dinner?"

"Dinner. What's got you so stressed?"

Not wanting to vent in front of Ben, she shrugged. "It's nothing."

Ben speared a piece of beef with his fork. "Must have been a bad text."

Caroline crossed her arms. "How do you know it was the text that upset me? Maybe it's you."

"Nope. You were relaxed until you checked your phone. Now you're glaring at me."

"I'm not glaring." But she relaxed her facial muscles, just in case.

"Tell us about it," Chris said before she shoved a forkful of salad into her mouth. "Maybe we can help."

Ben nodded.

So Caroline relented. As they ate, she explained the situation. "The organization can find a partner for me, but the teams who do that don't make as much money. At this point, all I need is someone physically able to dance, willing to do it, and in town for all four months of the event. Our list is shrinking."

Chris's forked clattered against her plate. "Are you serious?"

"Yes. Why?"

"You need an athletic guy with name recognition." She pointed at Ben. "You're eating dinner with *the* most famous guy in Traverse City right now."

Caroline looked at Ben. She'd been so focused on helping him adjust at Morrison she'd never considered him. He had more star power than anyone who'd danced in the past, and there was no doubt he could handle the physical aspect of it. Excitement coursed through her. "What about your knee?"

Ben snorted. "My knee gave way when a two-hundred-and-fifty-pound football player tackled me. Unless you think that might happen while I'm dancing, I'll be fine."

"You could still hurt it again."

"My knee's already blown. Even if I hurt it again, it's not like I'm going to miss out on the NFL a second time."

Good point. "People who've never heard of the dance-off might show up just to see you. And with your"—she motioned to his broad shoulders, shirt sleeves tight around his biceps—"you're better equipped for this competition than anyone." If he could keep a good frame, she could dance him through the rest. Instead of just competing, they could actually win.

"Caro." Chris snapped her fingers in front of Caroline.

"Sorry. What?"

Chris pointed at Ben.

"I'll do it."

His words hung in the air. Chris kept eating, but Caroline couldn't move. "You will?" she asked, willing herself not to hope but desperate to believe him.

"Sure. It's not like I have anything better to do with my time."

Not the enthusiasm she'd hope for, but at least it was a yes.

Chris piled more food onto her plate. "What would you do without me?"

What indeed. Ben's name alone would draw attention, and winning would certainly help secure Caroline's full-time job. Should she ask him to call some of his contacts or just be happy with his local celebrity status?

As she listened to Chris and Ben talk, ideas twirled through her head. No matter which one she followed, one thing was certain—Caroline and Ben would be seeing a lot more of each other.

Chapter 5

The whispering crowd reminded Ben of buzzing cicadas. Four years ago, that type of excitement recharged his batteries. He'd come alive as he talked about himself, his team, his plans.

No cameras or reporters had gathered to talk to him in the months since he, his coach, and his parents had told the world the hit to his knee had ended his football career. There hadn't been much to whisper about since then. In less than an hour, that would change.

In the week since he'd agreed to dance with Caroline, she'd checked in every day at work, but only for the appointed mentoring times. Apparently, she ran the whole program, so she kept her meetings with Ben brief before checking in on all the other new hires. She texted him, though. Schedules. Directions. Clothing questions. Why did he need shiny dress shoes?

Sitting beside her in the back of the theater, her arm pressed against his. "It looks like there's someone here from every northern Michigan news outlet," she said.

"Is that normal?"

Caroline shrugged. "I've never done this before."

"I thought you were a dancer?"

"I am, but I've never been in the dance-off. It's too time consuming."

"But you have time now?"

"I always have time for Pathways."

"When did you get so involved with Pathways?"

"When my Aunt Doris died."

"I didn't know you had an Aunt Doris."

"Technically, she was my mom's aunt. She was mentally handicapped and lived in a home most of her adult life. Instead of developing her talents, they stuck her in a house where she was never challenged. She never had the chance to live in a place like Pathways.

"Three years ago, my mom moved Aunt Doris in with them for the last few years of her life. I'd never seen her so happy." A sweet smile tugged at Caroline's lips as she stared past Ben. "I decided I would do anything I could to help handicapped individuals live their fullest lives possible. That's when I found Pathways, and I've been volunteering with them ever since." When she turned her attention back to him, her face radiated with joy. "I'll dance all day and night for Pathways if it'll help."

The sweetness of her smile nearly took his breath away. "I can't wait to dance with you," he whispered.

She sucked in a quiet breath. "Thanks."

"Don't mention it." He sincerely hoped she wouldn't because he hadn't meant to say that out loud. She was Chris's sister. She'd teased, mothered, and bossed him around for years. He shouldn't be flirting.

"Are you ready for tonight?" she asked, putting some space between them.

"I'm fine. Just trying to prepare myself for the attention."

She poked him in the arm. "You're the pro at this. What do you have to be nervous about?"

"I understand football. But dancing ..." It had seemed so simple at Caroline's apartment. Dance a few times, raise some money, and help a friend. At the theater, however, with the reporters and the cameras, it became real. Ben Allen was about to put on dancing shoes, and he didn't even know what dancing shoes looked like.

She patted his knee. "You'll be fine. I'm a good teacher."

"How do you know?"

"I've taught dozens of dance classes before."

"You have?"

"Mostly kids, but you'll catch on. You'll be a salsa master in no time."

An elegant, petite woman walked across the stage at the front of the room, and the buzz quieted. She stopped in front of a microphone and smiled. "Good evening, and welcome to the Dance for Hope's Dance-Off for Charity's media kick-off event. I'm Judy Jones, founder of the event, now in our sixth season."

Polite applause filled the room.

"Each year our fundraiser has drawn bigger crowds and raised more money, and we expect this year to do the same. We have six new-to-us charities involved, and one very special star who just might bring statewide attention to our event."

Ben's gut rolled. It was bad enough that all Caroline's hopes rested on him. He didn't want to carry the weight of the whole event with him too. If he turned out to be a terrible dancer, he'd let her down *and* the fundraiser. It had been less stressful trying to keep the Ball State offensive line out of the end zone in overtime of the Mid-American Conference Western Division finals. Of course, he knew how to sack a quarterback. Until a few moments ago, he thought salsa was just a Mexican condiment.

Judy introduced two people—the season's emcees—before starting with the charities. The plan was to introduce them along with their dancers and "stars" in alphabetical order. Pathways would be last, so Ben had plenty of time to think about how he might let everyone down if he didn't dance well.

Two more people walked onto the stage, but Ben didn't hear who they were. The voices around him jumbled together into a toneless noise. When something hit his shoulder, he snapped back to attention. "What happened?"

Caroline leaned toward him. "What's wrong with you?" she whispered near his ear. "You're pale."

"Getting nervous, I guess."

"Are you going to be okay?"

"I should be fine." He tried to remember another time when his feet had gone cold while his face flushed and his guts rolled all over themselves, but nothing came to mind.

"Good Lord." Caroline whispered something to the person next to her before grabbing Ben's hand and pulling him from his chair. She dragged him past a small group of people and into the theater's lobby. He sucked in a deep media-free breath. Caroline hit him again.

"What was that for?"

She stepped in front of him and poked him in the chest. "You need to get it together. You've got about eighty pounds on me, so there's no way I'm going to be able to drag you onto the stage." She crossed her arms as her sky-blue eyes scanned his face. "What's really going on and how can we fix it?"

"I'm nervous."

"Of what? You played in the Cotton Bowl in front of thousands of people with millions more watching on TV. Why should a room full of northern Michigan reporters bother you?"

"I don't know." He lied.

"Try again."

"Caroline." He forced his temper down.

"Ben." She stepped closer. "We can fix it."

"You can't fix my knee!"

She jumped back at his outburst, and he didn't blame her. Closing his eyes, he searched for calm. Not an easy thing to find when everything around him reminded him of what he'd always wanted and would never have, and every reporter in the building would love to ask him about it no matter how much he didn't want to talk about it. "None of those reporters will see me as a dancer. They'll see the NFL-never-was with a bum knee."

When he opened his eyes, she reached out and took his hand. "You can't change that, and I'm sorry. But you can prove to them you *are* a dancer. Show them there's more to you than football. If you'll trust me and let me teach you, I'll make a respectable dancer out of you."

"You promise?"

"A couple of practices a week and we'll be fine."

Two wouldn't be enough, but with Caroline's passion for Pathways, he was confident he could talk her into more. He hadn't been sure about transitioning from running back to defensive end in college, but lots of hard work had paid off. He could do it again. "I'll hold you to that."

"Good, because I stopped thinking of other possible partners after you said yes, and I'd hate to have to start from scratch again." She tugged him toward the door. "Come on. We can listen out here until they announce Pathways. Then we'll slip inside before they introduce us."

Ben let her guide him to a set of swinging doors where they watched through twin windows. He bent over slightly to look through the window on his side while Caroline's eyes barely cleared the glass on hers. The longer they stood there together, the more her confidence washed over him until he finally relaxed. When he shifted his left arm, her hand squeezed his. He'd forgotten she was still holding it.

When the fifth couple stepped onto the stage, she took a deep breath. "We're next."

She opened the door just enough for them to slip inside. A few people noticed them. Ben knew the instant one of the photojournalists recognized him—the camera turned from the stage and focused on him. He ignored the cameraman and followed Caroline's lead around the perimeter of the room. Toward the stage. Up the stairs.

"Dancing for Pathways charity, I'm thrilled to introduce two-time Michigan State Ballroom Champion Caroline Novak and her partner, All-American defensive end, Cotton Bowl MVP, and Traverse City's own Ben Allen!"

The room exploded in flashes as Caroline and Ben crossed the stage. They waved and smiled as the cameras followed their movements. The warm pressure of her hand in his guided him toward the lectern. Thankfully no one expected him to speak, so Ben focused on waving and smiling.

They joined the rest of the teams lined up across the back of the stage as Judy continued talking. Four nights of competition with their first one in only two weeks. That seemed soon.

Keeping his eyes forward and a smile on his face, Ben leaned down toward Caroline. "We compete in two weeks?"

"Yep."

"Is that enough time?"

"It will be."

"Way to spring that on a guy."

"I told you three times already." She jabbed him with her elbow. "Don't worry. You've got this."

Caroline forced herself to smile as the cameras flashed. She leaned into Ben. Two weeks. She had two weeks to teach him to waltz. She'd spent every free minute of the past week listening to music and choreographing the dance. She was ready. But was he?

She already knew how to waltz. Until that moment, it hadn't really occurred to her she was dancing with a complete novice. The onslaught of nerves caught her by surprise.

Judy finished talking and stepped back to join the row of dancers. Following her lead, the group stepped forward to smile and wave. After posing for some photos, Judy turned to the group, her face glowing. "And we're off! Just a reminder, our first competition is two weeks from Friday with a dress rehearsal the day before. On Thursday, every team will have thirty minutes with the live band and lighting to set up everything for the show. We don't want to give away any secrets, so we're going to start at six p.m. with a new team coming in every half an hour. Our seamstress is here tonight, so visit with her if you need any adjustments to your costumes."

Ben's nose brushed Caroline's ear. "I have to wear a costume?"

"We all do." Why did he think she'd asked him to pick out dress shirts? She patted his arm. "Don't worry. I'll help with that too. Did you find any colorful silk shirts in your closet?"

He laughed.

Caroline tried not to tense. "You at least have black pants and dress shoes, right?"

"Sure."

"Good. I guess it's time to get to work then."

"Excuse me?" A local TV reporter and cameraman rushed toward them. "Amy Innis, Northern Life TV. I was wondering if I could ask you a few questions about your involvement with the dance-off." Caroline opened her mouth to answer, but Amy's eyes were focused above Caroline's head. Closing her mouth, she stepped aside.

Ben flashed her a glance before turning to Amy. "I'd be happy to answer your questions."

Before Caroline could eavesdrop on their interview, Susan stepped in front of her and wrapped her in a hug. "I don't know how we can ever thank you for this."

"I'm happy to do it."

"Having you and Ben attached to our name is more than we could have hoped for, and what a fantastic year for us to have such an athletic team. Imagine what a win could mean."

"Doesn't it mean the same thing it always means?"

"Weren't you listening?"

Caroline's cheeks warmed as she shook her head.

"The fund matching? Caroline, the Klein Group is matching funds raised by this year's winning team. And this year we have a champion ballroom dancer and an all-American athlete. Imagine how much money we could raise."

She tried, but the potential overwhelmed Caroline's already overstimulated brain.

Susan hugged her back to reality. "Now that you're official, the dance-off has arranged for a photo shoot for you and Ben."

"We already had our headshots taken for the website."

"This is the official dancing photoshoot, with you two in

costumes and posing for the camera. One of the Pathways board members owns a local print shop, so we're going to have posters and cut-outs made."

"Cut-outs?" Like giant cut-out pictures of her and Ben? "They'll be all over town."

Fabulous. "Anything to help raise funds."

"Is there anything else we can do to help you and Ben?"

Not unless anyone could whip up a couple of giant silk button-down shirts. "I think we're going to be fine." She glanced back at Ben, who was now talking with a reporter for the local newspaper. "Just as soon as I can get him out of here."

Chapter 6

Caroline draped another garment bag on top of the four already filling the back seat of her car. After making sure everything was secure, she hopped in and zipped across town to the Allen house. She needed to see his closet for herself. She couldn't take another night of dancing-in-her-underwear nightmares.

Twenty minutes later, she pulled onto a long, paved driveway, slowing as she cut through the wide, green field toward the two-story farmhouse. The morning sun cast long shadows on the house and across the gray SUV parked in front. Recognizing Ben's vehicle, Caroline parked her compact car behind it.

She pulled a garment bag out of the car before knocking on the front door. A few moments later, Ben answered. Dressed in sweatpants, a T-shirt and bare feet, he looked like Ben-at-the-gym, but even with his tousled hair, her brain registered good-looking Ben instead. Time to shut that down. "Good morning. Can you get the other bags out of my car for me?"

"Sure." Without pausing for shoes or instructions, he walked to her car and pulled out the rest of the bags as if he was picking up a napkin. "Where should I take these?"

"To your bedroom. I need to see your wardrobe." His eyebrows pulled together, but he didn't say a word. Instead, he led the way inside, through a dark living room and back to the kitchen. His parents looked up from their spots at the breakfast table. Caroline smiled at them. "Good morning, Mr. and Mrs. Allen."

Mrs. Allen waved her off. "Please, it's Jennifer and Michael."

"Thank you for letting me come so early. Ben said it would be okay to come poke through his closet before work. I hope I'm not interrupting your morning."

"You're not interrupting anything," Jennifer said, "but you may want to keep your ears open for Annabelle."

"My little sister." Ben walked back to the table. Still carrying the garment bags, he handed Caroline a plate full of food. "She's beyond excited that I'm going to be dancing."

Caroline took the plate. "You made me breakfast?"

"My mom did, but she still feeds me like I'm playing football. There are always leftovers."

Caroline checked the clock hanging above the sink. "Do you think we could eat while I look at your clothes? I want to make sure we're not late to work."

Ben looked at his mom. "Are you okay with that?"

Caroline bit back a snicker. He needed his mom's permission?

"Of course. Just try not to—"

"Is she here? Is she here?" Footsteps thumped down the stairs moments before a blur of purple and turquoise streaked through the living room, stopping in front of Caroline. "Are you going to teach my brother to dance? Can you teach me? I've been taking ballet and tap, but I've never danced with a boy before."

Caroline looked down into wide, blue eyes framed by fountains of blonde hair. A slender nose like Jennifer. High cheekbones like Michael. A bright smile like Ben. "You must be Annabelle."

The young girl grabbed Caroline's hand and pumped it excitedly. "I'm twelve. I know, I'm a lot younger than my brother. He said you were going to teach him to dance. Can I watch?"

Ben wrapped an arm around Annabelle's neck and pulled her gently against him. "This is my little sister. Please forgive her. She's the performer in the family, and she got it in her head she might adopt you."

"Annie, what did we talk about?" Michael crossed his arms.

Annabelle sighed. "Not to be rude and to wait for an invitation." Her shoulders slumped.

Caroline smiled. She had fond-ish memories of her sisters at Annabelle's age. "Actually, you may be able to help me. I need to find clothes in your brother's closet that will match my dance costumes. You know what he owns. You can help me find shirts that will work."

The young girl's eyes somehow widened even more as she turned to face her parents. "Can I help, please? I promise I won't be rude, and I won't hardly even bother them."

Jennifer stacked the empty plates. "If it's okay with Caroline and Ben, it's fine with me, but you need to leave as soon as they ask you to."

"Yes!" Annabelle punched the air. "Let's go."

Caroline handed her plate to the girl. "You can carry my plate." She reached for another garment bag, but instead of handing them over, Ben gave her another plate of food.

"I'll carry the clothes," he said.

"I can carry them."

"I'm sure you can, but my parents are sitting right here, and I'll get a lecture later if I don't at least offer."

"I wouldn't want you to get in trouble with your parents," she whispered, taking the plate.

"I got the forks. Follow me!" Annabelle ran past them both. When she disappeared up the stairs, Caroline slowed her steps and leaned close to Ben. "You need permission to eat in your room?" she asked quietly.

"I told you my parents were different."

"Tell me more."

"My mom came out of a strict cult-like situation. She's a rebel in her family but super conservative by most standards."

"Oh." What would she think of Caroline's costumes?

At the top of the stairs, Annabelle stood in front of a closed door. Ben motioned her to the side. "Move, Annie."

"It's Annabelle. I'm not a little girl anymore." She flipped her waist-length hair behind her.

"It's seven in the morning, and I have to dig through my closet." He practically growled. "It's too early for this."

Annabelle looked at Caroline. "I hope you don't have too many morning practices. Mom says he's not a morning person. I say he's a grouch."

"Annie!"

She crossed her gangly arms. "Benjamin!"

Caroline looked down as she tried not to laugh.

Ben sighed. "*Annabelle* ... Please."

The girl hugged her brother. "Mom said to be patient with you. She said you might be fragile right now."

"That's it." He put Annabelle in a headlock.

She squealed. "My breakfast!"

Caroline laughed as she tapped her wrist. "We have an hour before I need to get ready for work."

Ben dragged Annabelle to the door and opened it.

Caroline froze. No wonder he kept the door closed. Piles of boxes and clothes covered the floor. Empty cups filled any empty shelf space. He hadn't even made his bed. "I'm not going in there."

Annabelle gasped. "Do you want my help cleaning?"

"No. I want more sleep." He pulled his sister down the hall as he looked over his shoulder at Caroline. "You can wait in Annie's room. I'll let you know when it's safe."

Ben tossed dirty socks into the basket in his closet before double-checking his room. A pile of athletic equipment filled one corner. He'd stacked all the dirty cups in a box by the door. The garbage was full but at least all the trash was in the can. His bookshelves were as organized as he could manage in five minutes. Three black garment bags sat on the bed.

Someone knocked on his door. "Are you ready for us?"

His gut rolled. Good grief. Women had visited him in his college dorm room, but no females besides his relatives had ever set foot in the bedroom at his parents' house. Even with his mom's permission, he still felt like a kid breaking the rules.

Another knock. "Come on, Ben. I want to see Caroline's dresses."

He scanned the room one last time, then opened the door. "It's better."

Annie set their breakfast plates on his desk before running to his closet.

Caroline carried her bag into the room. "I told your sister what color my costumes are so she can pull some shirt options for me."

Ben nodded as she walked past him. Annie pulled an arm full of hangers out of his closet.

"What exactly are you looking for?" He took the hangers from his sister, then laid them next to Caroline's bag. All button-down shirts.

"We're looking for anything that won't clash with what I'll be wearing." Caroline unzipped the first bag and Ben knew exactly why his sister was so excited. Shiny green material covered in sparkles filled the bag.

"That's a dress?" he asked.

She slowly lifted it out of the bag. The dark green material floated on the hanger. Lighter green beads swirled on the top while the bottom split into uneven ruffles. "This is one of my dance costumes," she said. "But I'll wear whatever costumes work with your clothes."

"Oh my gosh!" Annabelle reached for the dress. Ben clamped a hand on her shoulder, and she quickly pulled her hand back. "Can I touch it?" she asked. He hoped Caroline would agree because his sister trembled beneath his hand.

"I don't mind, but some of these dresses are pretty expensive and you were just eating bacon."

Annabelle ran from the room. Seconds later, the bathroom sink faucets turned on.

Caroline laughed. "She's cute."

"Is that what you call it?"

She swatted his arm. "Your sister's excited. I remember the first costume I bought. It's … special."

Ben tried to relate, but he couldn't get excited about clothes. "Okay."

Caroline smiled at him. "Remember your first sack?"

He could still feel the quarterback's legs in his arms. Ben nodded. "This is Annie's first sack. Got it."

Annabelle returned, her hands in front of her for Caroline's inspection.

"Thank you." Caroline handed his sister the first dress, then started unzipping the rest of the bags. Ben wasn't sure what he was supposed to do, so he ate while Annabelle oohed at each costume. Caroline even pulled out a short, red dress for his sister.

He pointed at it. "How'd you know to bring that?"

"What?"

"A costume for Annie."

"What?" She looked at him like he'd just suggested *she* sack *him*.

He pointed his fork at the red fringed dress his sister was twirling with. "The kid-sized dress."

Caroline laughed. "That's for Latin dances."

Ben studied the tiny dress his sister was hanging on his bookshelf. From the top of the straps to the bottom of the lowest fringe, it wasn't long enough to cover three shelves. The eggs settled like lead in his stomach. "That's really ... short."

"It's perfect for the cha-cha and the salsa. The fringe accentuates the twists and hip movements, and the length lets the judges see leg form and posture."

"I'll bet."

She stepped closer to him, the smile on her face widening. "You're blushing."

Ben faced her, a mixture of embarrassment and discomfort. "Yeah, because I just realized my dance partner's going to be wearing a glorified bathing suit." He tried to rub the blush off his face. "Do I, at least, get to wear clothes?"

"Yes, and I'll only wear that if we can't find something else that matches." She pulled out the last two dresses. Another short one with blue material and no fringe and a long, black, lace thing. "Will these be a problem for your parents?"

"No," Annie said. "My mom and I watch *Dancing with the Stars*. Your dresses are much more conservative."

Ben sat back as Caroline and his sister examined everything, Finally, she picked a black shirt off the bed. "This one might work for the second week. That's when we're doing the cha-cha."

Sounded Latin. Ben's mouth went dry. "What will you be wearing?"

She raised an eyebrow. "Do you really want to know?"

His gaze went to the red scrap of fabric on the other side of the room. "Probably not."

Annabelle stepped next to Caroline and took the shirt. "I'll put this by your cha-cha dress. What are you wearing for the first dance?"

"We're doing the waltz, so it should be a long dress."

"You should wear the purple one or the green one."

Annabelle hung his shirt in front of the red "dress," completely covering it. Ben shoveled food into his mouth as he tried not to think about what Caroline would look like in that red thing. She was still Chris's sister. His mentor. An older-sister-type figure. In a sparkly bathing suit.

"What about these?" Annabelle held up two dress shirts. One pale green and the other white with thin, blue pinstripes. Caroline inspected the shirts, holding them up to the light and in front of his chest. Annabelle pointed at the green one. "He looks really good in that one."

"Does he?"

"Yep. I heard one of the girls at church talking about it."

She had?

"We should give it a try then." Caroline took Ben's plate before handing him the shirt. "We're also going to need black pants, black socks, and black shoes. Can you grab those for me?"

"On it." Annabelle ran back to his closet.

Ben looked at his shirt. "Now what?"

"Now we try on the clothes and see how they look together."

Annabelle squealed. "You're going to try on your dress and everything? Can I help you get ready? I'll do your hair."

"Annie—"

"It's *Annabelle*."

Caroline touched his arm. "Unfortunately, we don't have time to do hair and makeup this morning, but I'll put on the shoes so we get a good idea of how it will look." Annabelle held up black pants and shoes. Caroline inspected them the same way she'd looked over his shirts before she finally nodded and pushed them into his hands. "Put these on, and don't forget the black socks. I'll change in Annabelle's room."

She took a pair of shoes out of a bag and the green dress from where it hung on his lamp, then the two females stepped into the hallway and closed the door behind them. Ben didn't know how long he had before they came back, so he changed fast.

He'd just tucked in his shirt when the door burst open. "Ben—"

His heart lurched. "Annabelle Louise Mikayla Allen!"

She froze in the doorway, her eyes the size of softballs. Before he could say another word, she jumped into the hallway and slammed the door shut. As soon as it clicked, she knocked softly three times. "Ben, are you decent? That's what I'm supposed to say. I'm never supposed to go into his room without knocking."

"Good plan."

He shook his head. Not many people saw this side of his life. Too late to do anything about it now. "I'm decent. You can come in."

This time the door opened slowly. Annie poked her head through the crack. A ridiculous smile filled her face. "You won't believe how beautiful she is, Ben. I want to learn to ballroom dance so I can wear dresses like this."

"Let her in, Annie. We're on a schedule."

His sister didn't even correct him as she stepped in and pushed the door wide open. Caroline twirled into the room, her green dress fluttering around her legs.

Ben's breath stopped.

The flowy material settled gently around her knees, but the rest of the dress clung to every curve of her hips, waist, and chest with long, sheer sleeves covering her arms in sparkles while displaying her athletic yet soft lines. Flesh-colored heels covered her feet, adding a few inches to her height while defining shapely muscles in her legs. That alone would have stolen his breath, but her hair—always in a tight knot behind her head—swung in waves around her shoulders.

He'd never seen anyone more beautiful.

Annie clapped as she bounced on the bed. "Isn't she pretty? Didn't I tell you my brother would like it?"

Caroline smiled as his sister. "It doesn't really matter whether or not he likes it. We just need to make sure this will work for the first dance." She refocused her attention on him. "Annabelle was right. That shirt looks nice on you. Now turn around so I can see the whole outfit."

Ben turned slowly, hesitant to take his eyes off Caroline. He wanted to appreciate the vision of her for as long as it lasted. When he finally finished his circle, she walked over and pulled at the bottom of his shirt, yanking it out from his waistband. His heartbeat spiked. "Can I help you?"

"Can this be untucked, or does it have tails?" He pulled the shirt out for her, and she frowned. "Are you married to the idea of this shirt, or would you mind if we altered it a bit? It'll be more comfortable for you to dance with it untucked, but it's a little long. We could have the costumer hem it for us. And shorten the sleeves. Can we cut the sleeves?"

"Whatever you want." And he meant it. He'd cut holes in the shirt and wear it inside-out if it meant he could keep looking at her.

"Then I think this could work. Let's go to Annabelle's room so I can see how we look side-by-side." He followed without question.

"Wow." Ben turned around at the sound of his mother's voice. She and his dad stood at the top of the stairs smiling. "You two look amazing."

"Thanks." Caroline stepped beside Ben and slipped her hand around his arm. "Do the greens work together? I don't want them to match completely, but they shouldn't clash either."

Dad pressed his lips together as he looked at Mom. She walked toward them and moved them under the hall light. "I think it should work. I'm surprised you found something in his closet."

"I'd like to have the costumer make a few changes, but it'll work."

Mom waved a hand. "Don't bother your costumer. Tell me what you need, and I can make the changes."

Caroline's eyes brightened. "You sew?"

"All the time. Now, what do you need?"

Ben tried to listen, but as soon as Caroline's hands touched his hips, his brain blew a fuse.

What was wrong with him?

Chris's sister.

Mentor.

Sister-figure.

He didn't have time to think about her. He still had to figure out where he wanted to go and what he wanted to do with his life. Traverse City and Morrison Insurance were fallbacks. He'd never planned to return, much less stay. Yet here he was, standing in his parents' hallway with Caroline's hands caressing his arms as she talked about sleeve length.

"Let me get my tape measure." His mom walked into her bedroom. Annie led Caroline into her room. Ben closed his eyes and sucked in the deepest breath his lungs would allow.

A hand smacked him on the back. "She's a beautiful woman, Son."

"Yes, she is, Dad."

"You work together?"

"Yep."

His dad laughed. "I don't envy you."

"Why?" Ben opened his eyes to look at his dad.

"Because I've watched you play through pain, suffer through bad games, and push yourself to meet recruitment standards you didn't think you'd make, but none of those ever inspired the panic I just saw on your face."

Ben's shoulders tensed at the thought of what his dad might have seen. "I'm a little nervous. I've never danced before."

"Sure." Dad smacked him again. "We'll blame it on the dancing."

As his dad walked toward his bedroom, Ben's mom stepped out with her sewing kit. "Let's find out exactly what Caroline wants."

What Caroline wants. That morning, Ben was sure he'd agree to anything.

Chapter 7

Nina Simone's "Feeling Good" played through Caroline's computer speakers as she stared out her office window. She visualized the dance again. In her head, it was spectacular. In reality, it depended on how well Ben held his frame. If he could figure out the turns. If he could remember the steps.

Someone knocked on her door, pulling her attention back inside. Ruth from accounting stood in the doorway. "Am I interrupting anything?"

Caroline shook her head. "Just my thoughts. What's up?"

"I thought I should tell you what's happening with Ben."

Oh no. Grabbing a pen and some paper, Caroline slid to the edge of her seat. "What's the problem?"

Ruth closed the door behind her as she stepped into the office. "He's been getting calls. All day."

"From?"

"Everyone. Local news stations, a couple of sports radio stations from downstate, a fan, and even some girl pretending to be his sister."

Caroline dropped her pen. "What? How are they getting past the switchboard?" How long would the fascination last, and would it interrupt their practices? "I'm sorry about this, Ruth. How can I fix it?"

"I don't expect you to fix anything. I just wanted you to know what's going on in case you get a call from my boss. It's been ... busy today."

Caroline nodded as her brain kicked into gear. "Thanks. If anything gets weird, or if anyone shows up, call security. I'll call John."

Ruth let herself out, and Caroline picked up her phone. She called John and filled him in on the situation. "I'm not sure what we can do," she said, but then she glanced at her clock and a plan formed. "I know Ben doesn't want any special treatment, and we're not supposed to give him any, but his morning's already shot for him. Can I take him out of the office for the rest of the afternoon?"

"For?"

"Dance practice. I'll come in over the weekend and make up the hours."

"Don't worry about that. Go ahead. Practice. I'll talk to the marketing department to see how we can capitalize on this attention."

She hadn't considered that angle. Maybe the attention would be good for Morrison, and she wouldn't argue with a boss who was letting her leave early.

After straightening her desk, she made her way to accounting. Inside, a few people waved to her as she moved toward the office in the back. Ruth sat behind her desk with Ben across from her, his back facing the door as he worked on a stack of papers.

Caroline knocked before stepping inside. "Hi, Ruth. I was wondering if I could take Ben for the rest of the afternoon."

"Of course."

Ben looked over his shoulder. "Can I finish this first? I'd hate to leave in the middle of something."

"Sure." Caroline took the empty chair beside him, and her brain began to whirl. How could they capitalize more on

Ben's fame? Could they direct all calls for Ben to the dance-off instead? Better yet, they could go to Pathways. Maybe Susan could schedule interviews for Ben in exchange for a "donation." Was that even legal?

A few minutes later, Ben capped his pen. "I finished through July of last year," he said, handing the file across the desk to Ruth. "I'll finish the rest tomorrow."

Ruth took the papers. "Thanks. I'll see you in the morning."

As he stood, he extended his hand across the desk. "Thanks again for your patience today. I appreciate all your time this week."

Ruth shook his hand. "You're welcome back next week, but I think you'll find another department better suited to your talents."

Ben finally turned to Caroline. "I'm all yours." He smiled, but he couldn't fool her. After their hours of mentoring together, she could see the strain behind his smile.

"Grab your stuff. We won't be coming back to the office."

He raised his eyebrows, but he didn't ask any questions as he followed her into the hall. He didn't say anything until the accounting door closed behind them. "Where are we going?"

"Today you're learning to dance."

"What?" He blinked twice.

Caroline hadn't expected him to cheer, but she certainly hadn't expected the vacant look. "It'll be fun. Even if it's not, it's got to be more fun than accounting."

"Probably."

Not very enthusiastic, but she'd take it.

Ben ran a hand through his damp hair, his breathing faster than he'd expected. Caroline clapped as she walked back to where she'd plugged her phone into the sound system. Two hours of framework, toe pointing, and one-two-threes, and she was as energized as when they'd started.

"Let's try it one more time," she said.

Ben held his hands up in surrender. "Not yet, not yet. Give my brain a chance to absorb all this information." He sucked in a breath to calm his surprisingly rapid heartbeat. Not once had anyone disturbed their practice. "How'd you score private time at the dance academy?"

"My former dance partner's parents own it. I'm considered part of the family." She smiled at him from across the room, her skin flushed and glistening. A long, yellow, see-through skirt hung from her waist, partially covering her knee-length black leotard. Not quite as girly as her dress, but it had a similar effect. When she wasn't bossing him around the dance floor, he had a hard time concentrating.

"Are you getting the steps? Would it be easier if I wrote everything out for you? Or I could show you your part and you could copy me."

"I can't even do my part, but you can do both?"

She cocked her head to the side. "I made up the dance. I'd better be able to do both parts."

"Good point." Ben shuffled off the dance floor and grabbed his water bottle. He doubted any man alive looked good in a sweaty T-shirt, shorts, and shiny black leather shoes. "How long did it take you to get used to all of these mirrors?"

Caroline clicked her way across the hard floor. "It's part of the experience. I watch my extensions and foot placement. It would be weirder if they weren't here."

"All I see is a sweaty football player in Dad shoes."

She laughed as she stopped next to him. They faced the mirror together. With her heels on, her head reached slightly above his shoulder. Even with the extra height, however, she was a fraction of his size. When his gaze reached the reflection of her eyes, she was looking at him, her head tilted.

Not sure how to respond to that look, Ben took the safe path. "Be honest. How am I doing?"

"Considering you've been dancing for all of two hours, you're doing great. Now, show me your frame."

Setting the water bottle down, he extended his left arm while his right arm hooked around an imaginary dance partner. Caroline raised her arms the same way, but her left arm wasn't quite as straight, so he crooked his elbow a bit until the lines matched.

She must have noticed something wrong because she stepped behind him and placed her hands on his shoulders. "Exhale." He obeyed. As he did, she coaxed his shoulders down and back. "Now don't move. Stand like this so you can memorize the feel of it."

As if he'd ever forget her small, strong hands sliding across his shoulders.

Her phone rang, ringing through the speakers. "I need to take this call." She jogged to the other side of the studio.

While Caroline took her phone call, Ben focused on his reflection. Arms. Shoulders. Toes. He watched his feet as he moved them across the floor. He wouldn't get as many bruises dancing as he had during football, but memorizing dance steps wasn't nearly as easy as remembering plays. Plus, no one cared how his hands and feet looked on the field.

He'd managed to work through the first part of their dance twice by the time Caroline returned. She had her purse and dance bag slung over her shoulder. "Do you mind if we take a break?"

"Sure. What's up?"

"I need you to take me to my car. I have to go to Pathways this afternoon."

Not sure what he'd do with the rest of his time, Ben said, "I'll go with you."

"You don't have to. I'll only be about an hour."

"It's not a problem. I'd like to meet the people I'm dancing for." He grabbed his bag and keys. "Let's go." Within minutes, they were in his truck and on the road. "You know, you told me why you got involved with Pathways, but what do you do there?"

"I help however I can. Sometimes I work in the office with Susan. I taught Erica how to use the stove and other basic skills. Today, we're helping them clean."

"How many women are there?"

"Four. Erica, Lucy, Liz, and Mary. Erica loves baseball, so there's a ninety-five percent chance she'll be wearing something Detroit Tigers or New York Mets. Lucy's classic OCD, so she'll probably follow me around making sure I put things in the right spots. If she's not keeping everything organized, she'll be watching C-SPAN."

Ben grimaced. "Why C-SPAN?"

"No one knows. She started watching it as a kid and got hooked. She's an excellent reference around election time."

"I can only imagine."

"Liz is our dirt freak, so today is one of her favorite days of the year. We deep clean every quarter."

"And Mary?"

"I haven't gotten to know her very well yet. She's new to the house and still pretty shy. Don't take it personally if she ignores you."

Finally Forever

They pulled into the driveway, and Caroline led Ben inside. A short dark-haired woman wearing a Mets T-shirt met them in the entryway. "Hi, Caroline. Deep cleaning started twenty minutes ago."

"I know. Susan called and told me the Jensens couldn't make it, so I brought my friend to help. Erica, this is Ben."

Erica looked at him as if seeing him for the first time. "You could be a baseball player."

"I'm actually a football player. I mean I was" She shrugged before turning around and walking away. He wanted to be embarrassed, but Erica's total indifference knocked him off balance. "I guess this is the place to be if I want a truly normal experience."

Caroline patted his arm. "You'll win them over. Give it some time."

He followed her into an outdated, mismatched house that smelled like Pine-Sol and felt like home. When he stepped into the kitchen, three sets of eyes turned to him.

Caroline joined the women. "Ladies, this is my friend Ben. Ben, this is Liz, Lucy, and you've already met Erica."

Liz walked right up to Ben and handed him a rag. "Thank you for helping us. You can clean the lights."

"Ben can clean all of the high stuff." Caroline walked over to a list lying on the counter. "It looks like you'll be dusting the tall light fixtures, tops of the windows, and ceiling fans." She glanced up at him. "You could sweep around the edges of the ceiling for cobwebs too."

"Anything you want, Boss." He saluted.

He headed straight for the dining room chandelier. Then to the living room ceiling fan. He wiped all the windowsills, the tops of the bookcases, and picture frames. Caroline and the ladies worked around him, pulling books and trinkets off shelves and moving furniture to sweep beneath it. After finishing the main living areas, Caroline escorted him into the bedrooms, where he cleaned everything higher than her head. Lucy popped in twice to see how things were going.

An hour after they'd arrived, Ben tossed his last dirty rag into a bucket. He made his way to the kitchen where Erica stirred something on the stove. Lucy sat in the living room watching C-SPAN. He didn't see or hear Liz or Caroline.

"Are you staying for dinner?" Erica asked.

"I don't know. I'd have to ask Caroline. Have you seen her?"

She shook her head. "Do you want a soda?"

"No, thanks, but I'll take some water."

"I can get it." Lucy jumped up from the couch and shuffled into the kitchen. She grabbed a glass out of a lower cabinet, filled it at the tap, and handed it to him.

"Thank you." She never looked at him as she handed over the glass. He took a sip.

"You're welcome. Are you Caroline's boyfriend?"

Ben choked on his water. What would make her ask that? "No, we're just friends."

"She never brought a boy here before."

It wasn't really a first—or third—date sort of experience, but he bit his tongue. "She probably wants to keep you guys all to herself."

"Ben!"

The panic in Caroline's voice punched him in the gut. He ran through the house and into the office, where she stood point at the ceiling. "What's wrong?" he asked, searching the ceiling for bats, bugs, or something potentially frightening.

"The fan."

"The what?" He focused on the wood paneled blades. "I already cleaned the fans." Irritation stomped down his panic.

"Did it look like that earlier?"

"Like what? It's a fan, Caroline." But as he took a deep breath to calm his racing heart, something about the fan looked ... odd. "It's crooked."

"Was it leaning when you dusted it?"

"No, I would have told you if the fan looked like it was going to fall on me." Which prompted him to tug on the back of her dress, pulling her out of the drop zone. Then he reached up to check the fan's integrity—he didn't want it falling on anyone else after they left. He barely touched a blade and the entire thing moved. He jumped back. "Maybe we should call an electrician."

"Electricians cost money. Pathways doesn't have a lot, which is why we're in the dance off." Ignoring the potential danger, she stepped beside him and inspected the fan. "What do you think happened?"

"If I had any ideas, I wouldn't have suggested an electrician."

"You don't have to be rude about it. Just make it"—she used both hands to push up the air in front of her—"make it stay."

He snorted. "It's not a dog." But with his limited electrical experience and above-average strength, he managed to push the base of the fan deeper into the drywalled ceiling. It stayed, but his Spidey sense tingled.

"Did he fix it?" Liz asked from the doorway.

Caroline glanced at him and raised her eyebrows. He'd give up his cleats to assure her, but he couldn't. "I wouldn't let anyone work at this desk until someone can check this out."

Her already small frame shriveled. "You're probably right." She turned him toward the door and ushered him and Liz into the living room. "I'll call Susan later."

"Are you staying for dinner?" Erica asked from the kitchen.

"We have to get back to dance practice," Caroline said.

Erica opened her mouth to speak, but something crashed behind them. Ben beat everyone to the office. The destruction in front of him stopped him faster than an angry lineman.

Caroline gasped.

Liz walked past both of them into the room. "I don't think he fixed it."

Disappointment and anger boiled inside him. "No, sh—"

"He tried." But Caroline's voice wobbled.

He couldn't blame her. The fan sat in the middle of the desk. Drywall hung from the ceiling and covered the floor. Dust flooded through the air. And mystery water dripped from the hole onto everything. "I think you might need more than an electrician."

"Then we'd better get back to the studio. I have a feeling winning the competition isn't going to be optional anymore."

Chapter 8

Caroline yawned as she fumbled with the studio key. Michigan summer mornings were usually bright, but a layer of clouds hid the sun and chilled the early morning air. By the time she finally managed to open the door, Ben's SUV pulled into the parking lot. She waited for him by the door.

He wore his black slacks, a white T-shirt, and flip-flops. The coffee tray in his hand instantly improved her mood. He offered her the tray. "It's the least I could do after the fan incident."

"It wasn't your fault."

"Technically, I know that, but I still feel bad. Besides, I needed the caffeine."

She let him enter first as she savored her first sip of hot coffee. Just enough cream, no sugar. When she stepped into the dance studio, Ben had the lights and stereo on. "Your enthusiasm is slightly annoying today," she said. "I thought you weren't a morning person?"

"I'm not, and I wouldn't call it enthusiasm as much as motivation. I hate losing, and now we have more reason to win."

"I knew you'd be a competitive partner, but not like this. Most other teams are only practicing a couple of times a week."

"Good. I was afraid we weren't practicing enough."

"I doubt anyone else is meeting ten hours a week."

Ben clapped his hands once. "Good. Practices aren't interfering with your schedule, are they?"

"I don't have other things going on right now." She set her bag and coffee on the floor so she could pull her dance shoes out of her bag. She kicked her sandals to the corner near Ben's shoes before meeting him in the middle of the room. "We have dress rehearsal tomorrow, so I think we should skip tomorrow's practice."

Ben finished tying his shoe before looking at her. "There's only two days before the competition. I don't know if that's a good idea."

"You know the routine, and you have a great frame. Taking a day off will be refreshing." Not to mention welcomed. Ben had insisted on daily practices for the past week and a half.

"Did you take time off when you practiced for your dance competitions?"

"This isn't a regular competition."

Ben crossed his arms. "You didn't answer my question."

She rolled her eyes. "No, I didn't take time off, but I also wasn't supposed to be fundraising. I don't only want us to be the best dancers, I want to raise the most money. I'm not sure if we're doing enough on that end." Sure, Susan had told her not to worry about it, but Caroline couldn't help it. Pathways' future—and possibly hers—depended heavily on how much money she raised.

"You're right." He sank to the floor across from her, stretching his legs in front of him as he leaned back on his hands. "I've been trying to practice like I would for football, but I never had to raise money for the team. How much time are we supposed to commit to fundraising? And what do we do?"

"The only thing we *have* to do is pose for pictures after dress rehearsal, but I feel like we should do more, especially now that their house will need a few thousand dollars' worth of repairs. The more money we raise, the less we'll have to worry about the ceiling and the better the chance Pathways will have to add a full-time, paid position to the organization."

"Is that the type of job you want?"

Caroline sat across from him and rested her elbows on her knees. "Not the type of job. *The* job. Does that make me a terrible person? I'm raising money for an organization so I can get a job there."

"Because you love them and want something better for them. I don't think that's terrible." Ben smiled. "If helping you get this job makes you a bad person, then I suppose I'm a bad person too."

"Why?"

"Because I want to help you get it."

Could he be any sweeter? She smiled at him, staring into clear blue eyes that she didn't tire of looking at, but after a few seconds, it morphed from sweet to uncomfortable. Why was he still staring at her? Warmth filled her cheeks. "Whether I work there or not, it won't happen if we don't raise enough funds for them to hire more staff, so we should probably start dancing." She hopped up and straightened her skirt. The last thing she needed was to lose herself in those eyes. She dug her phone out of her purse and plugged it into the stereo.

"Can we mix it up today?" Ben asked.

"What did you have in mind?" She looked over her shoulder.

He swung his arms from side to side as he twisted his body. "A warm-up. Something different."

"Like what? A jog?"

He snorted. "I don't know. Just different. We didn't always run the same plays in practice. That helped keep us sharp. Then we knew we had developed our skills, not just memorized plays. Is there a way to mix it up?"

Not a bad idea. She scrolled through her playlist and stopped at a contemporary pop song. "The tempo of this song is a bit faster, but the time signature is the same. Let's see if you really know how to waltz."

Caroline walked back to Ben. He presented his frame. She stepped into it, resting her left hand on his shoulder and pressing gently until it lowered. "Let's see what you can do, Mr. Allen. Lead away."

"I have to lead?"

"You're the man."

His back tightened. "Should I do our regular routine?"

She shrugged. "Lead me wherever you want me to go. It's your audible."

His muscles twitched beneath her hand.

"Don't overthink it. Just dance." He nodded, but his lips tightened. She squeezed his hand. "Relax. This is just for fun. And it was your idea."

"I'm already regretting it." Ben sucked in a deep breath. As he exhaled, his left hand pressed against hers. His right hand pulled her toward him, guiding her upper body as he took his first step. He found the song's tempo, moving her around the dance floor with more grace than she'd originally thought possible from a man his size.

He led her through their routine without missing a step. His feet didn't point as often as they needed to, and his shoulders occasionally tightened, but they'd work on that later. Turning off her performer's brain, she let herself enjoy the steps.

As they neared the end of their routine, the song kept playing. Caroline prepared herself to stop, but Ben pulled her closer. Led her into another step. Another spin. All basic moves, but perfectly in step with the song. Cradled in his frame, their feet waltzed as their arms relaxed, shrinking the frame. Pulling them closer together. The warmth of his body mingled with hers. His musky scent invaded her senses.

She tried to step back, but Ben held her in place. When she looked up, he was watching her. His fingers tightened on her back.

"Why don't you have other things going on right now?" he whispered.

"What?"

"You said you don't have other things in your life. Why?"

"I work."

"Everyone works. They still find time to have a life."

"I have a life." Sort of.

They stopped moving but didn't step apart. "What about your friends? Who do you go out with?"

"I have friends."

"I've been working with you for a month and dancing with you for two weeks, and you've never met anyone or rescheduled dance practice because of a night out. You even agreed to dance before work."

"I'm committed to the things I do. There's nothing wrong with that." In fact, the only thing currently wrong with her life was her little sister's friend psychoanalyzing it. "You're acting like I'm some old maid who's given up on life. My priorities are just different than yours."

"How do you know about my priorities?"

She didn't. She was so focused on work and the dance-off she hadn't paid attention to anyone or anything else for the past few weeks. "I don't, but spending a month together doesn't mean you know everything about me."

"I know, but I'd like to know more about you."

The building's heat must have kicked on because suddenly the dance studio was stifling. Except it was May, so the heat wasn't on at all. "I think we should keep practicing."

"Why are you so nervous?"

"I'm not nervous."

He flexed his fingers. "You're so tense I'm surprised you haven't snapped your spine. Why?"

"Nothing, now will you let me go so I can start our music?" But he didn't let go. Her arms trembled from the effort of holding them so stiffly, but she couldn't let herself relax. Everything about Ben said he was the kind of guy she could relax with, but she couldn't let herself. Not again.

"What did I do?"

"Nothing." And she wouldn't give him the chance to do it. Twisting her hand free from his grasp, she wrenched herself out of his hold. "You know, I think today's the perfect day to skip rehearsal." She didn't bother changing her shoes as she grabbed her things. "I'll see you tomorrow."

"Caroline—"

"The door will lock behind you. Don't forget to turn off the lights."

"Caroline—"

She didn't stop moving until she climbed into her car and took a deep breath. Pulled out of the parking lot.

Ben had grown into an amazing man, but she wouldn't let herself notice. She couldn't. Her heart couldn't take that kind of disappointment again.

Chapter 9

Ben checked the clock on his dashboard as he pulled into a parking space at the ballfield. Quarter after five. He had forty-five minutes before softball practice started, which meant he had about fifteen minutes before people started showing up at the diamond. Fifteen minutes before they recognized him and started asking questions.

He slid out of his truck and headed toward the third-base dugout. A breeze cooled the warm afternoon air as it carried the familiar scents of grass, dirt, and chalk toward him. Chris's car sat near the dugout, the trunk open. He couldn't see her, but the clanging bats gave her away. "Chris, you got a minute?"

She peeked out from behind the trunk, her blonde ponytail swaying. "Hey! What are you doing here? You look like you came straight from work."

Which he had because he needed help, but how could he start the conversation? "I don't know how to say this—"

"Then help me set up while you figure it out." She reached into the trunk and pulled out three bases. "Can you put these on the field?"

He took the bases and circled the field, his dress shoes thumping across the dirt infield. There'd never been any type of romantic chemistry between him and Chris, which he appreciated. She'd been a great resource when he had questions about the opposite sex, not that he had many. When he'd committed to football, he committed to it. He didn't have time to figure out which women were interested in him and which ones were interested in his status, so he'd given everything to the field.

And then the field had betrayed him. He could still hear his knee pop. Feel the burn of tendons tearing as the linebacker crushed him.

Just like that, football was behind him, and—out of nowhere—Caroline Novak was in front of him. Dancing with him. Searing the warmth of her touch onto his shoulder. He understood groupies, he'd seen enough of them with his teammates to know their motivations, but he couldn't figure out Caroline. And he wanted to.

By the time he made it back to the dugout, Chris was leaning against the chain-link fence watching him, arms crossed. "What's wrong with you?"

"I need your help."

"Follow me around the field while I stripe, and you can tell me who she is." She pulled the chalk cart out of the dugout and headed toward home plate.

He followed, matching her stride. "How do you know it's a woman?"

She laughed. "Because you've never needed help with your golf swing. What's going on?"

"I think I met someone."

"I'm sure you could meet dozens of someones. What makes this one special?"

"She's not interested."

Chris paused long enough to smirk at him. "Good. You need to work for it."

"Maybe."

"Don't be a baby. Not every woman in the world is going to fall all over you."

"Obviously, but this is ... different. Without football, I don't have anything else to focus on, so she's all I think about."

They headed up the third-base side, but Ben stopped and leaned against the fence as he admired the ball diamond. Hard-packed dirt crashed into thick, green grass. In high school, it had been his third home, behind the football field and his actual home. He knew exactly how many steps it took to reach first base from home plate. Where he needed to bend his knee and drop to the ground if he wanted to slide into second. How far he could stretch his arm and point his toe so he could snag a wild throw. The ball smacking into his leather glove as he caught the ball. One sniff of the air, and he remembered every detail of his life on the diamond, but it couldn't compare to the gridiron.

The thick hard pads strapped to his body. His fingers in the grass, twisting the tiny blades as he watched the offensive line, gauging the distance and planning his attack. Plowing through the tackle. Pushing past the guard, feeling his hands slip down a running back's hips and thighs as he tried to race past. Crushing the quarterback in a bear hug as they crashed to the ground.

He sighed. "I still can't believe I'm not playing."

Chris leaned beside him. "But you have the chance to be distracted, right? It might not be a bad idea, especially if she's not interested."

"Why?"

"If she's not interested, you'll have to try harder. You'll have to focus on her instead of yourself. It could keep you busy."

He wouldn't mind staying busy learning as much as he could about Caroline. He just needed to figure out how to keep her in the room with him.

"What's got you so worried about this woman anyway? You're great. She doesn't know that yet. Give her time."

"I think she knows me a little better than that."

"Then what do you want from me?"

Just ask her. He readied himself for a hit. "Why's Caroline so jumpy about men?"

"What does Caro have to do with this?" As soon as she finished the sentence, Chris's jaw dropped. "You're interested in my *sister*?"

"Why is that so hard to believe?" He crossed his arms, ready to defend Caroline. "She's amazing. Everyone at work respects her, and as far as I can tell, she's great at her job. She's an incredible dancer, the women at Pathways look up to her. She—"

"*I* know my sister's amazing. I didn't know *you* knew it. I mean, she's eight years older than we are."

His hope fizzled. "Do you think that's the problem?" Because he could change his attitude and his clothes, but he couldn't do a stupid thing about his birthday.

"I don't know what the problem is, and I don't want to know." Chris pushed the chalk cart away from him. "I don't want to get in the middle of this."

"I knew you wouldn't want me to ask, but I don't want to blow it again."

She stopped to look at him. "Again? Did you already try something with her?"

"You know me better than that. I told her I wanted to get to know her better, and she walked out." He pushed off the fence and walked toward his friend. "I'm not asking for all of Caroline's secrets. I just want to know if I did something wrong."

Chris propped her fists on her hips. "Why?"

"Because I really like your sister, and I'd like to know more about her."

"Why?"

"Because I have fun with her. I like being around her."

"Do you plan on getting married someday? Having kids? What if you could go back to the NFL? Would you?"

The inquisition nearly knocked him over. "What's going on here? You're acting as irrationally as your sister. Would one of you please tell me what's happening?"

Chris frowned. "It's not my story to tell. It's Caro's. But if you like my sister, the only tip I have for you is to be patient. And maybe try to help her forget the age gap. That's just weird."

Patience. He could do that. "Thanks, Chris."

"Whatever. If you're going to keep bothering me, then you need to help me set up."

"Can't. I have a photoshoot with your sister in thirty minutes."

"I don't want to talk about that anymore."

She returned to her chalk line while Ben headed back to his truck, smiling. He didn't know why Caroline needed his patience, but he could give it. In fact, he couldn't think of a better way to distract himself from all his free time.

As Ben stepped into the opera hall, Caroline was pacing the lobby. When she finally spotted him, his feet froze. Her eyelashes had doubled in size. Pink streaked her cheeks while green and gold glitter covered her eyelids. He didn't know what to say.

She rolled her eyes. "It's stage make-up. We're going to be under bright lights for some of these photos, so everything needs to be exaggerated."

"It's nice."

"It's ridiculous, especially in this outfit. It'll make sense once we're dressed and ready for the pictures."

"If you say so. Why are you ready so early? Am I late?" He checked his watch as he adjusted the garment bag on his arm. "I thought I was supposed to be here at six."

"You're fine. I'm the one who messed up."

"How?"

Caroline clasped her hands in front of her, shoulders back. "I'm sorry about our last rehearsal. It was early, and it took me by surprise. I didn't respond well. I'm sorry."

"Don't worry about it." He wouldn't. She'd just reinflated his hope.

"I'm so nervous about the dance-off, I can't seem to shut my brain off. I'm reading into things and creating make-believe scenarios." She shook her head. "Come on. I'll take you to the dressing room so you can change."

Reading into things? More like trying to pretend they weren't happening. She walked toward the double-wide staircase, but instead of following her, Ben stepped ahead of her and cut her off. "Wait a second. What exactly are you apologizing for?"

The pink spread from her cheeks down her neck. "Are you going to make me say it?"

"I want to make sure I know exactly what you're talking about."

Wrapping her arms around herself, Caroline looked at the floor. "I misinterpreted what you said."

"What do you think I said?"

"Do we have to talk about this here?"

"We have five minutes before we need to be upstairs, so yeah. Let's talk about this here."

She grabbed his arm and pulled him past the stairs, beyond the ticket booth, and back to a private corner of the lobby. "I thought you were hitting on me, okay? I feel stupid enough as it is. Could we please ignore this and pretend like it never happened?"

Ben shook his head. "I don't think so."

"Fine. Tease me. Harass me. Get it over with so we can go get our pictures taken."

"I *was* hitting on you, Caroline. Or I was trying to. I wanted to."

If she hadn't been wearing that ridiculous make-up, she would have gone completely white. Her eyes widened the same way Chris's had earlier. Caroline, however, took a step back, separating herself from him. "You can't be serious."

"Why does everyone keep saying that?"

"Who else said it?" She gasped. "Did you tell someone you hit on me?"

"I told Chris."

"That you hit on me?" Caroline clenched her teeth. "Why would you tell her that?"

"I wanted her help."

"Oh my gosh." She covered her face with her hands, turning her back on Ben as she faced the wall. "I can't believe you told my sister."

"I panicked. I needed help. I'd like to take you to dinner or hiking or whatever it is you'd like to do. I like spending time with you. I'd like to do it more often. I thought she could help."

She spun around and rushed him, standing toe-to-toe with him as she poked him in the chest. "We are not and cannot be anything more than co-workers and dance partners. For Pete's sake, you're my little sister's friend—"

"I'm not a child." Ben stepped forward, forcing Caroline to step back. "I'm younger than you. Big deal. We're adults, Caroline. Both of us. Tell me I'm rude or selfish or too into sports for you. Fine, then we might not work. But don't use age as an excuse, because that's all it is."

"Don't you dare tell me what I can and can't do."

Ben took another step. And another. "Why not? You've been telling me what to do for a month. I'm trying to ask you out, and you're *still* telling me what to do."

Caroline backed into the wall. Ben took one more step, crowding into her personal space. He stopped when his chin nearly touched her forehead. "You can't tell me how to feel, and you can't tell me what to do with those feelings. If you want to reject me, fine, but that's your decision. You don't get to make mine for me."

Her chest rose and fell quickly, her breathing fast. He braced himself for a fight, for more arguing and bossing around, but Caroline leaned her head against the wall and closed her eyes. "Can we talk about this later?"

His hope grew, but hesitantly. "That depends on what you mean by talking. And how late is later."

When she opened her eyes, dampness clung to the corners. "I'd love to wait until after the dance-off is over, but I'll settle for after the first competition."

Of course. The dance-off meant everything to her, and he wanted to support her. They needed to stay focused on the competition, and he was pushing things out of focus. "Okay."

"We can deal with this Sunday."

"By 'dealing with this,' do you mean you're going to tell me what to do, or can we talk like two adults?"

"You say your piece, and I'll say mine."

Not exactly promising, but certainly better than her walking out on him. "Fine. I'll call you Sunday after church." He stepped back. "Lead the way. I think we have pictures to pose for."

Chapter 10

Pushing another pin into her hair, Caroline secured the soft curls away from her face. The muffled applause of the audience thumped through the dressing room walls, but she focused on the reflection in front of her. Every strand of hair in place. Her make-up set. The green gown cinched and snug in all the right places. Everything was as good as it would get. Now to check on Ben.

As she stepped out of the dressing room, she prayed their performance would go better than dress rehearsal. She'd tried to prepare Ben for the changes, explaining how the lights and tables and stage would mess with his head even if they didn't directly interfere with their dancing. Despite her warning, he'd stumbled through the steps, unsure of himself and his footing. She'd only seen him briefly since then.

She walked through the backstage area looking for her partner. Her gut told her he wouldn't be in the wings with the rest of the dancers.

Her gut was right. Past the dressing rooms, down the hall, and across from the janitor's closet, Ben held a stiff frame as he danced by himself in the corner. His perfectly tailored shirt hung around the dark slacks that hugged his hips. His hair didn't move even though his feet did. He cleaned up as well as she did.

"How's it going?" she asked.

He kept dancing.

"Ben?" When he didn't respond, she touched his shoulder.

"Whoa!" He spun around, arms up and ready to strike.

Caroline jumped back. "It's me! Calm down."

Ben panted. "Don't sneak up on me."

"I didn't. Are you okay?"

"No. I think I'd rather face a three-hundred-pound linebacker."

"You're going to be great. I can't believe how fast you learned, not that I should be surprised. Ben Allen has yet to meet a sport he couldn't handle." She winked as she playfully punched his shoulder. "Now you can add dancer to your résumé."

"Sure." He nodded, but the tension remained in his back, shoulders, and face.

"You've got to relax." Caroline grabbed his wrists and shook his arms. "I've seen enough footage of you playing football to know you don't have a problem performing in front of people, so what's going on?"

"I've played football since I was eight. I've been dancing for two weeks."

"So has everyone else, and none of them are nearly as athletic as you. I wouldn't be surprised if you're the best amateur tonight." Or ever for the competition.

He nodded again but didn't look her in the eye. His arms stiffened as Caroline tried to loosen them.

"Ben ..." But what could she say that she hadn't already said? Panic squeezed her chest. She had to get him out of his funk and fast. They had less than twenty minutes before they danced. Cupping his cheeks with her hands, she forced him to face her, then waited for his gaze to settle on hers. "You can do this."

His jaw clenched.

"You're the best student I've ever had. I'm honestly impressed with how much you've learned."

He nodded, but nothing relaxed.

If words weren't going to work, Caroline had to get creative. Sending out a quick prayer for forgiveness, she slid her hands around his neck and locked her fingers together. Then she stepped toward him, letting herself lean into him. He trembled a moment before his arms relaxed. His hands wrapped around her waist, slid up her back, and pulled her close. Finally, his shoulders softened as he held her against his chest. He lowered his head as he lifted her off the ground, tucking her head into the crook of his neck.

Caroline let her eyes close as she absorbed the warmth and strength of his embrace. The fresh, clean scent of his skin. A tremor shook its way down her spine. Ben's arms tightened. She'd hugged him to help him relax—he clearly needed something to get his mind off his stage fright—but what was she doing to herself? She hadn't danced with a partner in five years. Hadn't been held by a man in any capacity in so long. Now her traitorous body begged her to hold on longer, but a round of applause announced that the first couple had finished. She needed to focus.

Unlocking her fingers, she let her hands slide along Ben's shoulders and didn't stop them as they continued down his arms. With a deep breath, he set her down. He loosened his hold so she could step back but didn't let go of her completely. She needed to step away—to break the connection between them—but she couldn't make herself do it. Couldn't step away from the comfort of a good man when she didn't know the next time she'd have a chance to step back into his arms. In two days, she'd tell Ben all the reasons why they couldn't do this again, but until then, she let him be a bit more than merely her co-worker and dance partner. A bit more than simply her friend.

Ben lifted his head and looked her in the eye. "I'm not sure if that's fair, using how I feel about you against me."

"Technically, I have no idea how you feel about me. I was just trying to get you out of your head and onto the dance floor. Did it work?"

The corner of his lips lifted into a crooked smile. "It did."

His ease inspired hers, so she smiled back. "Good. Then let's go someplace where we can move around a bit to warm up."

She tried to walk away, but his hands clasped her around the waist, holding her in place. He leaned forward, his jaw pressed to her temple, his mouth next to her ear. "You are the kindest, most thoughtful person I know. I won't kiss you now because I know you're not ready for that yet, but I want you to know that I'm thinking about it. And now you'll be thinking about it too."

When he stepped back, he winked at her, then walked away, practically strutting down the hallway. Caroline's legs wobbled without his arms around her. She leaned against the wall as her brain tried to piece together what had just happened. Sure, Ben had relaxed, but now her heart raced. Knees trembled. Skin tingled.

How was she going to survive the next three months?

"Ladies and gentlemen, Ben Allen and Caroline Novak!"

Ben inhaled as Caroline squeezed his hand. The singer crooned about birds in the sky. Once the band started playing, he would lead Caroline onto the dance floor.

The piano started. He smiled, lifted Caroline's hand in his, and stepped into the spotlight. When she smiled at him, pride filled his chest, pushing his arms into their proper positions and propelling him around the floor. Together, apart, twirling. One more time. One-two-three. Before he knew it, he dipped her. The band stopped. The crowd cheered. Exhilaration swept through him. It was almost as exciting as sacking the quarterback. An exquisite, feminine, sexy quarterback.

Caroline beamed, a brilliance in her eyes he'd never seen before. "You did it!" She threw her arms around his neck. "I knew you could!"

He picked her up and spun her around, laughing with her as the noise of the audience pulsed around them. All he wanted to do was run backstage to celebrate with her, but the emcee interrupted them. When Ben set Caroline down, she wrapped an arm around his waist and snuggled up beside him. The emcee asked questions and he answered, but all Ben cared about was memorizing the feel of the woman at his side.

All four judges gave them sevens. Not good by his estimation, but Caroline seemed thrilled, so he smiled. They finally made it backstage, then out into the lobby where four bouncing, cheering women met them, each of them wearing a shirt with his and Caroline's faces on them.

Warmth filled him, like the feeling he'd had when he first saw Annabelle. He let go of Caroline to greet the women of Pathways. He put his hands on his knees as he bent over to meet Erica's eyes. "I didn't know you'd be here."

She shook her head. "Susan said she wouldn't let us miss it. You were so good." She rushed over and hugged him.

Ben froze. Was that okay? He looked at Susan. She smiled. Well, then, maybe it was allowed. He hugged Erica back. As soon as he did, Liz and Lucy came at him from the sides until all three women hugged him together, squishing him between them. Something stuck in his throat when he tried to swallow.

"Are you trying to tackle my dance partner? He's not playing football anymore." Caroline stood next to Mary, but she looked at Ben. "How do you think he did?"

Lucy let go of him to hug Caroline. "You're so pretty."

"It's hard not to look pretty in this dress, don't you think?"

Liz and Erica finally released Ben, but they didn't move away, so he kept a hand on each of their shoulders. "I think we danced pretty well, but how's the fundraising going? How much money have we raised so far?"

Susan pulled a piece of paper out of her pocket. "When the night started, we had seven thousand pledged. There are over two hundred people here tonight, plus the people watching online, so it should go up. There's an extra thousand-dollar prize for the highest scores, and a new audience-favorite contest, which is another thousand."

Ben nodded. "Seven thousand's not bad, is it? I don't think I ever asked, but what's our goal?"

"Last year's top charity raised fifty thousand."

"In four months?" No wonder Caroline was so stressed about the dance-off. They could raise some serious money. "Seven's a good start then."

"Oh, our goal is higher than fifty." Caroline grinned like the Cheshire cat. "After all, we have Ben Allen on our team.

And now that everyone's seen how well you can dance, we have some great promotional material."

Her enthusiasm worried him. "What's the goal?"

"One-hundred thousand." Caroline beamed.

Ben waited for the punchline. "Are you serious?" Were they crazy?

Susan touched his arm. "You don't have to worry about it. All you need to do is dance. Our fundraising team and marketing volunteers have everything under control."

Maybe, but that didn't mean the pressure of their goal wasn't going to weigh on him, especially since they seemed to be resting all their hopes on his reputation and mediocre dancing abilities.

"Ouch!"

"Ow!"

Liz and Erica jumped away from him, each lady rubbing her shoulder.

Ben's gut clenched. "I'm sorry. I didn't mean to squeeze so hard."

"It's okay." Even though he'd probably left bruises on her shoulder, Liz looked up at him like he was her hero. "I'm glad you're dancing with Caroline. Can I dance with you next?"

"Excuse me, Mr. Allen?" An older gentleman in a suit and tie joined their small group. Behind him stood a younger man with a video camera. Ben immediately recognized them as a pair of TV journalists from downstate. "I'm Tim McCann, TV-27 Sports in Kalamazoo."

"Mr. McCann, of course. What brings you all the way up to Traverse City?"

"Western Michigan University's own Ben Allen, off the football field and on the dance floor. I'd love to ask you some questions about this event."

Liz walked away and rejoined the group of ladies. He didn't need to see her face to recognize her disappointment—her posture said it all. Ben smiled at Tim. "I'd love to answer some questions for you, but first I need to have a dance with my girl Liz. She's one of the ladies at Pathways, the charity we're fundraising for. Give me a minute, then you can ask all the questions you want."

When Ben approached Liz, her eyes had nearly disappeared as the smile consumed her face. "I need to warn you. I've only ever danced with Caroline, so I'm not sure if I'm going to be a very good partner."

He offered his hand, which Liz eagerly grasped. Because she stood several inches shorter than Caroline, he had to adjust his frame, but Liz didn't seem to notice or care. Taking short, slow steps, Ben led her through a modified version of the opening of his dance. Lucy sang a song he didn't recognize, but his legs remembered their patterns and he managed to guide his partner around their small portion of the lobby.

Finally, he lifted his arm and guided Liz beneath it, steering her in a slow spin before circling his arms around her from behind. He didn't fight the urge to drop a quick kiss on her cheek.

Caroline, Susan, Mary, Lucy, and Erica clapped like lunatics, cheering as if he'd intercepted a pass. Behind them, McCann and a handful of people applauded. Heat seared Ben's skin. Two-hundred people cheering for him on the dance floor hadn't meant half as much as this small group of supporters.

Liz stepped out of his arms, but not before flashing him that giant smile. All teeth and cheeks, it was just about the most wonderful thing he'd ever seen.

Caroline motioned toward the TV-27 Sports crew, but Ben shook his head. He didn't want to talk about dancing while his team celebrated without him.

He turned his attention to the reporter. "Mr. McCann, I apologize, but I think we're going to have to wait on the questions. I'd love to tell you what we're doing here, but we're still in the middle of the game. Catch me after everyone's done, and you can talk to me as long as you want."

"Sure, sure." The newsman stepped away, crowding in close to his cameraman to discuss something.

Susan rounded everyone up and escorted them back toward the hall. "Come on, ladies. We should go back to our table."

Caroline pointed backstage. "We have to hang out there until everyone's done. Then we'll all head out to the dance floor while they announce winners."

Susan offered a thumb's up. "Good luck."

Ben waved at each of the ladies as they disappeared into the audience. When Liz blew him a kiss, something inside of him melted.

Caroline slipped her hand around his arm. "Mr. Allen, what has gotten into you?"

"What do you mean?"

"Taking a new dance partner. Turning down an interview. Public displays of affection."

He shrugged, unsure how to express what he was feeling. "You said you wanted them to have new opportunities to do things. Isn't that why we're raising money?"

"One of the reasons."

"Do you think Liz has ever waltzed with a former football player before?"

"I doubt she's ever waltzed with anyone before."

"Good. Then she got to do something new today." So did he, and it felt amazing. How could he deny these women that opportunity again? When he looked at Caroline to tell her what he was thinking, tears filled her eyes. His insides flipped. "Oh, no. What did I do?"

"Nothing." She swallowed. "But I think you might be the kindest, most thoughtful person I know."

Hearing his words coming from her lips did weird things to Ben. Leaning close, he decided to test the waters. "Does it make you want to kiss me?"

"It does."

The world stopped moving. Everything around them slipped out of focus as Ben zeroed in on the woman beside him. She stepped closer, stretched up beside him, and pressed her lips to his cheek. "You're not just a good dance partner, you're the perfect person to be dancing with me for these girls. Thank you for doing this."

"You are so, so welcome."

Before his thoughts could run away with him, Caroline pulled him down the hallway. "Come on. We need to find out how we did and start planning for next month."

Start planning indeed.

Chapter 11

Sunday morning, Caroline paced the length of her apartment. The air was already warm, causing a thin layer of sweat to cover her neck. Or maybe her nerves had caused the slippery mess. Ben said he'd call her after church, but she didn't know what time that was, so she skipped her regular service to make sure she wouldn't miss his call. Even though she'd had a day to prepare, and even though she'd stayed home to figure out what to do about his declaration to kiss her, she still had no idea what she wanted to say to him.

She checked the time. Eleven fifteen. How much longer—

The phone rang.

Her feet stopped moving. It was probably him. All she had to do was answer it. If only she knew what to say.

The phone rang again.

She'd think of something. "Hello?"

"Hey, it's Ben."

"Hi." How original.

"Are you home?"

"Yeah, why?"

"I just pulled into your parking lot."

Caroline ran to the front window. Ben's SUV pulled into a parking spot directly in front of her apartment. She wasn't prepared for a face-to-face encounter. She was still in her red-and-white polka-dotted pajama shorts! "The door's open. I'll just be a minute."

She dashed into her bedroom, slamming the door behind her as she dove into the closet. Stripping out of her pajamas, she slid into the first clean outfit she could find—green capris and a peasant shirt.

The front door opened.

"Make yourself comfortable!" Caroline checked her reflection. No time for make-up. Not a problem. Let him see her *au naturel*. It might influence his mixed-up feelings. Running a brush through her hair, she tied it over her right shoulder. She wouldn't win any beauty contests, but at least she didn't look like she'd just climbed out of bed.

Brushing the wrinkles out of her shirt, she headed back into the living room.

"Your apartment's so pretty." Annabelle sat at Caroline's dining room table, her feet swinging from the tall seat. "I can't wait to have my own apartment."

Caroline looked at Ben on the other side of the table as she tried to figure out what was happening.

He shrugged. "Annabelle wanted to come when she found out where I was going."

"He didn't want to tell me. I had to steal his bagel until he spilled."

Caroline patted the girl's shoulder. "Don't feel bad. He didn't tell me either. Do you want something to drink?" Because she needed a second to figure out this new development.

"No, thank you," Annabelle said.

Ben shook his head as he pulled out the chair nearest Caroline, the one between him and his sister. "I thought we'd talk, then maybe we can treat you to lunch."

Caroline slipped into the seat. "And you wanted to talk about ..."

He sucked in a deep breath, his shoulders rising and falling in an exaggerated manner. "Staying focused on the dance-off. Not doing anything to jeopardize our chances to raise a hundred thousand dollars for Pathways."

A cool burst of relief washed over her. "What changed your mind?"

"Have you checked your email today?"

"No, why?"

He pulled out his phone. He tapped on the screen a few times before passing it to her. His email filled the screen:

> We got our final numbers last night. Between the money pledged, the $2,000 for being the crowd favorite and best dancers for the night, and the money raised in-house and online—are you ready for this? $16,500!
>
> I'm putting together a letter for the board and a press release for the papers, but I wanted to let you know first. I don't know how we can ever thank you enough for what you're doing. You're an inspiration and a blessing.
>
> Keep up the good work!
> Susan

Caroline reread the email. Then she read it again as she tried to process the information. "Sixteen thousand dollars? How is that even possible? That's more than some charities make in four months."

"They started live-streaming the event," Ben said. "They had a thousand people watching online."

"That's incredible."

Ben reached for his phone. "But it's not enough."

"What do you mean? We're almost halfway to last year's highest total."

"But we didn't even raise half of our goal."

"We have three more weeks. If we can keep this up, we'll blow right past that."

"We will, but"—he tapped his phone screen, then passed it back to her again—"we need to move the goal line. Susan accidentally copied me on this email."

> The electrician was right. The contractor inspected the damage, and it's worse than we thought. The fan fell because the ceiling and supports rotted because of a leak in the roof. The full report is attached. The short version is this:
> We need to replace the roof.
> Many of the tresses need to be replaced or reinforced.
> All of the wiring needs to be updated.
> The best-case scenario is $40,000.

"What?" Caroline's heart stopped, or maybe her lungs deflated. Whatever it was, her chest burned. And her head spun.

A small cool hand covered hers. She blinked her eyes into focus. Annabelle stared up at her. "Do you need some water?"

Caroline tried to smile. "I'll be okay. I'm just ... shocked."

"You're not the only one." Ben spun his phone on the table. "Susan emailed me again to apologize for copying me on the previous email and to assure me the board isn't upset. They're actually thrilled it happened now."

"Why?"

"Because we're raising tens of thousands of dollars to cover the cost. They won't have much extra money, but they won't go into debt fixing anything."

Caroline appreciated the logic, but it didn't stop her heart from breaking. Pathways' wish list would have to be put on hold. Again. Still, "Susan's right. This couldn't have happened at a better time."

"But what about your job?" A thin line appeared between his eyes when he frowned. "There won't be enough money to fix the house *and* hire a full-time manager. It's not enough to dance well anymore. We need to win so Pathways gets the matching funds. We need to get them the hundred thousand dollars. Or more."

Hope twirled in her heart. "It would change ... everything."

"That's why I'm willing to postpone *things* until after the competition. I need to focus on dancing."

"That's why I'm here." Annabelle grinned. "I'm going to help."

"Really?" Caroline tried to hide her surprise. "How's that?"

"Ben said I should come to rehearsals to record them. Then he can review the films at home between practices."

Caroline couldn't stop the laugh that bubbled in her chest. "You're making game tapes of our dance practices?"

The first hint of a smile pulled at Ben's lips. "It worked for football. I figure it can't hurt to try it with dancing."

"I don't think you have anything to worry about. You did better than anyone else. You don't have to beat the pros, you just need to dance better than the owner of a furniture store."

Annabelle sniffed. "Not if he wants to look good on TV."

"Annie."

She pressed her lips together as her brother stared at her.

"What do you mean?" Caroline asked.

He glared at his sister. "I didn't want to bring it up yet—"

"I am *so sorry*. I forgot you wanted to keep a secret, but it's such a good idea I wanted Caroline to know, in case she wants to help." Annabelle leaned across the table and grabbed her brother's arm. "It was an accident, I *swear*."

Ben sighed. "Do you remember Tim McCann, the sportscaster who spotted me at the dance-off?"

A half dozen reporters had asked to interview Ben Friday night, but only one from out of town. "I remember. From Kalamazoo, right?"

"His story aired last night." Ben tapped his phone, then handed it back to Caroline.

The TV-27 logo filled the screen, then a clip of Ben dancing with Liz.

> *Down but not out, northern Michigan's former football sensation traded in his cleats for dance shoes to use his college fame to support a worthy cause.*

Tim McCann narrated the three-minute feature, which started with a clip of Ben dancing with Caroline before cutting back to Ben and Liz. The reporter summarized Ben's football career and the dance-off.

> *Allen isn't focusing on what he can't do on the field. Instead, he's doing whatever he can to help the women of Pathways House, a nonprofit organization dedicated to providing quality supportive housing and essential support services for adults with developmental disabilities.*

The screen showed Susan, the girls, and some of the board members cheering for Ben and Caroline.

Ben's face filled the screen again.

> *These women are capable of so much more than anyone realizes, but because it may take them longer to learn or do something, they've been overlooked or ignored. I had the chance to work with them—not because they weren't capable, but because they weren't tall enough to change some of the lightbulbs in their house—and I can admit that they surprised me. They make their own money, run their own home. They don't need handouts, they just need a chance.*
>
> *Any funds we raise can help in so many ways. We can upgrade their house, hire someone to be their full-time*

support system, maybe even finance another house so we can help more people. You'd have to ask the board exactly how they plan to use the funds. All I know is I want to help them raise as much as possible because they deserve it.

McCann kept talking, but Caroline stopped listening. Tears blurred the video as Ben's words replayed in her head. She wiped the tears away as she swallowed back the emotion. "That was beautiful."

"Did you see how many people have viewed that clip?" Annabelle asked.

She blinked again as she tried to focus on the screen. "One-hundred thousand views? Are you serious?"

"That's just since it aired yesterday," Ben said. "It's already been shared almost a hundred times on social media. Give it a few days and some of the other news outlets will pick it up. I've already sent the link to Western's athletic department and public relations office."

"Why?" She passed back his phone. "Why would they care about a Traverse City fundraiser?"

"They don't. They care about me. They've already invested a year on my career. Now they can keep it going." Ben leaned back and crossed his arms.

"I have two options here. I can stay quiet and hope we raise enough money. That would be the easiest thing for me, the guy who didn't pay anything for his college degree. I didn't even have to pay for books, and almost every time I went out to eat, someone offered to treat me to dinner. Or I could suck it up, let people see me doing something completely foreign and uncomfortable, and earn money for a bunch of ladies who have had to fight for every opportunity in their lives." He shook his head. "This isn't about me. It's about them. They deserve to have someone sacrifice something for them."

Caroline couldn't help herself. She slid off her seat and slid her arms around Ben's neck. "You really are the kindest, most thoughtful person."

"I'm kind too, and I can be thoughtful," Annabelle said. "It was my idea to videotape the practices."

Caroline stepped away from Ben and hugged his sister. "I think it's a great idea."

Annabelle bounced in her seat. Her blonde curls hopped around her shoulders. Every muscle in her face tightened.

Ben laughed. "Fine. Tell her."

"I'm not just making practice videos! I'm going to edit them into promotional videos to send to all the major Michigan television stations." Annabelle squealed.

"You can do that?"

The preteen huffed. "Of course I can. I've been making videos since I was a kid. And this is really important to Ben, so I'm going to make sure they're the best videos I've ever made. I've been watching *Dancing with the Stars* online to see what they include in their segments, and Ben said he'd see if it would be okay to go to Pathways to record. I bet they would like being in the videos."

"I don't even know what to say." Gratitude, awe, affection, wonder, and a dozen other emotions filled Caroline's chest. "I'm a little overwhelmed by all of this. Have you talked to Susan yet?"

"Annie and I came up with this plan last night. You're the first person we've told."

"We didn't even tell my parents, but don't tell them that." Annabelle leaned close and whispered, "I wouldn't want them to feel bad."

Caroline chuckled. "Your brother must be a great role model because you are a remarkable young lady. I bet you're a great little sister."

The twelve-year-old's eyes widened. "I am. Can I call you sometime?"

"Sure."

"Why would you need to call her?" Ben asked.

Annabelle rolled her eyes as she wrapped an arm around Caroline. "Sometimes a girl just needs to talk to a girl."

Ben lifted an eyebrow. "What about Mom?"

"It's not the same. I bet Caroline doesn't talk to her mom about everything."

"She's right. Sometimes there are things you want to tell your sister." A catcall sounded from Caroline's phone. She sighed. "And sometimes your sisters torture you in ways no one else can."

"Is that Chris?" Annabelle pushed herself up, straining to see Caroline's phone.

"No, that's her attempt to make me crazy."

Ben smirked before grabbing the phone. His face went blank when he looked at the screen. "Who's that?" A man with tan skin, brown eyes, and a baseball cap smiled at them.

Caroline shook her head. "I honestly don't know."

Annabelle took the phone from him. "Oh, he's cute. Why do you have his picture?"

"Because Chris thought it would be funny to put a dating app on my phone. I asked her to remove it, but instead, she turned the notification into a catcall." Caroline swiped twice on her phone and the picture disappeared.

"How many dates have you gone on?" Annabelle asked.

"None."

"Why not?"

"Because I'm not interested.

Ben cleared his throat. "So it's not just me?"

She shook her head. "It's nothing personal."

Annabelle cocked her head to the side. "What's nothing personal?"

Caroline tossed her phone onto the couch. "You know what? We need to plan our schedule so Annabelle can be at our practices."

"Do I get to go to all of the practices?"

"That's what we need to talk about."

"Ben said we could go out to eat. Are we going out now?"

Ben pulled his keys out of his pocket and tossed them to his sister. "Go ahead and cool my truck off. We'll be down in a few minutes."

"Yes!" Annabelle ran out of the apartment without glancing back.

Caroline ran a hand through her ponytail. "I'll need a few minutes to get ready."

"Why?"

"I wasn't expecting company. I need to brush my hair, put on some make-up—"

"Don't. You look beautiful."

Heat worked its way up Caroline's face. "You don't have to try so hard."

"I'm not trying. I'm being honest." Ben walked around the table to stand beside her. "You looked great in your dance costume, but this is you, and you're stunning."

She couldn't look up at him. How was she supposed to respond to that?

"You need to know—I meant what I said. I want to focus on raising money for Pathways. I don't want anything to distract us, but I also meant what I said before. I plan to get to know you better."

"Weren't you listening?" She crossed her arms. "I'm not interested."

"In men as a species, but I'm not all men, and sooner or later you'll let me show you." Ben patted her shoulder. "Come on, now. Annie's waiting."

Chapter 12

Ben couldn't stop his smile as he stepped out of Caroline's apartment. On the way over, he had almost talked himself into ignoring his attraction to her. He was so glad he'd failed.

Work Caroline and Rehearsal Caroline had nothing on Casual Caroline. He didn't even know how to describe the blue of her eyes in that outfit. And her hair. He clenched his fingers as he tried to imagine how soft it would feel.

Ben stepped into the sunshine, literally and figuratively. As the midday sun warmed his face, Caroline's confession warmed his spirit. It wasn't that she wasn't interested in *him*, she wasn't interested in anyone. He just needed to find out why. Then he could figure out a way to change her mind.

Annie waved at him from the front passenger seat of his truck. He slid into the driver's seat and pointed to the back. "Sorry, sport. You have to sit in the back."

"Why? Caroline didn't even come down."

"Give her a second. She'll be here."

Annie gave an exaggerated sigh, but she unfastened her seatbelt and climbed between the seats. As her foot disappeared, the door to the apartment building opened.

Caroline stepped outside still wearing the green and blue outfit with her hair across her shoulder. The fact that she hadn't changed encouraged him. As she climbed into the passenger seat, Annie's head appeared between the seats.

"Where are we going to eat? I'm starving," his sister said.

Caroline shrugged. "I was going to have leftovers, so anyplace would be an improvement."

"Bennnnnnnn ..." His sister grabbed his arm and set her chin on his shoulder.

"We ate there Friday."

"That was two whole days ago."

He looked around her so he could see Caroline. "Do you like Thai food?"

"I love it."

"Woo hoo!" Annie punched her arms in the air before flopping back into her seat.

"Then you two really could be sisters. It's the only thing she ever wants to eat when we go out." He put the truck in gear and pulled out of the complex.

"How often do you eat there?"

"We've gone there the last six times we've been out." He glanced at his passenger. "I have a hard time saying no to her."

Caroline chuckled. "You at least like Thai food, don't you?"

"In moderation. Annie doesn't understand moderation yet."

His sister's head popped back up in between the seats. "Why aren't you interested in dating boys?"

Ben pointed back. "Seat belt." She disappeared. Ben listened for the soft click. "And manners."

"But Caroline said I could adopt her as a sister. That's the kind of question I would ask a sister. She's my new role model. Don't you want me to learn from her mistakes?"

Caroline snorted, but Ben stifled a groan. "You don't have to answer her."

"I know, but she has a point. I have two younger sisters. Chris and Carmen both know why I'm not interested. It might help *Annabelle* to know the full story."

And give him the information he needed. "If you insist."

Caroline twisted in her seat, giving Ben a tight smile before facing Annie. "I was engaged before. Twice."

The girl gasped, masking his own. "When? What happened?"

Caroline took a long breath. "The first time I was in college. I dated Brett for two years, and he proposed to me during my senior year. We were going to get married the winter after we graduated, but I found out he'd been lying to me."

Ben strangled the steering wheel.

"What did he lie about?" Annie asked.

"His family. I wanted to put an engagement announcement in the newspaper, but he kept coming up with reasons not to do it. We got into a huge fight. He finally admitted that he couldn't put his name or picture in the newspaper because his mom was sick, and he didn't want her to know where he was."

"Seriously?" Ben hadn't meant to interrupt, but—what the heck?

"And that was just the beginning. He had a brother serving time in prison, and his dad hadn't talked to him for years, but Brett lied about everything. I didn't mind his family history, but after that I never knew if I could believe him. We broke up a few weeks later."

"Were you sad?" Annie whispered.

"For a long time." Caroline's voice cracked. "I was your brother's age when that happened, and it took me two years before I trusted anyone enough to date again."

Years?

"I met Chad when I was twenty-five. We dated for almost a year before he proposed."

"Did he lie too?" Annie's voice wavered.

"No, Chad was always honest with me, but he couldn't commit."

"What does that mean?"

Caroline shifted in her seat. Ben glanced at her quickly enough to see her stiffen. "Well, he wanted to, uh ... act like we were married without getting married."

"You mean he wanted to have sex?"

Ben nearly drove off the road. "What do you know about sex?"

He checked the mirror in time to see Annie roll her eyes. "Some of the girls in my class have sisters in high school, so they're always talking about it. I asked Mom. She told me all about it."

The air in the truck thinned. Ben would have to live at home until Annie was twenty-one to make sure no one else tried to "explain it" to her.

Caroline touched his arm. "Are you okay? You're turning purple."

"No, I'm not okay. My twelve-year-old sister knows about sex. Last year, she wanted to be a mermaid." He scrubbed his face. "There's no going back now."

Annie patted his shoulder. "Manners, Ben. Don't interrupt. Caroline's telling a story."

"Don't say sex again, and I won't interrupt again." He didn't have to see Annie to know she was rolling her eyes again. "Go on. I'll try to stay quiet."

Caroline let go of him and refocused her attention on his sister. "Since you're obviously old enough to know what I'm talking about, I won't sugarcoat it. Chad asked me to marry him, but he never wanted to set a wedding date. He asked me to move in with him, wanted me to cosign loans with him, he even wanted to adopt a dog and talked about having kids, but he wouldn't set a wedding date."

"Why didn't you just do all the married stuff without getting married?"

"Because I was raised to believe the wedding comes first. Statistics prove that when people move in together and start a family and *then* get married, they have higher rates of divorce, but when they get married first, more marriages last."

"Then why wouldn't he pick a wedding date?"

Caroline shook her head. "I still don't know. He never gave me a reason, and he got mad whenever I asked. After four months, I realized he wasn't going to commit, so I broke the engagement."

"How old were you?"

"Twenty-six."

"How old are you now?"

"Thirty."

"You're older than Ben? You don't look that old."

Caroline chuckled. "Thank you."

"That was four years ago," Ben said. "You haven't dated anyone since?"

"I've been a little gun shy since the second broken engagement."

"Sure, but four years?"

"I'm ... nervous. There was a lot of heartache." She swiveled to face forward again, her voice quiet. "A lot of self-doubt."

Ben wanted to tell her he was nervous too, but Annie asked, "Do you think you'll ever get married?"

Something he wanted to know too.

"I'm still hoping I'll find forever with someone, but it hurts when you think you're going to spend the rest of your life with someone, and then you don't. It doesn't matter how old you are. A broken heart hurts the same if you're sixteen or twenty-six." Caroline cleared her throat before facing Annie again. "And that's why it's important to protect your heart. You don't want to date someone and hope for the best. You need to get to know a boy first, make sure he's good and honest and—"

"Kind and thoughtful?" he asked.

"Ben's kind and thoughtful."

He caught Annie's eye in the mirror and winked.

Caroline sat back in her seat and stared out the window. "Yes, he is."

"But he's a lot younger than you too. That would be weird."

"Or exciting." He glared at his sister in the rearview mirror. "I might be younger, but I have my perks. I'm an All-American football player."

She crossed her arms. "You *were*."

Her words hit harder than an angry guard.

"Oh look, we're here." Caroline pointed to their left. Sure enough, the Thai Garden sign blinked on the side of the road.

Part of Ben wished he had a few more miles to find out more, but another part of him rejoiced his sister wouldn't be able to give Caroline any more reasons to reject him.

He parked, and Annie and Caroline jumped out. "Let's get food first, then talk about the videos," she said. "I have so many questions."

Caroline wrapped her arm around Annie. "I have answers."

Ben kept a safe distance as he followed them inside. While they strategized for the dance-off, he'd strategize a way to win over Caroline.

Chapter 13

Caroline walked through the dance steps, tapping her toes and heels on the smooth floor. A motor rumbled outside the studio, slowly getting louder. She recognized the hum of Ben's truck.

The front door opened, and a whirl of energy rushed into the studio. "Hi, Caroline. Where do you want me to set up the camera this week? Should I get a different angle? What do you want me to focus on?"

"Hi, Annabelle." She gave the girl a squeeze. "You should ask your brother what he wants. He's the one watching the tapes."

"Anywhere you want is fine." Ben shuffled into the room. "It's not the angle that's the problem."

"Don't get down on yourself," Caroline said. "It's only been a week and the cha-cha's difficult."

"I know, but …" He stopped when he spotted Caroline. The corner of his mouth quirked.

Her face flushed. "But what?"

"Your hair is down."

"I wore it down last week." She combed her fingers through the strands of the ponytail she'd worn since the Sunday of "the talk." The Sunday when Ben couldn't stop staring.

"I know, but I'm still getting used to it."

Maybe she'd been wrong. "Does it bother you when we're dancing? I can put it back up." She raised her arms to fix it, but Ben stopped her with a head shake.

"Don't. I like it."

"As long as you're okay with it." Another vehicle rumbled outside. Caroline dropped her hair as she looked at the clock. Tony was early. She only had about sixty seconds to run her idea past Ben. "I think I have an idea for helping you learn the hip motion for the cha-cha."

"I'm willing to try anything." He threw his sandals into his bag. "The only thing we have on video is you repeatedly telling me I'm not doing it right."

"That's not true." Was it?

Ben slipped on his dance shoes. "No, you're much nicer than that, but it's the same principle."

"Hopefully, we can change that today."

The door opened. Tony smiled as he stepped inside wearing a dance studio T-shirt with his dance pants and shoes, per the usual. "Am I late?"

"No, you're early," Caroline said, the familiar rush of friendship and affection flowing through her.

He walked right to her and gave her a hug. "You know how I am about punctuality."

"I do. Thanks for doing this." When they parted, she turned to Ben. He'd made his way toward them, face blank as he looked down at Tony. Several inches separated them in height and width, but Tony didn't flinch. "Ben, this is my former dance partner, Tony Caldwell. He agreed to come in today to help you with your hips."

Ben's jaw twitched as he extended his hand. "Thanks for your help. I appreciate it."

"Anything for Caroline." Tony accepted the handshake and winked at her.

Ben sighed. "You're going to make me dance with him, aren't you?"

Caroline laughed. "No, but I think I figured out the problem. You've been watching cha-cha videos, but they aren't doing *our* dance. I think there's a disconnect because you don't know enough about the individual dance steps to figure out which ones are the ones we're using."

"How's Tony going to help with that?"

Caroline slipped her arm through Tony's. "He's going to dance with me and Annabelle's going to record it. We'll do our dance. Then, when you're watching the video, you'll see exactly how each step should look."

"That might help, but how's he going to learn the dance?"

Tony clapped Ben on the back. "Caroline emailed me the steps. We'll run through it a few times to make sure I've got it, then record it. I'll stick around afterward so I can see where you're having the most problems and see how I can help."

Annabelle slowly approached them, her hands clasped behind her back and her eyes on Tony. "I'm ready whenever you are."

Caroline slipped an arm around Ben's sister. "Annabelle, this is my former dance partner, Tony. Tony, this is Ben's younger sister and our videographer, Annabelle."

"Hi." The young girl smiled, her cheeks a rosy pink.

"It's nice to meet you, Annabelle." Tony bowed. "Why don't you show me where you set up so I know where we should dance?"

"Okay."

As Tony followed her to the other side of the studio, Ben stepped beside Caroline. "What's wrong with Annabelle?"

Caroline chuckled.

"What?"

"I think your sister has a crush on Tony."

Ben straightened his back. "That's ridiculous."

"Why? She's crazy about the whole dance competition, and Tony's a legitimate dancer. And he's a good-looking guy."

"If you say so."

She tried not to smile as she patted his arm. "Don't take it so personally. You're good looking too, but you're her brother. That would be completely inappropriate."

"Now you're just being weird."

"I was going for helpful."

"Do you really think Tony can help?"

"I do. He's an amazing teacher. First, he and I will dance so you can see how it should look. Annabelle will record it. Then, while you and I practice, Tony will dance behind you. He'll help with posture and sway while you work on the dance steps. You'll get a feel for how the rest of your body should be moving while your feet do."

Ben's lip twitched. For a second Caroline thought it might curl—maybe a smile or maybe a snarl—but he managed to push down whatever emotions were affecting his facial muscles.

"We're ready!" Annabelle waved.

Tony clapped as he strode over. "All right, let's get started."

Caroline smiled up at Ben. "Time to see what we can do."

Ben scowled as he watched the television.

Annie sighed. "Tony's such a good dancer."

"Yeah, he's amazing." He really was. And Ben … well, he was a football player in dance shoes.

Caroline had been right about everything. It took Tony two practice runs to learn a dance Ben hadn't learned in a week. Tony and Caroline danced across Ben's parents' television screen, moving in perfect synchronization. More than that, their faces told a story, switching from passion to excitement to intrigue with each step. Ben looked constipated when he appeared on screen.

And, weird as it was, moving around the floor with the short dancer's hands on his hips had helped Ben calculate exactly when to sway, twist, and dip. Tony had even helped Ben figure out how to keep his right shoulder down. Apparently, Tony was the Midas of the dance world, turning Ben's dance moves into pure gold.

At least, Ben hoped they would turn into gold. At the very least, he'd improved from awkward to tolerable, but Tony had offered to come back anytime he could. Ben didn't want to need any more help, but he also didn't want to disappoint Caroline or the girls.

A pillow smacked him in the face. "What the—"

"Stop being cranky."

He threw the pillow back. "Why do you think I'm cranky?"

"You keep groaning and huffing and—" Annie scrunched her nose and twisted her lips. "You're distracting me."

"Sorry." He lifted his hands in surrender. "I didn't mean to interrupt this experience for you."

"Shh. I want to watch this again."

As Annie restarted the dance, Ben's phone dinged. Swiping the screen, he noticed a new email from Tim McCann. He could watch the perfect dance team anytime. Might as well see what McCann wanted.

> Ben,
> My boss loved the story about you and the fundraiser. She'd like me to cover the rest of the events. I'll be there the morning before each competition to talk with the people at Pathways. I'd like to schedule some extra time to talk with you and find out more about your post-football life. I'm happy to communicate with you by email but wondered if you would mind sharing your phone number with me so I can call you if needed.
> I'm looking forward to learning more about this event. Thanks for your time.

Interesting. Ben sent a quick reply with his phone number before scrolling through the rest of his unopened emails. Newsletter, junk mail, email from unknown senders.

Finally, a reply from the Western Michigan athletic department.

> What an incredible story. We can't wait to talk to you about it. It's perfect for the alumni newsletter.

The newsletter would reach tens of thousands of people. Perfect.

Further down the mailbox was a reply from Western's public relations department, along with two more from local stations. He hadn't told Caroline about his attempts to contact people in case they didn't work out, but maybe he should reach out to more people.

His phone rang, startling him. Ben bobbled it before finally sandwiching it between his hands. When he regained control, Caroline's name flashed on the screen. "Hey, what's up?"

"I'm sorry to bother you on a Saturday. I know we said we'd take weekends off, but I have a quick question for you."

"Shoot."

"How would you feel about skipping practice Wednesday night and going bowling instead?"

"Like a date?" He smiled at the possibilities.

"No." Or not. "The girls have been asking about you, and they haven't gone on an outing together in a few months. They all like bowling, so I thought we'd kill two birds with one stone."

And if they were out in public, Ben could send the time and location to a few reporters. Maybe take a few publicity shots. Anything to help spread the word. Plus, he'd be with Caroline. Even if no reporters showed up, that would be worth the night out. "Absolutely. When and where?"

"Slap Jacks at six? We usually get pizza while we're there, so don't eat. We'll fill up on bowling alley food."

"Can't wait."

"Thanks. I'm not going to tell them about it until the day of—in case anything happens and we have to cancel. I don't want to get their hopes up."

"I'll make sure not to mention anything to anyone between now and then. Are you sure you want to cancel practice, though? We should reschedule."

"I know you're worried, but you've already made a ton of progress. A night off won't kill us. And I know you're watching the video. I can hear the music in the background."

Ben winced. "Technically, I'm not watching it. Annie is."

"I told you she has a crush on Tony."

"Let's not talk about my twelve-year-old sister's love interests. I'm still trying to recover from the sex talk."

Caroline laughed. "Be honest. Who's watched the video more, you or her?"

"I'm not sure, but she's watched it with me every time I've turned it on. She even came into my bedroom when I was watching it on my laptop."

"Is she learning anything?"

"Just that ballroom dancing is the best thing ever, and she needs to learn how to do it if her life's going to be complete." Caroline laughed again, the cheerful tone ringing through the phone. "You have a great laugh."

"Ben—"

"I know. Waiting until the dance-off is over, but that doesn't mean I can't compliment you."

"Who are you complimenting? Is that Caroline? Can I talk to her?" Annie abandoned her armchair and hopped onto the couch beside him.

"I'm talking to her."

"But I have so many questions for her." She reached for the phone.

He turned away. "Then call her on your own time."

"Ben, come ooooooooonnnnnnn."

"You could just give her the phone," Caroline said. He heard the smile in her voice.

Ben snorted. "Why should I make it easy for her?" And give up his chance to talk with Caroline. Annie huffed as she walked away. "That got rid of her."

"Little sisters aren't easy to get rid of. Trust me."

"Maybe not, but it bought us a few minutes of peace."

"That's what you think. You just haven't"—her voice cut out—"experience. Hold on." Caroline's laugh filled the line. "That's my call waiting. It's your sister."

"What?" Ben looked around the living room. Annie stepped into the doorway from the kitchen, the cordless house phone at her ear. "Smooth move, Annie."

She smirked. "It's Annabelle."

"I don't want to get in the middle of this family dispute, but I sort of feel like I should answer this call."

Even though everything in him wanted to keep talking, Ben knew Annie had given him the perfect out. "Go ahead. You two talk. I have some plotting to do."

Annie's face lit up. "Caroline? I've been watching the video of you dancing all week. How do you spin without getting dizzy?"

His sister drilled his dance partner, but Ben didn't have time to concentrate on their conversation. Opening his email, he started a new message.

Promotional Opportunity—Ben Allen's Post-Football Life.

Chapter 14

Caroline parked the minivan in front of the bowling alley. Lucy climbed out first and practically ran across the sidewalk. She opened the front door for everyone, waiting while Caroline checked the van for wallets before locking it. Once they were all inside, Lucy led the procession to the register.

The middle-aged cashier held up his hand. "You're already taken care of. Just tell me what size shoes you need, and you can head to lane fifteen."

"What do you mean we're taken care of?" Caroline asked. "Who paid?"

"The young guy on lane fifteen. Said to treat you all to two games and shoe rentals."

She looked down the alley. Ben and Annabelle sat under number fifteen.

Everyone put on their shoes before navigating the maze of tables and chairs until they reached the Allens. All the girls called out their greetings, and Liz snuggled up to Ben for a hug. He smiled during it, but his gaze was on Caroline, which she knew because she watched him the entire time. After his hug with Liz, he walked toward her.

She crossed her arms. "You didn't have to pay. All the girls work. They have enough money."

He crossed his arms. "Hi, Ben. Thanks for the bowling. That was really nice of you. Why don't we buy dinner for you and your sister?"

Caroline sighed. "You're right. I'm sorry. Thank you, it was incredibly generous of you."

He shrugged. "I wanted it to be as much of a date-night-out for them as I could make it."

"I'm sure they'll be talking about it for days." And she'd be thinking about it. Kind and thoughtful, that was her Ben. No, no—that was Ben. *Just* Ben.

He took a step closer, leaning toward her as he did. "I have a confession. Tonight might get a little interesting, and I was hoping some free bowling might help you not get too mad at me."

Her chest constricted. "What did you do?"

"I may have told people we were going to be here."

"What kind of people?"

"Media people?"

"Is that a question? Are you not sure if you told media people, or are you not sure if you should be admitting to it? Who and how many?" She needed to call Susan.

As she reached for her phone, Ben wrapped his fingers around her arm and pulled her over two lanes. "When you called me Saturday, I'd been checking emails. All the people I contacted about the dance-off wrote me back to schedule interviews. I thought our bowling night might make a good promotional opportunity for the dance-off."

"*You* called the press?" One half of Caroline's brain started clapping. The other half tried to silence the warning bells ringing in her ears. Both sides demanded she call Susan. Caroline pulled out the phone and dialed.

"Did I do something wrong? They were at the dance-off. I thought this would be fine."

"At the dance-off with the executive director and family members. What if they accuse us of using the girls for financial gain?"

"Would they?"

"I don't know. I also don't know if we can—or should—speak on behalf of Pathways. What if we say or do something wrong?" They could tank the fund-raising efforts or her chance at a job. Anger and anxiety tangoed in her chest. "You can't make decisions for everyone."

"I'm not trying to, but Ben Allen will draw a lot more press than Susan, whose last name I don't even know."

Voicemail. Caroline hung up and sent a text. "Maybe it'll be fine, but we need to check."

A young, dark-haired man in a blue jacket approached Lucy. Caroline jolted, but Ben grabbed her arm. "Do you know him?" she asked.

"David Andrews, 7&10 News. I created this mess. I'll take care of it."

"And what are the rest of us supposed to do?"

"Bowl. I won't let them talk to any of the girls unless you give me the okay."

Not ideal, but it would do. "I suppose I'll follow your lead then. You're the press pro, after all."

"Exactly, which is why you wanted me on your team in the first place."

She couldn't argue with that, though she didn't have to argue.

Mary was at the end of their lane ready to bowl her first frame while Annabelle and Erica looked at the menu. Ben walked straight for the reporter as calm as if he was going to greet a friend. As promised, the reporter never approached the girls. Between frames, her phone pinged.

What a great opportunity! The girls can decide for themselves if they want to chat.

Please thank Ben for this! Susan.

Just in time, because Caroline heard Lucy talking about the Detroit Tigers and Erica explaining what she picked for dinner. She looked at the reporter in time to see Liz blush when asked about her dance with Ben.

They were four frames in by the time David left, but they only enjoyed a few minutes of quiet before another reporter showed up, this time from someplace downstate. Caroline tried to be discreet as she watched Ben turn on the charm. Once again, the reporter spent most of his time with Ben, but Liz and Annabelle were more than willing to offer their stories as well. Caroline appreciated the publicity, but the evening was about the girls, not Ben. Would they care?

The third reporter arrived as they started their second game. The woman couldn't have been much older than Ben. Caroline had just rolled a spare when the reporter approached her.

"I'm Kelly Wyman, WWTV-13 Grand Rapids. You must be Ben's dance partner."

"Yes, I'm Caroline Novak." *I have a name.*

"I wondered if you might be willing to answer a few questions for me. On camera."

"Um, sure. What do you need me to do?"

The young brunette pointed to where her cameraman stood. "If you wouldn't mind standing over there, we have some good lighting set up." Caroline followed Kelly to a well-lit area and stood in front of the camera. Kelly clipped a microphone onto Caroline's shirt before stepping out of the camera's shot. "Does the microphone feel comfortable?"

Caroline nodded. "I think so."

"Great. We'll edit this when we get back to the studio, so just answer honestly."

"Okay." As if she'd lie about a fundraiser.

"How does it feel to be dancing with Ben Allen?"

Of course. Caroline wanted to be honest—frustrating, fun, wonderful—but she didn't know how the reporter would edit it. Instead, she said, "It's different."

"How so?"

"I'm used to dancing with men who've trained for years. This is all new to Ben, so I'm having to teach him everything. He's also a lot bigger than any of my former dance partners." And younger. And interested.

"How would you rate his skill level?"

"For someone who's never danced before, he's doing really well."

Kelly winked. "And how's the chemistry?"

Caroline's blood cooled. "Excuse me?"

"How's your chemistry with Ben?"

"Uh ... good?" How had Ben answered that question?

Kelly raised her eyebrows.

Caroline opted for total honestly. "Listen, I've known Ben since he was a kid. We know a lot about each other. It was easy to get comfortable, but that doesn't mean it's chemistry."

"Why did you ask Ben to dance with you?"

"Honestly?" Because he could bring a lot of attention but she couldn't.

"Please."

"He wasn't my first choice."

Kelly perked up. "Why not?"

"Like I said, we grew up together. Even though he's a star football player, he's always been my younger sister's friend. Plus, he'd recently been injured. I wasn't sure if he'd be interested."

"How did you convince him to participate?"

"I didn't have to convince him. He volunteered."

"Why?"

Caroline pointed at Ben. "You'd have to ask him."

"Any other thoughts on what it's like dancing with one of college football's former superstars?"

Caroline cringed. Was that really how the media would label him for the rest of his life? "I don't know about former football superstar, but Ben Allen the man is a star in his own right. He's sacrificing his time and privacy to raise funds for a bunch of women he met a few weeks ago. I don't think there's anything 'former' about his superstar status."

Kelly smiled. "No, of course not. Thank you for your time."

"Thank you for giving our event some publicity." Caroline unclipped the microphone before the camera guy could approach her and smacked it into his palm. Why would Ben voluntarily contact these people? And how had she ended up defending him? This was his mess.

As she walked toward her group, Ben pointed at their lane. "It's your turn. Everyone decided to eat while we waited." She stepped toward their lane, but Ben caught her arm. "Did you mean that?"

"Mean what?"

"About my superstar status?"

"Oh." She hadn't realized he was listening, not that it would have changed what she said. It wasn't like she had anything to be ashamed of. "Yes. I meant it."

He smiled, then glanced at her lips.

She glanced at his lips.

His smile widened. "You'd better go bowl."

"Don't let it go to your head." She walked away, listening to him chuckle behind her. Great. Now he thought he was winning her over. All she had to do was hide the fact that he was.

Chapter 15

Caroline stifled a yawn. She sat behind her desk and drained the last of her venti coffee, already planning to grab another at lunch. Too much bowling followed by too many dreams of Ben's lips had left her tired and frustrated. If the coffee didn't help, she'd see about an IV.

The phone rang, and she groaned. Eight o'clock was too early for a work call, but she answered anyway.

"Caroline, it's Anne from Human Resources."

"Anne, what's up?"

"John wants to get started on the new training as soon as possible. When can we meet to review the options?"

Caroline opened her email. A new one from Anne sent at nine o'clock the night before. She scanned it. Winter strategic planning retreat. Christmas party reminder. New management leadership training in the fall. Wow. "Options for which event?"

"All of them."

"I've had the Morrison Center reserved for the Christmas party since last Christmas, so that's not a problem. Let me read your email more carefully. I should be able to get some bids for the other events in the next couple of weeks."

"How about Monday?"

"That's only five days from now, including Saturday and Sunday. I can contact people, but I can't make them respond to me by then."

"Next Friday then."

Even though Anne couldn't see her, Caroline forced a smile. "Next Friday should be fine."

"Perfect. Ten a.m. in the conference room."

And that was that. Caroline hung up the phone as she read through the email. Good grief. The company was adding two new training events to the calendar during Caroline's busiest season in years. As usual, John wanted three options for each event, but according to the email, he wasn't sure if he wanted to go out of town, so Caroline needed to come up with local and out-of-town options. Lodging, meals, activities, not to mention finding the right training program.

All on top of mentor evaluations, the end-of-the-summer picnic, and the mid-year employee volunteer hours. Plus the dance-off and the Pathways grant she hadn't started yet. She was going to need more than coffee.

Chapter 16

Monday morning, Ben pulled into an empty parking space at the Morrison building. He snagged his lunch from the passenger seat before heading into the office. He'd be working with the marketing department this week. It had to be more exciting than accounting and underwriting. While he appreciated the chance to experience all the company's departments, he wasn't sure how much longer he'd survive the boredom.

"Hey, Ben! Wait up!"

He scanned the parking lot until he spotted a stocky man waving at him. Late thirties, maybe early forties with a bit of a stomach, but he moved easily enough. His clean-cut hair didn't move as he jogged the last few steps between them. Familiar, but Ben couldn't place the man.

"Scott Wahr, the Michigan Minute."

Ben clenched his fingers. "I'm not interested." Real journalists he could handle, but not the sneaky, gossipy kind. The Michigan Minute fit into the latter category. "And don't pretend like you know me." He turned his back on the man and marched toward the office.

Scott followed. "I just have a couple of questions about your new girlfriend."

"I don't have a girlfriend."

"So you're single, then?"

Dang it. Ben hadn't meant to give away any information. "No comment."

"Is it true the dance-off is a ruse and that you're secretly experimenting with dance therapy to mount a football comeback?"

"No comment."

"Does your girlfriend know you're planning to go back to the NFL when you're back in shape?"

Ben laughed. Where did they come up with that stuff? "No comment." Only a few more feet to the door.

"So you're not serious about the job offer with the Detroit Lions?"

Job offer? He couldn't ask, though. It would only encourage more questions. But what had he heard?

"So you *are* considering the job?"

"I didn't say that."

Scott stepped in front of him. "But you didn't say no comment either."

Ben rolled his eyes. "Fine. No comment." He stopped in front of the insurance building's double doors. "I need to go to work now. I trust that you won't follow me. I'll talk to security to make sure."

Scott opened his mouth to say something, but Ben didn't want to hear anymore. He stepped into the building. The receptionist eyed him from behind the desk, her gaze darting between him and the man outside.

"Good morning, Bridget. Will you do me a favor and not talk to that man about me? Even if he just wants to confirm that I work here, please say 'no comment.'"

Bridget picked up her cell phone and snapped a picture of Scott. "I'll pass along his photo. Make sure no one says anything."

"Thanks. I owe you."

Normally, Ben checked in with Caroline before he switched departments, but he didn't bother going to her office. He'd send her a text after he settled in at marketing.

He rode the elevator up two floors, and when the doors opened, a young man Ben recognized as an intern was waiting for him. "Hey, I'm Cole." The two shook hands before moving down the hallway. "The head of the department wanted to greet you himself, but they had an unexpected meeting this morning, so he sent me."

"I appreciate the welcome. How do you like working in marketing so far?"

"I love it. It's a small department, so I've had the chance to learn a lot." They entered an office similar to the accounting department but with fewer desks. Light gray cabinets and drawers with darker gray desktops. The same black leather chairs. They might work for most people, but Ben's giant build didn't quite fit.

Cole pointed to an empty desk along the far wall. "The meeting should be over in an hour, two tops. There's a marketing manual on the desk for you. It's more of a history of the Morrison marketing strategies. Just something to familiarize yourself with before everyone comes back." The intern returned to his desk on the other side of the office.

Ben sat and flipped through the marketing book, but nothing about it appealed to him. Not when he had access to a computer and there was a rumor about a job with the Detroit Lions. Just to be safe, he flipped open the history book while the computer started up. He did try to read the guide, but he couldn't shake Scott's words.

He logged in and searched for his name. Four hundred thousand results. He added "Detroit Lions" to the search box. Two hundred thousand. 'Ben Allen's Detroit Lion's job offer.' One hundred and fifty thousand. Most of the top results were the same as the previous search, but those weren't the results he wanted. If he'd gotten a job offer, it would be on the first page. No, he wanted to read the rumors.

He clicked through a few pages to find the more obscure articles. It wasn't until page four that he found something remotely related. The Big MAC Blog—All Things Mid-Atlantic Conference. Ben found the football tab and searched. In a post titled "Now What," the author speculated as to what some of the conference's top football players should consider doing if they didn't make the NFL cut. He recognized all the players' names. At the bottom, he found it.

> **Former Western Michigan University standout Ben Allen may have already found his calling. After a career-ending injury on the field, he's now on the dance floor raising funds and working with disabled women in his hometown. It's not just that the guy can dance (which, apparently, he can—he won the first month's dance-off). Videos like this one show that he also has a way with the ladies, even with their disabilities. With that kind of patience and heart, he could still make a career for himself in the NFL. Many teams—like Detroit's own Lions—run programs for disadvantaged and disabled youth. If Allen can redirect the skills he's learning on the dance floor, he might just be able to make it in the National Football League after all.**

A mixture of hope and frustration swirled through his chest. After the injury, his coach had mentioned recruiting and coaching positions with college teams, but Ben wanted to play. In the back of his mind, he knew many of the pro teams had charitable arms, but he'd never heard anything about full-time work with them, not that he'd have considered them anyway.

But that was before. Ben searched for volunteer opportunities, NFL foundations, and any other word combinations he could think of. Most of the team sites mentioned camps and charitable programs, but they didn't provide a lot of information. Just the basics about how players and teams served their communities. Open jobs for volunteers, but nothing about who ran the programs or how.

Then again, why should there be? Fans went to team websites for stats and schedules. How many people cared about summer kids' camps? Ben hadn't cared until Scott Wahr brought it up.

Did he care now?

He scrubbed a hand over his face. What was he doing?

He was a football player, not a coach or recruiter or camp organizer, and it wasn't like anyone had offered him one of those jobs. He looked at the marketing history. He closed the web browser and turned off the monitor. Time to accept what he couldn't change.

Caroline checked the time again. It was 5:20 p.m. Still no email. The hotel's event manager hadn't technically promised she'd send the retreat bid by the end of the day, but she'd said she'd try. Caroline couldn't be mad about not receiving something that had never been guaranteed, although it certainly would have helped keep her on track. Oh well. She'd come in early so she could edit the new employee handbook before the bids rolled in.

By the time she finally left her office, it was after five-thirty. She couldn't handle another fast-food meal, which effectively eliminated time for dinner. Her stomach growled. Skipping dinner wouldn't be such an issue if she hadn't already skipped lunch.

When she opened the car door, a hot blast of air greeted her. After turning on the air conditioner, she dumped her purse onto the passenger seat. Pens, wallet, hairpins, and receipts. Empty wrappers. Hiding under a notepad, she spotted the sharp edge of a foil package. Perfect!

The protein bar was smooshed like a pancake, but she didn't care. She peeled the wrapped off the melted bar, then licked the wrapper clean. Never had semi-sweet chocolate and dry, peanut-type filling tasted so good.

Someone knocked on her window.

Caroline dropped the melted bar onto her lap, chocolate-side down. Ben waved. She ignored the bar and rolled down the window. "What are you still doing here? We have practice in less than thirty minutes."

"I'm on my way there now. Why are you still here?"

She sighed. "Working late."

Ben pointed at the bar on her lap. "Is that your dinner?"

"What's left of it." She picked it up, leaving a smear of chocolate on her skirt. What a waste. She would have enjoyed eating that.

"Do you want to meet later so you can eat?"

"I don't have time to eat."

Ben frowned. "You need to eat."

"I did." She waved the wrapper in front of him.

He shook his head. "I'll see you at the studio."

Caroline put her car in reverse and backed out of her parking spot. When she pulled into the studio parking lot, her breath hitched. She didn't even remember the drive. She'd driven it often enough that she could have made it there in her sleep, but part of her worried that she actually *had* driven while sleeping. She didn't have time to worry about it, though. Ben would be pulling in soon, and she still needed to change.

By the time she stepped out of the dressing room, Ben was stretching in the dance studio. He didn't say anything, so she didn't. Instead, she walked to the stereo to queue up the music. A large meal replacement bar sat on the shelf beside the cell phone dock. Some of the tension eased out of her back when she saw it.

Kind and thoughtful. She was in trouble.

Chapter 17

The cool water washed over Caroline. After three tense dance rehearsals, she needed to cool off and refocus. Hopefully, Ben was doing the same, because tomorrow night they had dress rehearsal, and they had to be better. Each week the competition got a little better, so they had to as well. She needed to think of a better way to motivate him, which she'd do after her shower and a quick snack. She hadn't skipped any meals that day, but protein shakes and peanut butter sandwiches weren't cutting it.

After rinsing off the stress of the day, she ignored the sink full of dishes and opened the refrigerator. She cringed. She had planned on going grocery shopping until the need for a cold shower overwhelmed her. She could put together a mayo, mustard, and pickle sandwich, but nothing about that sounded good.

Things didn't look much better in the pantry. Pasta but no sauce. Rice. No beans. Canned peaches.

Caroline didn't have time to go shopping and she didn't want to leave the house at 7:30 at night. She hadn't touched the Pathways grant proposal since before starting dance rehearsals, and she still had bids to compile for Anne.

Time for backup. She pressed a number on her phone and waited. After three rings, Chris answered. "What's up?"

"What are you doing right now?"

"Watching a baseball game. What are you doing?"

"Standing in my kitchen hoping for a visit from the food fairy."

"What do you need?"

"Everything, but right now I'd settle for a twelve-inch Italian meat-eater's sub with provolone cheese."

"Want me to grab you any eggs or milk or anything?"

"Yes, to all of it."

"I'll pick up a few necessities and bring them over."

"Thank you." Caroline hung up, then noticed a missed video chat with Carmen. When was the last time they'd talked? Caroline couldn't remember. It wasn't easy coordinating schedules across time zones. It was definitely too late to call Germany, so she settled for a text.

> CAROLINE: SORRY I MISSED YOU. CRAZY AT WORK. COMPETITION NIGHT COMING UP! SHOULD SETTLE DOWN IN A FEW WEEKS. WILL TRY TO CALL BEFORE THEN. :)

That wouldn't make up for the weeks without talking, but Caroline felt good about making an effort. Sort of.

Pushing the guilt aside, she grabbed a can of soda from the fridge and sat in the corner of her couch. If she could write the grant proposal over the weekend, she could review it and finalize it in the next couple of weeks.

Wait, she couldn't write the proposal over the weekend. It was the art fair. She and Chris helped their mom every year. She couldn't skip that. Maybe if she helped Saturday, they wouldn't care if she skipped Sunday. Then she'd have a full day to write, after grocery shopping and cleaning. And doing the laundry. She was down to her last three pairs of clean underwear.

The true weight of her responsibilities pushed her deeper into the couch. She needed to re-evaluate her schedule. But first, she needed to print out the grant information.

She jotted notes on the page, searched for supporting research, found a few unrelated links that would be perfect for the employee retreat, and even googled music for next month's dance.

Someone knocked on her door.

Caroline didn't have time to set aside her laptop before Chris walked in. "How did you get here so fast?"

"So fast?" Chris tossed her a bag. "I was going to apologize for taking so long. What happened here?"

Caroline glanced at her clock and gasped. "Nine o'clock? I still have so much to do."

"Does that include cleaning because this place is a dump?"

"I know."

Chris set a larger bag on the counter. "I would expect to find Carmen's apartment like this, but not yours. Are you sick or something?"

"Not sick. Tired." Caroline set her computer aside and tore into the bag on her lap. She bit off a chunk of sub. Soft, crusty bread melted in her mouth seconds before she bit through layers of spicy meat. "This is amazing." Chris pulled milk, bread, eggs, coffee, cream, and cookie dough out of her bag. "You're my hero."

"That's sad." Chris put the groceries away before turning on the faucet. "Seriously, what's going on here?"

Caroline sighed. "I overcommitted myself." Again.

"So bad you can't even buy yourself food?"

"I keep meaning to go shopping, but I've been working late and then practicing, and by the time I'm done, I'm either so hungry I buy fast food, or I'm so tired all I can think about is going to bed."

"You hate fast food."

"I know. My stomach hates me right now."

"Order groceries."

"That still takes time, and I have to be here when they arrive."

"No, you don't."

Caroline groaned. "*I do.* There's a food thief in the apartment complex."

"Got it. Why didn't you ask anyone for help?"

"I did. I called you." Caroline tore off another chunk of her sandwich as Chris filled the sink with water and dish soap. "I didn't realize how bad it was until tonight."

"I don't know how this hasn't made you crazy. You're going to make yourself sick if you try to keep this up."

"You don't know that."

Chris thunked a plate in the dish rack. "You were sick every Christmas and spring break when you were in college. After every major dance competition, you got sick for a week. And when you decided to throw an over-the-top surprise party for Mom and Dad's anniversary, you insisted on doing everything yourself even though you were working and training, and you got so sick you couldn't even make it to the party. You push yourself until you make yourself sick. You have a very specific MO."

"My MO?"

"*Modus operandi*. I watch a lot of *Law and Order* reruns, but that's not the point. What if you push yourself so hard you get sick before the final dance-off?"

Valid question, but not a concern. "I've danced sick before."

"I'll bet Tony didn't appreciate it."

He hadn't. In fact, he'd refused to talk to her for a week, even while they practiced. He'd led her around the floor without so much as a hello. "It's not the best for dance partner dynamics, but I can do it."

"That's selfish."

The words smacked Caroline across the face. "Excuse me? I'm raising money for a nonprofit organization. How is that selfish?"

"Have you asked Ben if he wants to dance with you while you're sneezing all over him? Maybe the other dancers don't want to dance through your germ cloud."

"Ben's so competitive that he played football with a broken finger. He'd probably dance sick too."

"That doesn't mean he wants you pushing yourself to the point where you collapse."

"Don't be melodramatic. I'm not going to collapse."

Chris's face darkened as she banged dishes around. "First of all, you don't know that. With your history, you might. Secondly, why is it okay for you to help people and do things for others, but they can't do the same for you? Ask for help. Hire a housekeeper. Stop being a martyr."

Caroline's temper simmered as a dozen comebacks ran through her mind, but Chris had a point, not that Caroline would admit it out loud. Instead she said, "I'll try to make changes, but next week."

"Why wait?"

"The art fair. We can't miss it."

Chris grunted. "Shows how little you know about our mother. She would want you to rest."

"I've known her the longest, so I'm pretty sure I know her better."

"Obviously not, because I won't be at the art fair this weekend, and it was her idea."

"What?" Caroline almost dropped her sandwich. She was half shocked, half jealous. "Why?"

Chris's hands slowed in the dishwater. "There's a special training this weekend in Chicago. School districts have been seeing a lot of positive results after implementing high-intensity fitness into their curriculums. An expert's flying in from Virginia to talk about how it's impacted their district and to give tips on how to introduce it to others."

"Chris, that's incredible. Isn't that what you've been trying to do at school?"

"Yes, but I haven't had any luck. The athletic director is stuck in his old-school rut, and he doesn't want to hear anything about it."

"Is he going with you to the conference?"

She rolled her eyes. "Of course not, but I gave the information to the superintendent, and he's interested. He likes the idea of being the first district in the state to try something like that. Two other board members are going too, and they want me there so I can answer questions."

"How long ago did you find out about the conference."

"Six weeks ago."

"You're just telling us now?" Caroline's jealousy morphed into frustration.

"No, I'm telling *you* now. I told Mom about it as soon as I found out, and I told her I was going to skip the conference and meet with the board when they got back. She told me if I did, she'd withdraw from the art fair so I wouldn't have a reason to stay home."

"She did?" But they planned their summers around the art fair. Why hadn't anyone told her?

"Yes, and if you'd tell her about everything you've got going on and how tired you are—and especially how disgusting your apartment is—she'd let you out of this weekend."

Caroline slouched, trying to imagine a weekend with nothing to do. She couldn't. Even if she skipped the art fair, she'd spend the time working and feeling guilty about abandoning her mom. If she had been proactive like Chris and told her mom about her schedule earlier, maybe she could have found someone to fill in for her.

Chris sighed. "I can feel you guilt-tripping yourself into not calling Mom."

"It's the right thing to do." Wasn't it?

"For you. I should just call Mom and tell her what's going on."

Caroline's pulse spiked. "Don't you dare."

Chris held up her hands, a dishcloth dripping in one hand. "Don't worry, I won't tattle. But you need to tell her."

"I'll think about it."

Chris shook her head as she wiped down the counters. Caroline took advantage of the silence to finish her sandwich. It was the fuel she'd need to stay up and work. She'd call her mom later. Maybe.

Chapter 18

Thursday evening, Ben left the marketing office and made his way toward Caroline's. She sat at her desk, arms crossed on top of it with her head resting on them. Her ponytail fell forward, partially covering her face. He knocked lightly on the door frame. "Caroline?"

Her head popped up. Unfocused eyes looked around the room until she spotted him. "Ben, hi. What can I do for you?"

"Wanted to see if you want to grab some dinner before rehearsal. We could talk about which reporters are coming tomorrow, maybe decide if you want to talk to anyone."

She smiled—a real smile that lightened her face and crinkled the corners of her eyes. "I appreciate the offer, but I think I'm going to be here until I leave for rehearsal. I need to work on the Pathways grant proposal for a little while. After five, Morrison's quieter than the library."

He tried not to frown. Another late night meant … "Are you going to have time for dinner?"

She rolled her eyes. "Yes. I brought food with me."

Probably another meal replacement bar. He'd parked next to her car yesterday and noticed a pile of wrappers and Taco Bell bags on the floor. Not the greatest diet, but at least she was eating. Although, he could make sure she ate something of substance. "I'm going to head out then," he said. "I'll see you soon."

"Sounds good." She turned her attention to the papers on her desk.

Ben pulled out his phone and dialed a familiar number as he headed out of the building.

A white, Styrofoam container landed on Caroline's desk, startling her. Ben settled into the chair across from her with his own container. "What's this?" she asked.

"Dinner."

Her back tensed. "I told you I have dinner."

He glared at her. "A protein bar?"

"Peanut butter sandwich."

"Better, but it's not a Solito's wrap with homemade potato chips."

Her mouth salivated. "You went to Solito's?" She didn't wait for him to answer before she popped open the lid. There it was—the turkey pesto avocado wrap stuffed with spinach, shredded carrots, and Swiss cheese inside a rolled, grilled whole-wheat tortilla. Forgetting manners, Caroline bit into the wrap like her life depended on it. Perfection. "You're an angel."

"No, just a guy trying to make a good impression."

"Mission accomplished."

He winked.

She blushed. "This doesn't change anything."

"Of course not."

But the smirk on his face didn't match his words. "This isn't a date."

"I know. When we finally go on a date, you'll know. Trust me."

The anticipation that tickled Caroline's nerves surprised her, but she didn't want to think about it. Instead, she took another bite before reviewing the proposal draft she'd sketched out. She hated the redundancy of grant proposals but who was she to argue? If someone wanted to give Pathways ten thousand dollars, she'd write it in Sanskrit if they asked. After she figured out Sanskrit.

Ben crunched on a potato chip. She peeked up at him. From someplace, he'd produced a novel, which he read as he ate.

How was he the same kid who used to belch with Chris in the basement? And why had Caroline been avoiding him outside of dance practice? This was the most relaxed she'd felt in over a week.

She made notes on the proposal while she ate. It didn't take long to work her way through the first page, then the second, and onto the third.

"We should get going."

"What?" Caroline looked up, startled to find Ben sitting in the same chair and slipping a piece of paper between the pages of his book.

He pointed at the clock. "We should go."

Where had the hour gone? And how had she gotten so much done in such a short amount of time? "Wow. I'm glad you were watching the clock." She swept her papers into a pile. "You don't need to wait for me. I'll meet you at the opera house."

"I'll at least walk you out." Ben cleaned up their takeout containers while she gathered her things. In no time at all, her office was clean, and they were stepping into the fresh air. Another perfect northern Michigan evening.

When he headed to his truck, she reached into her car to grab her costume out of the backseat. The four-block walk would be good for her soul. With each step, the sunshine and energy of the city revitalized her soul. The soles of her shoes smacked quietly against the pavement as the slow-moving traffic buzzed around her.

Caroline stopped and closed her eyes, soaking in the atmosphere. It was already June, and it was the first time she'd stopped to soak in summer. She'd have to start taking her work home and onto her deck. Maybe she could figure out how to dance outside too.

Not wanting to be late to rehearsal, she reluctantly opened her eyes and continued on. As she left the parking lot and stepped onto the sidewalk, she smiled. Ahead of her, a tall, dark-haired man carried a Western Michigan University gym bag. "I guess great minds think alike," she said.

Ben turned, already smiling. "Parking downtown at this time of day is terrible. I didn't feel like fighting for a spot that's even further away from the opera house than the Morrison building."

She jogged to catch up. "Okay, maybe we don't think alike. I wanted to enjoy the weather."

"Me too. I miss being outside." He slowed his pace until she reached him, then they fell into stride with each other.

"I was just trying to think of a way we could practice outside."

"Is that possible?"

"Not unless someone wants to get hurt, or you want to build a dance floor in your parents' yard."

"I'm not sure I can talk them into that, but Annie would love it."

They walked together in silence, sidestepping tourists as they wove through town. When they crossed a busy intersection, Ben's hand pressed against the small of her back, guiding her through the meandering throng of people. She didn't need his help, but a wave of comfort enveloped her as he offered his assistance anyway.

It was a good thing her schedule didn't leave much time to think about Ben, because she was realizing how much she enjoyed thinking about him. And being with him. If she had the time, she might enjoy spending more time with him too, but to what end?

Her ex-boyfriends had done some damage to her confidence and ability to trust, not that she should compare Ben to either of them. Though several years younger, he was clearly a better man than both of them combined, but that didn't mean he would be in a few months. Brett and Chad had both presented the best versions of themselves at the beginning. What if Ben was doing the same? Caroline didn't know if she could survive another broken heart, not that she and Ben were even dating yet.

No, they weren't dating. Period. Man, she needed some sleep.

"What are you doing this weekend?"

Finally, a chance to refocus her thoughts. "I'm working with my mom at the art fair."

"Does she still make those inspirational signs?" They arrived at the opera house, and Ben opened the door.

"Yep. Chris usually works with me, but she's leaving town tomorrow, so it's me and my mom. I thought about asking if she could do it without me, but I think I'd like to spend some time outside this weekend."

"That sounds fun."

"It is. We look forward to it every year." They climbed the stairs together and walked backstage. As they neared the corner where they would split to go to their respective dressing rooms, Caroline's mind whirled with possibilities. Before she could reason with herself, her mouth rebelled against her better judgment. "Would you like to work the art fair with us?"

The corner of Ben's lips twitched. "I'd love to."

"It's not a date."

"Of course not."

"I'll text you the details later." She hurried away, trying to forget the pure joy on Ben's face. Her body worked on autopilot as she dressed for rehearsal. By the time she made it to the auditorium, Susan and Ben stood talking near the Pathways table. Something had Susan excited—her hands flapped so quickly she could have flown around the room. As soon as she saw Caroline, she rushed toward her.

"Caroline, I don't know how he did it, but that Ben of yours ..." Tears filled Susan's eyes. "We've received forty thousand dollars in online donations."

Caroline grabbed the back of a nearby chair to keep herself upright. "What?"

"That's just since last month."

"That's on top of the sixteen thousand?" Caroline did sit down this time.

"And that's just the total as of this morning. Who knows how much it is now?" Susan's face glowed in the dim ballroom as she pressed her hands against her chest. "We can fix the house. I don't even know what to say. We thought we'd have to give up some of the wish list, but I had no idea ... I never could have expected ..." Susan bent and hugged Caroline. "Thank you."

As quickly as the hug started, Susan stepped away, wiping her eyes as she returned to the Pathways table. Ben made his way to Caroline. He looked unreasonably good in black pants and a black shirt. It was his eyes, though, that captured her attention. They shifted back and forth as he looked at her. Heat spread through her cheeks, and she silently thanked the stage manager for keeping the lights low.

"I've never seen Susan so excited," she said. "I don't know how you did it, but thank you."

"I didn't do much. The press and public relations committees are doing most of the hard work. I'm just answering questions and posing for pictures."

"And changing the lives of at least four women, probably more." And if they could win the dance-off? Caroline's mind spun at the thought.

"Ladies and gentlemen, if you could please make your way to the stage, we'll run through the schedule and get you out of here as quickly as possible."

Instead of moving toward the front of the ballroom, however, Ben stepped toward Caroline. With the stage lights behind him, she could barely see his face. He stopped mere inches in front of her. The warmth from his presence tickled her skin. "As happy as I am to help the women of Pathways, and I'll forever be grateful to you for introducing me to them, I would do all of this just to see you smile."

His confession knocked the air out of her lungs. Before she could figure out how to breathe again, he turned around and walked away.

She was in so much trouble.

Chapter 19

Something clanged. Something else clattered. Caroline groaned as she swatted at her nightstand. She must have hit everything on the nightstand *except* her alarm clock. Peeling her eyes open, she scanned the bedroom until she found it across the room on her dresser, where she'd put it the night before, so she'd have to get out of bed to turn it off.

Her stupid love of the outdoors had done this to her. She could go outside and enjoy the weather without having to get up at the crack of dawn for an art fair. She peeked at the clock again. Okay, eight o'clock wasn't the crack of dawn, but it was too early for a Saturday morning, and yet still too late to help her mom set up the booth. She should have been there an hour ago.

Rolling out of bed, Caroline shuffled to the dresser and turned off the alarm. Why was it still ringing? Wait, was that her phone? There was no way she'd find it before voicemail picked up, so she decided to get dressed.

She was brushing her hair when her phone rang again. Running into the living room, she dumped out her purse. "Mom. What's up?"

"Just checking in. You said you'd be here by seven."

Oops. "Are you sure?"

"Yes, I'm sure. Are you okay?"

"I'm fine, but late, apparently." She swept everything back into her purse. "I'm on my way."

"Don't worry. Everything's under control here. I was hoping you could pick up some coffee on the way."

"Sure."

"A large coffee with two creams and a large, iced vanilla coffee, please."

"You need two?"

"One for me, one for Ben."

Caroline's heart trilled. "Ben's there?"

"He picked me up at the house this morning and helped me set up the booth."

A kaleidoscope of butterflies swarmed Caroline's stomach. She tried to steady her voice. "How nice."

"Hurry up now. Ben brought doughnuts, but we're waiting for the coffee before we enjoy them."

"I'll be right there." Caroline's hands shook as she disconnected the call. What was she getting herself into?

She dropped her phone into her purse, locked the apartment, and headed to the coffee shop. The line moved slowly, but she was back in her car with three cups of coffee by eight-thirty. Even though the art fair was barely a mile away, it took another fifteen minutes before she found a parking spot and her mother's booth. Ben and Mom sat in stadium chairs in the shade of a nearby tree.

Shoppers wandered around the park. Only a dozen or so customers visited the dozens of booths, but thousands of people would go through by the end of the weekend. Caroline stepped under her mom's canopy as two women stepped out.

"Hi, honey." Mom smiled as she stood. "Better late than never, I suppose."

"Sorry about that. At least, I brought caffeine." She hugged her mom. "Are there still doughnuts?"

Finally Forever

Ben reached under his chair and picked up a waxed paper bag. "I didn't know what everyone liked, so I bought chocolate frosted."

"Any doughnut is a good doughnut."

Mom took her coffee and started walking away. "I'm going to find Donna's booth. Can you kids cover this while I'm gone?"

"We'll be fine, Mom."

Her mother gave a quick wave before disappearing around the corner.

Caroline sat next to Ben and handed him his coffee. "Still trying to convince me you're not a morning person?"

He passed her a pastry. "Extremely motivated."

Not sure how to respond, she bit into the treat, but Ben's proximity dried out her mouth. She chugged her coffee, but the burning liquid scalded her tongue. She spit everything out as she tried to cool her mouth.

"Are you okay?" He patted her back, but his hand made her more uncomfortable. She wheezed in a breath. "Caroline?"

"I'm fine." She sputtered, trying to breathe in cool air while dislodging doughnut bits from her airway. "It's been a long time since I had a doughnut. I'll remember how to eat it eventually."

He laughed as he handed her a bottle of water. "It's like riding a bike."

"Thanks." Her hand trembled as she gripped the bottle.

"Are you sure you're okay?"

"Would you believe me if I said I was nervous?"

"About what?"

She sipped the water as she prepared herself to confess. He deserved the truth. "I'm nervous about you."

He smiled.

She rolled her eyes. "Go ahead. Soak it up."

"I'm not soaking anything up."

"Then why are you smiling?"

"Because you're human."

Not the response she'd expected. "What's that supposed to mean?"

"You're smart and considerate. You're generous with your time. You're beautiful. And you're nervous about being alone with me at an art fair." He leaned toward her. "Now that I know you're not perfect, maybe I can convince you to overlook our small age difference and give me a chance."

She leaned away from him. "I'm never going to be perfect."

"I'm never going to be older than you."

She laughed despite her nerves. "How can you be this mature when you're just out of college?"

"My parents deserve all the credit."

"How's it going living with them?" She couldn't imagine living with her parents again, especially ones as conservative as Ben's.

But he relaxed in his chair. "I had two options. Go into debt renting a place I couldn't afford or live with my parents for a few months while I save up some money."

"You don't have a savings account?" So much for a responsible young man.

He shook his head.

"How have you not saved any money?"

"What money? By the time I was old enough to drive, football was everything. I trained year-round, so I never had a summer job, and I didn't have time for one during the school year. Then I went to college, and football *was* my job."

That had never occurred to Caroline. "I thought my dance training was intense, but at least I was able to work while I trained. I can't imagine finishing college with nothing."

"There are pros and cons. I might not have any money, but I also don't have any student loan debt."

Her heart palpitated. What would that be like? "My student loan payments are almost as much as my rent."

He let out a low whistle. "I can't imagine trying to pay that off with what I make at Morrison."

"I can't imagine living with my parents. Was it hard moving home again?"

He slouched in his chair as two older women entered their booth. "It still is. I was expecting to be living in my own apartment in the city paid for by NFL money, not down the hall from Annabelle."

"How are you doing with that?"

"Some days are easier. I keep reminding myself that in less than a year, I'll have enough saved to move out."

"You really didn't have anything?"

He shook his head. "When I was twelve, I started saving for a truck. I paid cash for it when I graduated."

"That's impressive."

"I wanted to spend the money years ago, but even after Western offered me a full-ride scholarship, my parents reminded me I couldn't spend money like I had a professional contract until *after* I signed a professional contract. Until then, I was a poor college student like anyone else. It used to irritate me because I thought my folks didn't think I could make it in the pros, but now I'm thankful."

The shoppers each picked up some artwork, so Caroline stood to help them. She tried to make small talk, but she wasn't paying attention. Ben's story kept replaying in her mind. What a completely different experience from her own and not at all what she'd expected to hear.

"Honey, are you okay?"

"Excuse me?" Caroline blinked away the brain fog as she refocused on the customers.

"My change?"

She looked at her hands, which still held cash that was not hers. "I'm sorry. I got lost in my thoughts."

"I can imagine it's hard to concentrate with a young man like that hanging around." The silver-haired woman winked at Caroline. "Put him out front, and you'll have women stop by just to say hi to him."

Heat consumed Caroline's face. "I'm sure he'll be flattered to hear you say so." She slid each hand-painted sign into its own bag before handing them to their new owners. "If things get slow this afternoon, I'll move his chair."

Both ladies laughed as they carried their goods to the next booth. When Caroline walked back to her seat, the smirk on Ben's face confirmed that he'd heard the whole conversation. Not willing to stroke his ego, she dropped back into her chair and stuffed a doughnut into her mouth.

"I wonder how much money I could help your mom make today."

Caroline rolled her eyes. "Now you're going to use your fame to sell motivational signs?"

"No, I'm using my fame to help raise money for Pathways. I'd be using my good looks to help your mom."

Ignoring him, she pulled out her phone. "I haven't checked my email yet. Did Susan send an update with last night's totals?"

"Not that I saw, but last month, she didn't send the official count until Saturday afternoon."

"Caroline, sweetheart, could you and Ben run to the hardware store for me?" Mom whooshed back into the booth. She sat in the empty chair on the other side of Caroline as she waved at passing customers.

"What do you need?"

"A tarp."

"Why?"

"It's not for me, it's for Donna. I'm concerned about her paintings. Her tent's not big enough for her to keep everything under it, so she has some paintings and reproductions in a crate behind it. If we get any rain, they could get ruined."

Puffy, white, cotton-ball-like clouds floated overhead. "I don't think it's supposed to rain this weekend."

"You never know, and Donna's working by herself, so she can't go get a tarp. I told her I'd bring one back for her, but I really should be at the booth." Mom reached into her pocket and pulled out a twenty-dollar bill. "It doesn't have to be big. A four-foot by four-foot tarp should be big enough."

"I'll be back in a few minutes." Caroline started to stand.

"Take Ben with you."

She froze. "Why?"

"You never know when you'll need help."

With a tarp? Caroline glared at her mom.

She winked.

Caroline's patience stewed. After two failed engagements, her mother should know better.

"I can drive." Ben's voice pulled Caroline back into the moment.

Mom smiled. "Take your time."

Chapter 20

Ben had to stop himself from whistling as he and Caroline walked down the sidewalk and away from the art fair. Not that he wanted to skip the art fair—he'd enjoyed everything about it so far—but he was about to be alone with Caroline. No work. No dancing. Just the two of them being Ben and Caroline.

She stopped walking at an intersection and looked up at him. Her hair hung like a curtain around her shoulders. He'd never seen it like that before, and he'd been having a hard time not staring at her, trying not to memorize the way her tresses moved with her and around her.

"Ben?"

"Yeah?"

"Which way?"

"Which way what?"

"To your truck?"

Oh, right. He needed to focus. "This way." He took advantage of the opportunity to rest his hand on her back and guide her to where he'd parked. "You look nice this morning."

She ran her hand over her hair, pulling it over her shoulder and twisting it around her hand. "Thanks. So … how's Annabelle?"

"Sleeping. She was pretty wound up last night. I have no idea what time she finally went to bed."

"I'm always wound up after a competition. What about you?"

He shrugged. "I've only done this twice."

Fair. "What did you do after football games?"

"Half the time I was traveling, so I listened to music on the bus. The rest of the time, I went home and tried to catch up on classwork."

She looked at him, eyebrows raised. "No frat parties?"

He cringed. "Houses full of drunk people? No thanks."

"So you did homework?"

The disbelief in her voice irritated him. When they reached his truck, he yanked the door a little harder than necessary. "Contrary to popular belief, football players still go to class, but we also train and practice full time, which means staying up after games and skipping parties." He tamped down his annoyance as Caroline climbed into the car. He should have opened her door, but he needed to calm down. He slid into his seat, still stewing.

"I'm sorry."

That turned down the heat a bit as he pulled out and headed to the store. "More players earn their degrees and get jobs than the ones who make it to the NFL. It's just that they aren't the ones who make headlines. I'm used to people misjudging me, and I usually don't care, but ..."

She swallowed. "But you do now?"

He parked and turned off the truck. Those brilliant eyes twinkled at him. No bright blue eye makeup or black lines on her lids. Just her crystal-blue, God-given eyes surrounded by glowing skin framed by chocolate-brown hair. And two full, pink lips.

Lips that had already asked him to wait but then invited him to the art fair. He'd been right not to date in school. He didn't understand women.

Shaking his head, Ben hopped out of the truck. "We'd better get that tarp and get back." He didn't wait for her—couldn't wait for her—as he headed toward the store. He needed space to figure out what was going on.

Quick footsteps padded behind him, getting louder until Caroline appeared beside him. "Is everything okay?"

Hardly. He didn't know what to say, so he said, "Fine."

Her steps faltered, but she kept his pace. "Are you sure?"

Mindful of the people around them, Ben took Caroline's hand and led her across the parking lot to the side of the store and out of the public's view. He might not get her alone like that again, and he wanted answers. "What do you want, Caroline?"

Confusion clouded her face as her eyebrows pulled together. "A tarp?"

"With me. What do you want with me? I thought you invited me to help this weekend because you were done pretending like you aren't interested in me, but ..." He closed his eyes, trying to rein in his frustration. "You obviously have ideas about what kind of person you think I am, so why did you invite me here?" Opening his eyes, he focused all his attention on her. Their size difference made dancing interesting, but he'd never been as aware of it as he was in that moment. Slowly lifting a hand, he touched the ends of her hair, wanting to touch her but not wanting to scare her. And needing to make sure she knew exactly how he felt.

"I like you. I want to take you out to dinner and watch movies with you. I want to see what could happen between us, and I thought maybe you wanted that too, but ..."

Caroline wrapped her arms around herself. Her gaze dropped to his chest. "I like you too," she whispered.

The air around them stilled.

She shuddered as she took a long breath. "But I've had my heart obliterated. Twice. If I let this get serious and I'm broken again ..." When she finally looked at him, her eyes misted. "If we start something and it fails, I don't think I'd recover because"—she swallowed—"because I already care more for you than I ever did for Brett or Chad."

"Caroline." He didn't know what else to say. She'd given him the most amazing gift with that admission, and he wanted to return it. "I've never dated before."

Her eyes snapped up to his. "You've never been on a date?"

"I've been on a few, but only because someone else asked me. I've never asked a girl out."

"Why not?"

"I never liked anyone enough to spend my free time with them."

"But you want to spend your free time with me?"

"I'm trying to free up more time so I can spend it with you."

The faintest curl pulled at her lips. "I have baggage."

He risked a step closer. "Nothing about you feels like baggage."

"I might want to go slow."

He smiled. "I've waited twenty-three years to finally ask a girl out. I can be patient."

One more step. Close enough to wrap his arms around her, to pull her against him, but he satisfied himself with rubbing his thumbs across the tops of her hands. A tremor rippled through her fingers. "I have some free time tonight," he said. "Would you like to go out with me?"

"Yes."

His lips begged to taste hers, but he pushed back the urge and instead pressed a kiss to the back of her hand. "I'll pick you up at seven. Now let's get that tarp."

Chapter 21

Caroline checked her reflection one last time. What was she so worried about? It was dinner with Ben. She'd eaten with him before, and he'd assured her several times it would be a casual date. That did nothing to calm her nerves.

Not wanting to appear too formal or too eager to impress, she'd already tried on and discarded four outfits. Now she was back in the same outfit she'd worn to the art fair. Maybe she should reconsider.

Someone knocked on the door.

Not someone. Ben.

Caroline ran a hand over her French braid, making sure it was secure as she walked across the apartment. With a deep breath, she opened the door to the unknown.

Tall, tan, and handsome, Ben smiled at her. "Hi."

Her heart fluttered. "Hi."

"Are you ready?"

"I am. I think. I don't know because I don't know where we're going. Do I look ready?"

"You look amazing."

She drew in a calming breath. "Then I guess I'm ready." She grabbed her purse and keys. "Do I need to bring anything else?"

"We'll be outside if you think you'll need a coat."

"I should be fine."

Ben stepped aside so she could lock her apartment, but he didn't go far. Summoning every ounce of gumption she could muster, she slipped her hand around his bicep. "Where are we going?"

"That depends. Do you want options, or would you like me to pick a place?"

"Options." She needed something she could control.

He led her down the stairs and out to his truck. "There's a band playing on the deck at this restaurant in Elk Rapids, or there's the patio at the new restaurant downtown. There's also a baseball game tonight if you want to go."

The first two sounded romantic, but the baseball game sounded fun. Was he hoping she'd pick one over the other? "What do you want to do?"

"I want to go wherever you want to go, but if I was by myself, I'd go to the game."

Caroline smiled. "Good, because I'd like to go there too."

"Then we'll go." It took ten minutes to get to the ballfield and another five to get inside. Ben led her to the concession stand. "What would you like for dinner?"

"It's a baseball game. I think we're required to eat hot dogs and peanuts."

"Agreed." While he ordered their food, she watched the teams warm up until he handed her a cardboard tray with a large soda, a foil-wrapped hot dog, and a bag of peanuts. A small plastic cup contained a variety of single-serve condiments. "Can I get you anything else?"

"This is great, thanks."

He motioned to the left. "Then follow me."

They sat past third base behind the home team's dugout. The stadium was less than a quarter full, so the empty seats around theirs provided a bit of privacy amid

Finally Forever

the crowd. After the national anthem and starting lineups, Caroline settled into her seat with dinner on her lap. The muted slap of the baseball in the catcher's mitt reminded her of the hundreds of softball games she'd watched Chris play. Games where she often saw Ben with his friends or her parents.

He settled beside her. "Be honest. Did you pick the game because I said I wanted to come, or do you want to be here?"

Caroline squirted mustard onto her hotdog. "And pass up a chance to eat the best hot dog in Grand Traverse County?" To make her point, she stuffed half of the hotdog into her mouth.

Ben laughed. "Do you come to many games?"

"Not as many as I'd like. I love the ballfield, though. Even when there's a big crowd, there's something peaceful about being here."

"There's definitely a different atmosphere on the ball diamond than on the football field."

"That's right. You played baseball in high school, didn't you?"

He nodded as he bit into his hotdog.

"But football won."

"It did, although as soon as my knee gave out, my first thought was that I should have stuck with baseball."

"Do you regret playing football?"

He looked her in the eye. "I don't regret anything that got me here."

How did he do that? "You know, for someone who's never dated, you certainly are smooth."

He leaned onto the armrest between them, testing the boundaries of her personal space. "I've had years to save all my best lines." His gaze flickered to her lips. "I tried not to think about it before, but I'm suddenly quite anxious to practice everything I've missed out on."

Aware of his gaze, Caroline licked her lips. Ben sucked in a quiet breath. She'd never been overly flirty before, but seeing the influence she had on Ben, she understood why other women embraced the skill.

Maybe her age and experience gave her the confidence. If she was honest with herself, maybe she was as anxious as Ben to practice the whole dating thing. Ben didn't know what he was missing, but Caroline did. She could still remember the warmth of cuddling on the couch and the security of having a strong arm wrapped around her.

And the sweetness of a first kiss.

Neither of them moved as a bat cracked on the field. People cheered and music pulsed through the speakers, but Ben and Caroline looked only at each other. His hand cupped her cheek as he leaned forward. To encourage him, she closed the distance between them until she could smell the relish on his breath.

"I'm going to kiss you now."

She nodded.

His lips brushed hers, the barest of touches, yet every nerve sparked to life. Caroline's eyes fluttered closed, and he kissed her again. Ben's hand slid across her skin to the back of her neck, his fingers threading into her hair, his lips softly tugging at hers. When he finally pulled away, Caroline shivered. He may not have dated much, but the man could kiss.

When she opened her eyes, he dropped another soft kiss against her lips. "I had planned to do that when I took you home. I didn't mean to kiss you in public."

She smiled. "I hadn't planned to kiss you at all."

"At least I'm being honest."

"I *am* being honest. I may have thought about kissing you, but that doesn't mean I was planning to."

He smiled. "Good thing I planned ahead."

Heat filled her cheeks, but she didn't look away. "Maybe we should watch the game."

He faced the field, but not before dropping an arm around her shoulders first. Caroline chuckled at the stereotypical move, then she leaned into him. Regardless of what happened later, she'd enjoy what was happening now.

Ben ran his fingers through the ends of Caroline's hair. It was softer than he'd expected, yet it slid through his fingers like liquid. He couldn't seem to stop touching it.

She didn't complain. Actually, she hadn't said anything since the sixth inning. Somehow, she'd managed to fall asleep against him despite the cheering, the music, and the hard plastic seats. He'd loved every minute of it. He'd have to wake her up soon, though. There were only two outs left.

The home team's relief pitcher threw another strike, and the small crowd roared.

Caroline flinched.

Ben looked down at her as her eyes fluttered open. "Hi," he said.

She pushed herself up, looking around. "I'm sorry."

"Don't be. I don't mind."

She straightened her clothes and patted her cheeks. When she ran her hands through her hair, she looked at Ben. "What happened to my braid?"

"I couldn't help myself." He handed her a black elastic band, not in the least bit sorry.

She took it back and twisted her hair up into a sloppy bun. "Why didn't you wake me?"

"You've been tired for two weeks. I figured you needed rest. Besides, it's kind of flattering to know that you're comfortable enough with me to fall asleep."

She blushed. "You're a very comfortable person. Thanks for being my pillow."

"Anytime."

He missed her nearness when she moved to the edge of her seat for the last few minutes of the game. Time sped up as the home team won, and he led her out of the stadium. The ten-minute drive back to her house took ten seconds. He tried to think of a way to stretch their time together, but she climbed out of the truck while he was thinking. Before he knew it, they stood on the landing by her door. He stayed on the step below her to keep Caroline at eye level.

She twirled a piece of hair. "I'd invite you in, but it's after eleven, and I haven't cleaned my apartment recently."

"I'll see you tomorrow then?"

She cringed. "What?"

He braced himself for battle. "At the art fair."

"You don't have to—"

He covered her mouth with his hand. "I'm helping, Caroline. And I'd like to take you to dinner afterward."

"I don't—"

He raised his eyebrows.

She rolled her eyes, then pushed his hand away. "I'll see you at the art fair, but I *need* to work on this grant proposal tomorrow night—I should have been working on it tonight—so no dinner."

Ben wanted to convince her to skip the art fair to work on the proposal tomorrow, but she would never go for it. Now that he'd spent a non-dancing evening out with her, he wasn't sure he could just go home and wait until she had free time, especially since it didn't sound like she had much. He grinned. "Fine, but I'd like to take you out again sometime this week." He shuffled closer. "I had fun tonight. I'm hoping to repeat the experience."

Her cheeks turned pink. "I had a good time too."

He wrapped his arms around her and pulled her close until she rested her head on his shoulder. The gentle puffs of her breath warmed his skin. He could have stayed like that for hours. Instead, he loosened his grip and stepped back a step. "I suppose this is when I should kiss you good night."

She smiled. "I suppose so."

"And tell you that I'll call you later."

"That sounds about right."

"But then this would be like any other date."

Caroline shrugged. "I guess it's pretty standard."

Ben took another step back. "You don't get to be a professionally recruited football player by settling for standard." One more step back.

Caroline crossed her arms. "That's it?"

"I'll see you tomorrow."

"Sure ... okay." She pressed her lips together and pulled her keys out of her purse.

Perfect. "Caroline?"

"Yeah?"

He smiled at her. "I'll bet you spend the rest of the night thinking about me."

"That's presumptuous."

"Maybe, but now aren't you curious to know what that goodnight kiss would have been like?"

She gaped.

He winked. "I'll see you tomorrow."

Chapter 22

Sunday morning, Caroline sat on the edge of her bed watching the alarm clock. As soon as it hit seven o'clock, the alarm wailed. She turned it off and rushed to the bathroom.

Ben and his stupid non-kiss.

He was right. She'd thought about it most of the night, and as soon as she opened her eyes, thoughts of what hadn't happened flooded her mind.

After a quick shower, she dressed in her most flattering blue, sleeveless shirt—the same color as her eyes—and white shorts. She dried and curled her hair until it bounced around her face in soft waves. Rosy-pink blush on her cheeks. Light gray and blue eye shadow, liner, and mascara to highlight her eyes. Clear gloss accentuating her lips. She smiled at her reflection. Today *she'd* give *Ben* something to think about.

When she walked up to her mom's booth, her mom whistled. "Wow, look at you. I don't suppose this has anything to do with Ben coming today?"

"He's Chris's friend. And how did you know he'd be here?"

"He called to see if he could bring anything this afternoon. I've always liked him." Mom picked up her portable worktop and calligraphy pens. "I need to work on some new pictures now."

The morning flew by as Caroline sold and moved drawings. When the sun was high in the sky, her stomach growled. "Mom, I need to eat. Do you want anything?"

"Whatever's fine."

Caroline cut across the park to the food court as she tried not to think about Ben. The line crawled forward. She tapped her foot, anxious to get back to the booth before he arrived. She wanted to control the surprise. By the time she returned, Ben was sitting in the chair beside her mom, and next to him sat Annabelle.

Annabelle saw Caroline first, jumping out of her seat and waving. "Caroline! I hope you don't mind that Ben brought me. He said it would be okay."

"It's fine. If I'd known you were going to be here, I would have bought you an elephant ear too."

The girl shook her head. "I don't want to get oil on my hands. Your mom said she'd show me how to do calligraphy."

"That sounds like fun."

Mom pointed at the food. "Let Ben have that. I'll eat later. Now, young lady, you come over here." Her mom and Annabelle huddled their chairs around a small tabletop.

Ben stood as Caroline approached. He didn't take his eyes off her.

Maybe this approach would work better after all. She offered him some food. "Want one?"

He stared at her silently.

"Ben?" She batted her eyelashes, relishing her success. "Is something wrong?"

"You look ..." He swallowed.

"I look what?"

He shook his head. "There aren't words."

She stepped close and handed him a plate. "I wanted to make sure you'd be thinking about me later."

He blinked, then he tipped his head back and laughed. When had that sound become so sensual? When he calmed, he looked past her. She followed his gaze. Mom slowly drew a line across a sheet of paper as Annabelle copied her technique.

With both of them occupied, Ben kissed Caroline. "It's good to see you again."

He must have led the after-church crowd to the art fair because Caroline had only taken two bites of her food before the stream of customers started. Ben turned on the charm, smiling at each visitor and answering as many questions as he could. As customers bought pictures, Caroline filled the empty spaces with other copies of her mom's work.

For as much as the morning had dragged on, the afternoon raced by. Annabelle wrote her favorite quote in shaky calligraphy, and Caroline's mom helped her pick an eggplant-colored mat to frame the artwork. Before Caroline knew it, the local church bells tolled five o'clock. Annabelle folded chairs while Ben took down the tent and Caroline packed boxes full of artwork.

"I'll bring my car around." Mom took off.

"I can't believe I learned how to do calligraphy. This is so cool." Annabelle showed Ben. "Are we going anywhere else today? It's okay if we don't because I want to go home and practice some more. Caroline's mom gave me two pens and some paper. She said she'd give me lessons."

Caroline chuckled as Annabelle rambled.

Ben rolled his eyes. He motioned toward his sister. "Did you talk this much when you were her age?"

"I did, and there were three of us."

"I can't imagine." He dropped a kiss onto her cheek. "Thanks for giving her something to talk about."

It took a second for Caroline to register the silence. When she looked at Annabelle, the girl was staring at them, her face expressionless. Caroline shot a glance at Ben. He was busy trying to fit the tent back in its bag. She jabbed him with her elbow. When he looked at her, she pointed at his sister.

He turned to Annabelle. "What?"

Annabelle stared at Caroline. "Did my brother kiss you?"

"Yes."

"Are you two dating?"

Caroline's stomach fluttered. "Yes."

The girl's forehead wrinkled. "Do you guys kiss a lot?"

"Um ..." What should she say?

"Because I don't get it. Skyler tried to kiss me at school once, so I pinched him. It just looks so sloppy and gross."

"It is." Ben zipped up the tent bag. "You should avoid it until you're at least twenty-five."

Annabelle planted her fists on her hips. "You're not even twenty-five yet. I don't think I should be talking to you about this anyway. You're a boy. You probably don't understand kissing the way girls do."

Caroline tried not to laugh as her mom's silver minivan backed up near them.

"I can't thank you kids enough," Mom said as she climbed out. "I'll be home in no time."

Ben picked up three boxes. "Do you need any help unloading?"

"No, no. Gary will be there. He'll help."

Caroline carried the chairs to the van. Ben managed to move everything else in two trips. Her mom hugged everyone before climbing in and driving away. As she did,

Annabelle wrapped an arm around Caroline. "Ben says we need to go home."

"That's probably a good idea. I have a lot of work to do tonight, so I won't be very good company." And she didn't want to revisit the kissing conversation.

"Thanks for letting me come today."

"Thank you for coming."

"I'll start walking to Ben's truck so you guys can kiss if you want." Annabelle shuffled away, her calligraphy supplies clutched to her chest. Heat engulfed Caroline's face.

Ben groaned. "I don't know what my parents are going to do with her. I'm ready to send her to a convent for the next ten years. I don't know how your parents survived three daughters."

Caroline laughed. "You're a good brother to worry, but if your parents are raising her the same way they raised you, I don't think you have much to worry about."

"I hope." He sighed. "I should let you get to work."

"Thanks." She meant it, but not completely. The last thing she wanted to do was go home and work. Especially now that she had options.

Ben kissed her cheek. "Just in case Annie's watching. I'll see you soon."

"Practice tomorrow at six?"

"Sure." He winked before jogging after his sister. Caroline watched until they walked out of sight. Then she picked up her purse and headed home.

She loved her apartment and the view, but it had never been so depressing to walk through her front door. In the two weeks since Chris had been there, the sink had refilled itself with a stack of dirty dishes. Dirty footprints and spilled food marked the tile floors. The once thin layer of dust had grown into an opaque film covering her furniture. And that was just the living room. A pile of laundry covered the guest room bed.

Laundry!

Caroline ran to the utility room and lifted the washing machine lid. A waft of musty air pushed her back. She couldn't even remember when she'd put the load in the machine, not that it mattered. Peeling the towels away from the sides, she started the machine again. She'd have to leave herself a note so she didn't forget to dry them.

After changing into running shorts and a T-shirt, she entered the guest room to attack the rest of the laundry. She was sorting through clothes when someone knocked on her door.

It was like the universe didn't want her to finish the grant proposal. Ever. "Just a minute!" After making sure the laundry piles didn't fall, Caroline shuffled to the front door and opened it. Joy forced up a smile. "Ben."

His arm snaked around her waist as the other hand threaded into her hair, pulling her against him to kiss her. Her heart thundered—shocked, relieved, and thrilled to be with him, wrapping her arms around his neck. His lips claimed hers repeatedly. Caroline surrendered, clinging to him as she shuddered in his arms.

When he finally relaxed his hold on her, his lips slowed in their caresses, but he didn't pull away. His breath came quickly, matching the ferocious tempo of her pulse. He smiled against her lips. "I've been thinking about that since last night."

She returned the smile. "Thank you for not kissing me like that in front of your sister. I'm not sure how I'd explain that one." As quickly as the thrill arrived, it faded. "Not that

Finally Forever

I wouldn't take a kiss like that anytime, but what are you doing here? I told you I can't do dinner tonight. I have—"

He pressed his lips to hers again before taking a small step back. "I know, you have the grant, but I have a confession. I've been talking to your sister."

The last ember of thrilling died out. "About us?"

"Not intentionally."

"What does that mean?"

He led her to the dining room table and pulled out a chair. "It means we were talking, and she might have mentioned her late-night sub delivery to you."

"And?"

"And she asked me to stop over to see how you're doing. She said you can get singularly focused and not see what's going on around you." Ben scanned the apartment for the first time since stepping inside. "I see what she means."

Embarrassment engulfed her. "I would have cleaned if I'd known you were coming."

"I think that was Chris's point. She doesn't want you to worry about it, so she sent me over to help."

"What?" Caroline didn't know if she should scold or thank her sister. Either response would have to wait until after the humiliation of Ben scrutinizing the layers of filth in her apartment.

"I also brought you dinner."

Relief consumed her as she finally sank onto the chair. Between his help and Chris's interference, she might just survive the summer. The relief bubbled up in her eyes.

"Where do you want me to start? Do you want to eat first or ... are you crying?"

Caroline sniffed as she shook her head.

He wrapped his arms around her. "Will you let me help?"

She nodded. "Thank you." She hugged him back, letting his energy soak into her.

"Are you hungry? Do you want to eat first?"

Caroline leaned back to look at Ben. "Why are you doing this?"

He pushed a strand of hair away from her damp eyes. "Because I want to."

"But why?"

"I like being with you, even if that means cleaning so you can work. Maybe if I help out, you'll have some free time for another date."

Closing her eyes, Caroline leaned her forehead against Ben's chest. "You're too much."

He kissed the top of her head. "I hope it's a good too much."

"It is." Forcing herself away from him, Caroline stood and wiped the tears from her eyes. "I'm going to get to work. Then we'll eat. Maybe we can salvage some of tonight for a movie."

"I'd like that." Ben headed to the kitchen as Caroline gathered all her grant and research papers. She sat at the table to work, but her gaze kept making its way to Ben. His broad shoulders and narrow hips moved easily through her kitchen, cleaning dirty dishes while pans heated on the stove. He glanced over at her, and Caroline blushed to have been caught watching him.

This wasn't going to work.

Restacking her papers, she gathered them to her chest before heading into the kitchen. Ben stopped. She rested a hand on his forearm and stood on her toes to brush a kiss against his cheek. "I'm having a hard time concentrating, so I'm going to work in my bedroom until dinner's ready. Is that okay?"

"Of course. Do whatever you need to."

She took her work into her bedroom but left the door open. Something about the sound of Ben's movements calmed her heart. After spreading her work out across her bed, Caroline closed her eyes and listened to the amazing man in her kitchen. What had she done to deserve him?

Caroline yawned, stretching her back and arms to loosen her tight muscles. Her room was still dark, so it had to be early. Or late? Rolling over, she looked at her clock. One o'clock. In the morning?

She bolted upright. How could it be morning? Ben was cooking dinner. She was working on the grant. Things needed to be done!

Jumping out of bed, she peeked into the living room. Her clean living room. Light from the parking lot brightened the space. Turning on the nearest lamp, Caroline tried to figure out what had happened.

The dirt-free tile squeaked beneath her bare feet. Pillows straightened. Blankets folded. Coasters stacked on a recently dusted coffee table. Everything shined or sparkled. Not a speck of dust to be seen. Diagonal stripes marked her carpet. She'd slept through the vacuum cleaner?

She checked the bathroom. The familiar scent of lemons and bleach tickled her nose. All her make-up and hair products were still on the counter but were neatly organized. She lifted the lid and checked behind the curtain—he'd even cleaned her toilet and shower.

Her stomach roared.

Too bad she'd slept through dinner. Someone else's home-cooked meal would have been amazing, but she had yogurt in the refrigerator. Making her way to the kitchen, she admired Ben's thoroughness. He hadn't just cleaned her dishes—he'd put everything away.

When she opened the refrigerator, Caroline almost cried again. Stacks of full plastic containers lined her shelves. A note hung from one of them.

> **You fell asleep before dinner was ready. I served it up for you so you can grab and go this week. My mom also sent some of her baked oatmeal. That's in the containers with the blue lids. I hope you slept well. I'll see you tomorrow. Ben**

The sweetness of his note and his help that weekend turned her resolve to mush. She didn't even know why she'd been so reluctant. She'd known him for more than a decade. If he wasn't a good guy, Chris wouldn't be his friend. But Caroline didn't need Chris's opinion. She saw it every day she and Ben were together. Everything about him impressed her. His football success more than proved his ability to focus and commit. Now he was focusing all that commitment and energy on impressing Caroline.

And it was working.

Chapter 23

A rainbow of folders covered Caroline's desk. Mentor program. In-house training. Out-of-town training. Manual updates.

She loved staying busy, but did it all have to happen during the dance-off?

Before tackling the manuals, Caroline checked her email to make sure no other last-minute changes had rolled in.

And there it was from the Human Resources department. *Can you edit this and add it to the end of our handbook?* Caroline clicked on the link. Twelve more pages? She printed them. Might as well edit them first, then she could figure out if she really needed them.

When she closed the company email, a little envelope appeared on the bottom of her computer screen. She hovered her mouse over it.

Susan@Pathways.com, subject: Dance-off & Grant

Caroline didn't hesitate to open the email, her pulse rising. Had she missed a deadline?

> I can't believe it!
> You and Ben have set a new fundraising record for the dance-off. We raised $25,000 in one month! I cannot tell you how excited and grateful we are. The board is revisiting our wish list for Pathways, and we have

you to thank for that.

Speaking of funds, are you still working on that utility grant? One of the board members asked about it Friday night, and I forgot to ask. You're already doing so much for the organization, you shouldn't have to work on that too. If you've already started it, can you send me everything you've completed? The board will finish that for you. You and Ben just keep dancing!

Caroline reread the email as an invisible chain slipped from around her neck. She didn't have to finish the grant proposal. She could think of a dozen things she *should* do with that extra time, but she also knew what she *wanted* to do. Clicking the forward button, she typed Ben's name into the recipient line.

I don't know what to say. THANK YOU!

She clicked send and returned to the Human Resources Manual. Anne had included a note: *The information here is good, but the tone is wrong. Can you make this less formal?* That would take some time.

Her cell phone dinged from inside her desk drawer. Odd. No one called her on her cell during the workday. She opened the drawer to check it.

Ben: Lets celebr8 2nite. Dance 2morrow?

Rolling her eyes at Ben's lazy texting, Caroline punched at her screen.

Caroline: If we don't practice, we won't have anything to celebrate next month.

Ben: Rest is important. Take u 2 dinner?

Caroline: We did that Saturday night and I slept through dinner last night. What else have you got?

She drummed her fingers against the smooth desktop while she waited for the ping.

Ben: Boat ride?

He had a boat?

Caroline: Yes! Where? When?

Ben: Pick u up at 6? Can eat on the water.

Caroline: Sounds good, but I can meet you.

Ben: My d8. My rules. C u at 6.

Caroline tucked her phone back into her desk. She didn't know Ben's family owned a boat. Chris had never mentioned it. Maybe it was a new purchase, not that it mattered. She'd never eaten dinner on the water. She only had to wait—she glanced at her clock—three hours.

Trying to push Ben's invitation to the back of her mind, she looked for ways to make an HR document more casual. It only took an hour to mark out some ideas, which allowed her plenty of time to give the rest of the manuals their first edits. When she finished the last one, it was five minutes before five. Close enough. If she left now, she'd have time to freshen up before her date. She didn't bother straightening her desk before she grabbed her purse, turned off the lights, and rushed out of the office.

The late June air greeted her as she stepped outside. The heat and humidity would make for an amazing night on the water. Someone honked. She jumped as a car pulled out of its parking spot, narrowly missing her. Oops. Waving to her coworker, she jogged out of the way and to her car. It had been a long time since she'd left work early. She'd forgotten how busy the parking lot could be.

She hopped into her car and rolled down the window. Squinting against the sun, she reached for her sunglasses. She'd need to remember to take them with her.

Her mind wandered as she crept through the slow-moving parking lot traffic toward the road. What should she wear on the boat? Maybe a light jacket. Or a bathing suit under her clothes, just in case.

Someone honked behind her. Caroline waved as she checked the rearview mirror. Hitting the accelerator, she pulled out of the parking lot.

A horn blared.

Brakes squealed.

She looked left in time to see the black grill of a truck driving straight into her door.

Chapter 24

As Ben stepped outside, a car horn blared. Seconds later, metal crunched. It sounded close. Looking around him, he spotted some commotion at the far end of the parking lot. That couldn't be good. He walked toward his truck, scanning the parking lot as he walked. He'd passed Caroline's car that morning when he arrived at work. She always worked late, so it should still be there. Except it wasn't.

What were the chances?

Forgetting his truck, he headed toward the growing crowd at the end of the parking lot. Several people milled around talking on their phones. As he got closer, the air thinned. A black pick-up truck had crunched in the driver's side door of a small red car.

Caroline's car.

He covered the distance in seconds, trying to get to her.

A strange man leaned through the driver's window. "Just try to stay still. The cops will be here soon."

Ben yanked the man away. "Caroline?"

Blood covered her face, but she gave him a wobbly smile. "I'm okay."

He fought back the vomit as he grabbed the door. "We have to get her out. Move the truck!" Something wrapped around him, pulling him away. "Let go of me!"

The stranger from the car stepped in front of Ben and pushed against his chest as other forces pulled him from behind. What were they doing? Caroline was bleeding!

"We can't get her out yet," the stranger said.

"We have to try." Ben pulled against his captors, but they held firm. He strained to see the car—to see Caroline. He couldn't leave her there!

The stranger grabbed Ben's shoulders. Ben tried to look around him, but the man was quick. "I'm an EMT. I've seen dozens of car accidents before. She's going to be fine. It was a low-speed impact, but somehow the truck is stuck to the door. We're waiting for a metal cutter."

"A what?" Ben shifted his attention from the wreck to the man in front of him. Who cared about the metal? "She's bleeding. Back the truck up and get her out!"

"The blood's from a head wound. Those bleed a lot, but that doesn't mean it's serious. She's responsive, which is a good sign, but her left arm hurts. If we try to pull the truck away, we could jostle her and hurt her arm even more. That's why we're waiting for the metal cutter. Until it gets here, I need you to step back."

"But she's my, my ..." Dance partner? Girlfriend? Reason to go to work in the morning?

Someone spoke, but Ben didn't register the words. He couldn't tear his eyes away from the crumpled metal. Caroline was in pain. How much longer would she be in there?

From somewhere off to the side, John Marsh stepped in front of Ben, clapping a hand on his shoulder. "Are you okay, son?" Ben blinked as he tried to concentrate on the CEO, but he needed to get to Caroline. "I think you can let him go now."

"Let who go?" Ben finally focused on John as the tension around him loosened. One, two, three men released him as they returned to their cars. "Where did they come from?"

John tried to steer Ben away from the accident, but his legs wouldn't move. The distant wail of sirens drew nearer. "Come on, son. There's nothing we can do to help."

"I know." The words cracked in his throat. "But ..."

Somehow Ben found himself sitting on a bench half a block down the street with John beside him. Police cruisers, a fire truck, and an ambulance surrounded the area while police officers directed traffic out of the parking lot. John talked to someone. Hours seemed to pass as Ben waited, hoping for any sign of Caroline. Finally, a red truck appeared, and more uniformed responders jumped out. Within minutes, the sickening crunch of metal filled the air.

"Ben!"

His gaze snapped in the direction of his name. Down the street, from the opposite direction of the crash, Chris jogged toward him. He jumped to his feet. "Chris!"

She wrapped him in a bear hug. "I came as soon as John called. Are you okay?"

He squeezed his friend, fighting for some type of control. "I'm fine. It's Caroline. She's trapped in her car. She's bleeding. She's ..."

Chris tightened her arms around his waist. "They'll take care of her." She stepped back, framing his face with her hands. "We don't know what's going on yet, so we're going to stay positive until we hear something. Got it?"

Chris's bossy teacher's voice managed to soothe Ben's nerves. Metal groaned. He turned in time to see the door peel away from the car's frame. Three people rushed in with a stretcher. Every muscle in his body tensed.

John returned from somewhere and handed Ben a business card. "She's awake and answering questions. This is the card for the first officer on the scene. He'll find Caroline at the hospital later. They're getting her in the ambulance now."

Chris extended a hand to John. "Thank you for calling me. Do you have any idea what happened?"

"Nothing's official, but it sounds like your sister pulled in front of the truck. Thankfully, the speed limit's low here. I'm going to stick around to make sure the rest of the employees make it home okay and to help the police in any way I can. Will you call when you know how she is?"

"Of course. Ben and I will go to the hospital now." Chris dragged Ben down the street. "I'll drive."

Ben wanted to argue, but the ambulance screamed as it pulled onto the road. The longer he fought with Chris, the longer it would take him to get to Caroline. "Fine. Let's go." While he didn't exactly feel safe in Chris's sedan, at least it wasn't a shoebox on wheels, and Chris knew how to handle it. She slipped in and out of traffic, making the short drive to the hospital even shorter.

Once they arrived, it took every ounce of Ben's discipline to stop himself from demanding answers and charging through the halls. No one seemed to be in any hurry to get them information as they walked from one area to the next, giving their names and waiting.

They'd been at the hospital for thirty minutes before Chris and Caroline's parents arrived. Chris met them at the door, wrapping her arms around both parents at the same time.

Ben followed her but tried to respect their privacy. Mrs. Novak dabbed a tissue under red, puffy eyes, and Mr. Novak stood as straight as a telephone pole. Ben nodded at both of them. "Mr. and Mrs. Novak."

"Thank you for being here with Chris," Mrs. Novak said. "We called Carmen. We'll call her again as soon as we know how Caroline is. What have you heard?"

Chris shook her head. "Not much. They're taking her in for x-rays and a CT scan. She hit her head, so there was a lot of blood, but they don't know how bad anything is yet."

Mrs. Novak took Ben's arm and led him to a couch. "I don't want to imagine the worse, so we'll hold on to hope until the doctors come out, okay?"

"That sounds like what Chris said." He sat next to her on the too-small, low-backed couch. Desperate for a distraction, he asked, "How did you end up doing at the art fair?"

"It was my best year yet." She patted his hand. "I don't think it hurt having a handsome young man working my booth all weekend."

"If I'm still around next year, maybe I can help again."

Chris sat on the couch across from them. "Are you leaving?"

"I don't have any plans to, but I never had plans to come back, either." And he never planned on Caroline.

The double doors to the emergency department opened. A gray-haired female in a white coat scanned the room. When her gaze landed on their small group, she walked toward them. Dread, fear, and anticipation ripped through his veins, threatening to strip away his composure. He clung to every shred of dignity as Mrs. Novak clung to his hand.

"Christine Novak?"

"Yes." She stood. "These are my parents. How's Caroline?"

"She's stable, but she's sore."

Relief crashed into Ben's chest as tears filled his eyes. *Stable*. He'd never heard a more beautiful word!

"How bad?" Mr. Novak asked.

"She's going to be fine. She managed to get her arm up to cover her head, but that put the force of the truck into her left arm. She didn't break any bones, but her shoulder was dislocated. We've strapped her arm to her chest to prevent any more damage. She also sprained her elbow and wrist. We didn't see a break, but she's still quite swollen, so I'll have her come back for x-rays. She's going to be very sore, and the shoulder will need a few weeks to heal, but she should be fine."

"What about her head?" Ben asked. "I saw her in the car. Her head was bleeding." He would never forget the blood.

"A small cut. Her CT scan came back clear."

The tension rushed out of the room as Ben sank back against the couch. Mr. Novak asked to see Caroline, and Mrs. Novak released Ben's hand, but he didn't follow them as they followed the doctor. They needed to be with her, and he needed to calm down.

Chris stopped in front of him. "Are you coming?"

He shook his head. "You and your family should see her first. I'm not even sure if I'm allowed back there."

She slugged him in the shoulder. "Do you want to see my sister?"

"Yes." More than he'd expected.

"Is she going to want to see you?"

"I hope so." Man, did he hope so.

"Then come on."

He followed Chris through the sterile hallways. What was he going to say to Caroline? If he hadn't suggested boating, she wouldn't have been in the parking lot so early. She would have missed the truck completely.

And what would her parents think? Had she told them about him? Would he have to have that conversation now? Did he need to ask her dad for permission to date her?

When he stepped into her room, every worry dissipated. Caroline's long hair framed her pale face. Above her left ear along the hairline, he spotted a small row of black stitches. A sling hugged her left arm to her body. Mrs. Novak sat beside the bed brushing the hair out of Caroline's eyes. Mr. Novak stood behind his wife, his knuckles white as he gripped the back of the chair.

"They're going to keep me for a few hours, then release me. They want me to take a few days off work, but I'm going to be fine."

Mrs. Novak touched her daughter's cheek. "I'll stay with you for a few days."

"You don't have to do that. I just need to rest."

"You can rest with me there. I don't want you home alone the week after a major car accident. You'll need someone to drive you around. Help around the house."

"I'll take care of her." Ben took a step closer to Caroline, unable to stay away any longer. "I don't know if I can be there during the day, but I'll go over every night."

"And I can hang out during the day since I don't have to be at school for anything." Chris patted her mom's hand. "I know you still have orders to fill from the art fair. You take care of those. Ben and I will make sure Caro's fine."

Their mom shook her head. "The orders can wait."

Caroline sighed. "Mom, it'll be okay. I know you mean well, but it might not be a bad idea to let Chris and Ben help. They're both taller and stronger than me, so they can help me around if I need it. Your back still gives you problems. I wouldn't want you to hurt it again trying to help me."

"If I need help, I'll call your father."

Mr. Novak let go of the chair and rubbed his hands across his wife's shoulders. "Caroline has a point, Pammy. We call

Chris anytime we need to move furniture. Neither one of us will be much help outside of cooking and cleaning."

Their mom sniffed. "All right, but I'm going to go home and cook all your favorite meals. I'll bring them over tomorrow, so you won't have to cook anything for at least a week." She stood and faced Ben. "I'm trusting you to take care of her."

He nodded. "Thank you."

She tried to smile, but her lips barely curled up. "Now that I've seen my baby, I need some chamomile tea. Gary, will you escort me to the cafeteria?"

Mr. Novak kissed Caroline's forehead before meeting his wife by the door. He made eye contact with Ben before giving a stiff nod. "We'll talk."

"Yes, sir."

As soon as the couple left, Ben pulled the chair as close to the bed as possible, desperate to touch Caroline and assure himself that she was real and whole and okay. She reached her right arm across her body, grimacing.

"Don't." He reached for her good hand and guided it back to her healthy side. "You're going to be sore enough. Don't try to push it now."

Chris stood at the end of the bed. She forced the same sad smile her mom had tried. "You freaked me out, Caro."

"I freaked myself out. I'm sorry to mess up your night."

"Are you sure the doctors are going to release you?"

"Yes. They haven't found any major injuries, but they want to make sure they check me for everything before I leave."

"Then, I'm going to go make sure Mom's okay." Chris tossed her car keys to Ben. "Give me your keys. You can take Caroline home in my car tonight. I'll have my parents drop me at your car, and I'll drive it over tomorrow."

He pulled his keys out of his pocket and tossed them to her. "You're leaving already?"

"I'm sure we'll come back for a few minutes, but my mom's a worrier. It'll be better for everyone if we can get her home and keep her busy."

"Thank you." Caroline tried to sit up, but she only managed to get an inch off the bed before she cringed.

Ben slipped an arm behind her shoulder. "Let me help."

She shook her head. "I think I'll lie back down."

He slowly lowered her to the bed, letting his hands linger on her shoulder.

Chris and Ben made plans to help Caroline before Chris left. As soon as she did, Ben pressed the lightest kiss to Caroline's lips.

She sighed. "I'm sorry I ruined our date."

He sat back, but he couldn't let her go. Being careful to avoid her stitches, he gently pushed the hair back from her face. "Don't apologize. Don't worry about anything. Please, just rest and focus on getting better."

"Okay." She closed her eyes. "I'm so tired."

"Are you okay to sleep? Do you have a concussion?"

"I don't think so. I don't remember the doctor saying anything about having one." A small smile pulled at the corners of her mouth. "I'm not sure about you anymore."

"Why's that?"

"Because you purposefully let people hit you for years. Why would anyone do that?"

"First of all, I did most of the hitting. Secondly, I never tackled a truck." And he'd never been as terrified as when he saw that truck and her car, but he wouldn't burden her with that now. "Will you rest?"

The smile melted off her face. "Will you be here when I wake up?"

"If you want me to be."
Caroline nodded as she closed her eyes.

Chapter 25

Ben opened the passenger door. Caroline grimaced as she tried to unfasten the seatbelt with her right arm.

"Let me do that," he said.

"I'm sorry you have to do everything for me. I feel so helpless."

He unbuckled her. "You survived a car accident. You're allowed to be helpless for a while." Sliding his left arm behind her shoulders, he took her right hand in his. "Go ahead and turn slowly. Let me know if you need help."

Her lips pinched together as she started to swivel, managing to turn halfway toward the door before stopping. "I expected my left arm to ache, but I didn't realize my entire left side would hurt."

She tried again, but Ben couldn't stand seeing the pain in her face. Letting go of her hand, he slipped his arm under her knees and lifted her out of the car.

"You don't need to carry me."

"I know." It barely took any effort to kick the car door shut and carry Caroline to her building. "Rest tonight and you can struggle tomorrow."

"I don't want anyone to coddle me." But as she said the words, she rested her head against his shoulder.

It took some shifting, but Ben managed to get Caroline through the apartment and into her bedroom. She hadn't made the bed that morning, so he set her on the unmade side before turning on the light.

She groaned as she connected with the mattress.

His gut twisted. "I'm sorry."

"It's okay." She didn't open her eyes, though.

As he draped a blanket over her, she sighed. The doctor had given her a hefty muscle relaxer before they left the hospital, so she'd be asleep in no time. He should probably settle himself on the couch and get some sleep too, but he wanted to watch her for a while longer. Make sure she was okay.

The bruise on her left cheek had darkened. The jagged red lines of each scratch screamed against her normally smooth skin. Hopefully, none of them would scar.

Her breathing deepened, her chest rising and falling beneath the blanket as her face relaxed. Ben picked up her right hand, careful not to move her too much as he kissed the marred skin.

Three months ago, the idea of moving back to Traverse City had nearly sent him into depression. Nothing about it appealed to him. All he'd wanted was a way out of town.

Now, the only thing he could think about was staying close to Caroline. Sure, she'd bossed him and Chris around as kids, but they'd deserved most of it. Even then, he'd admired her. She was mature and responsible and beautiful, and now she was trusting him to take care of her. He wasn't going to blow it.

Keeping his hand on top of hers, Ben slid to the floor and leaned his head against the bed. He'd stay there for a few more minutes, just in case.

Caroline's neck ached. She reached for her pillow, but hot knives stabbed her in the shoulder. She tried to rub the pain out of her neck and arm, but every move sent pain screaming through her.

The accident.

The truck.

She opened her eyes, looking for the monster grill, but the soft light from her bedroom lamp surrounded her. She was home, and she was safe, but her heart thundered. Tears flooded her eyes as the adrenaline faded and her emotions caught up to her.

And the pain. Every muscle in her body cried out for relief. She cried. With each sob, her body jerked, causing more pain.

"What's wrong?"

Caroline gasped as Ben's face appeared from beside her bed.

"I didn't mean to scare you. I must have fallen asleep on the floor." He still wore a button-down shirt and dress pants, though both were wrinkled. His short hair stuck out in several directions.

"You don't have to sleep on the floor. I have a bed in the guest room."

"I know, but I wanted to be close in case you needed anything." Ben pushed himself up until he sat on the edge of the bed. The movement rocked the mattress, which moved her, which started a new wave of pain. "What hurts?"

The tears welled up again. "Everything. I didn't think it was going to be this bad." She managed to push out the words. "I don't know why I'm crying. I think it's just all catching up to me. And everything aches."

"The doctor said you might hurt for a few days. I'll get you some ice and a muscle relaxer."

She hiccupped through the tears, trying not to grimace. "I don't have muscle relaxers."

"The hospital sent some. I'll be right back."

He left the room, and Caroline tried to rearrange herself. Her muscles rebelled, begging for relief but fighting against her as she tried to provide it. Ignoring the pain, she shifted her weight, giving her neck and shoulders a break.

Ben returned with a glass of water and an ice pack. "What hurts the most?"

"My left shoulder."

He handed her the water and some pills. "Two of these should help."

"Thanks."

Her body shifted as Ben sat down again. "It'll probably be easier to ice your shoulder if you stay lying down."

"I've had injuries before. I know how ice works."

"Sorry. You've been through a lot today. I just wanted to help."

Caroline sighed. "I know." She accepted the pack and set it on her shoulder. It took a few moments for the chill to penetrate her skin before starting its work. "Thank you."

"Do you need anything else?"

She shook her head. "I'm hoping to fall asleep as soon as these pills kick in. Why don't you go sleep in the guest room? It'll be a lot more comfortable."

"I'm sure it will be, but I'll stay here until you're done icing. Then I'll leave you alone. I promise." He watched her closely, the lines of his face harsh and straight.

She tried to smile. "I'm not trying to get rid of you, but I don't want both of us waking up sore tomorrow. There's a perfectly good bed in there."

"I'll check it out later." He shifted slowly, which limited the jostling. "I'm happy to sleep on the floor too, but I'll do whatever makes you happy."

"I'm happy to have you here."

His eyebrows pinched together. "Are you really?"

She found his hand with hers and squeezed his fingers. She tried to hold back a yawn but couldn't find the energy to fight it. "Can we talk about this later? I'd like to talk about it. Later."

Finally, he smiled. "Whatever you want."

If only he knew.

Chapter 26

The pain started in her shoulder, then spread to her arm, neck, and back. Caroline tried to get comfortable again, but too much of her body ached. If it hurt this much to lie in bed, she might as well get up.

Pushing herself up, she spotted herself in the mirror and winced. A bruise had appeared overnight, and dried blood caked her hair. She still wore the same clothes she'd worn to work the day before, except several drops of blood had darkened the left shoulder. Reaching across her head, Caroline found the stitches.

What a night. She'd have to call into work, then call the insurance company to find out about her car. Someone must have found her phone at the crash because it now sat on her nightstand. She tapped the screen. Another missed chat with Carmen, but she'd left a message.

Caroline opened the app. Her sister's round face with cropped dark hair and chocolatey eyes filled the screen. "Mom and Dad called—are you okay? They said you'll be fine and I don't need to come home, but I need to hear it from you. Are they just telling me you're okay so I won't worry? I'll probably be in rehearsal when you get this, but leave me a message, okay? No texts. I want to see you for myself. Love you."

For a second, Caroline considered brushing her hair and attempting to use some makeup to hide her bruise, but Carmen wanted honesty and she deserved it. It was hard for all of them living on separate continents and missing out on each other's lives. The least Caroline could do was show her sister what everyone else in the family saw.

She tapped the screen. Her bruised, stitched face appeared. She smiled. "Thanks for checking on me. I'm going to be fine. In fact, I'm already home. My shoulder hurts, but it'll heal, and once I get a shower, I'm sure I won't look so bad. I'll email you later with all the details. Love you too."

Standing slowly, Caroline tossed the phone onto the bed, then managed to open her door before stopping. Ben filled her entire couch, his feet propped on the armrest. He breathed deeply, not quite a snore but loud enough that she could hear him from across the room. The sight of him sleeping stirred something in her chest.

She glanced at the clock. Six-thirty. She wouldn't wake him yet. He'd probably slept less than she had, and he still had to go to work. The least she could do was offer him caffeine.

Moving as quietly and carefully as possible, she started a pot of coffee, savoring the rich aroma. As soon as she got a cup in her, she'd try the shower. Until then, she couldn't decide if she should stand in the kitchen or sit at the table. Both options seemed equally painful.

"I should be doing that."

Caroline sucked in a breath as she turned to face Ben. "You have got to stop doing that. How is someone so big so sneaky?"

Instead of answering, Ben stepped closer. "I've never been accused of being sneaky. How are you feeling?"

"Like I've been hit by a truck."

His face clouded over. "That's not funny."

"It's a joke." She nudged his arm.

"Maybe in a few weeks it'll be a joke, but not yet." He swallowed, his gaze dropping to the floor.

Caroline's heart cracked. Ignoring the aches, she slid her good arm around his waist, stood on her toes, and kissed his cheek. "I'm fine. Really, really sore but fine."

He didn't move.

"What's it going to take to convince you that I'm okay?"

"I know you're okay. I don't know why I'm still upset."

Caroline suspected, but she didn't want to hope. Instead, she leaned against him and took some of the weight off her left leg. "Try not to worry too much. My mom will worry enough for everyone. Maybe you can just try to help me forget about the pain."

Ben finally wrapped his arms around her, though not as tight as he normally did. "You're right. I'm complaining about how your accident made *me* feel while you're the one living through it. Talk about self-centered."

"You're not self-centered. You slept on my floor and my couch to take care of me last night. Neither of those must have been comfortable. Why didn't you sleep in the guest room?"

"I tried, but there are piles of clothes on the bed. I wasn't sure what to do with them."

"I'll have Chris help me with the laundry today."

"And by help you mean you'll have her do the laundry for you, right?"

Caroline rolled her eyes. "I'll let her carry the laundry, but I'm not letting her put my clothes away. Her closet's a disaster."

He leaned back to smile at her. "How can a closet be a disaster? It holds your clothes. What could go wrong?"

"I won't bore you with the details. You'll just have to trust me that I have very high closet standards."

He ran a finger along her jaw as he smiled. "I'll add that to the list."

"What list?"

"The list of interesting things I'm learning about you."

Nervous energy fluttered in Caroline's chest. "You keep a list? What kind of things are on this list?" Though she wasn't sure if she wanted to know.

"You like colorful purses."

Caroline couldn't hide her surprise at his observation. "I wouldn't have expected you to notice something like that."

"I also know that you're addicted to soda, and you eat junk food when you're stressed. You read western romance novels. You never wear high heels. And you listen to me when I compliment you."

"What do you mean I listen to you?"

He touched the hair behind her right ear. "You stopped wearing your hair in the tight bun."

He'd noticed, but she said, "And you think that's because of you?"

"Isn't it?"

She didn't admit to it, but she could feel the blush climbing up her face. Ben didn't say anything. He simply kissed her.

The coffee pot beeped.

Caroline stepped back, not because she wanted space between them, but because she needed a shower, and she wasn't sure how long it would take. "I'm going to grab some coffee, then a long, hot shower." She tried to get some coffee, but Ben held on to her wrist.

"You can't take a hot shower."

"I need a shower."

"That's fine, but you need to take a cold shower."

"That sounds terrible."

"I know, but you need to avoid heat for at least seventy-two hours."

Caroline groaned. "Then I'll be out in two minutes."

"What do you want for breakfast?"

"A hot shower. You should go home and get changed."

"I'll leave when Chris gets here."

"You don't have to do that. She won't be here for hours, and I don't want you to be late for work."

"I don't care."

"But *I* do. Now let me get my coffee."

Ben grabbed two mugs while Caroline got the creamer. She filled her cup and headed toward the bathroom. Ben made a noise in the kitchen, but she didn't dare turn around to see what was happening. The sight of a handsome man in her kitchen made her consider possibilities she'd long given up on.

As she closed the bathroom door, Caroline moaned. Though everything in her being wanted to run a hot shower, Ben knew what he was talking about. The man had spent more than half his life hitting people. That didn't make the thought of a cold shower more appealing, though. Especially with how slowly she was moving.

Caroline ran her cold water. Carefully removing her clothes and sling, she stepped into the uncomfortable stream. She moved as quickly as she could, but by the time she climbed out, she could hardly control her shivering. Cold, wet hair clung to her back. She tried wrapping it in a towel, but it slipped off. She tried again, but her shaking arm could barely pick up the towel, much less twist it. She'd figure it out later.

Holding the towel between her left arm and her body, Caroline managed to cover herself. Cracking open the door, she looked for Ben. He stood with Chris in the kitchen. Praise the Lord.

"Ch ... Ch... Chris, can, can you h ... h... help me?"

They both turned, so Caroline ducked behind the door.

"I'll step outside." Ben's voice carried through the bathroom door a moment before the apartment door opened and closed.

Chris knocked. "Let's get you changed."

Caroline wasn't thrilled about her sister helping her dress, but she needed to stop the shivering, so she opened the bathroom door. Chris didn't say anything as she escorted her sister to the bedroom. For as much as Caroline hated the awkwardness of the situation, her tension eased once the cold hair was off her back and she'd slipped into cotton capris, thick athletic socks, and a worn Detroit Tiger's T-shirt. After securing her arm in the sling, Chris wrapped an oversized zippered hoodie around Caroline.

"Let me get your blow dryer and I'll take care of your hair."

The front door opened. "Is everyone decent?"

Caroline examined her discolored reflection. "Sort of."

"Can I come in, or should I stay outside?"

"I'm covered. Come on in."

The door closed. After a few soft footsteps, Ben appeared at the bedroom door. His eyes widened.

"Do I look that bad?"

He grinned. "No. You look like Chris."

"She should. Those are my clothes." Chris carried the hairdryer into the bedroom. "I wasn't sure what she'd have here that was clean, so I came prepared."

Ben looked between the two of them. He opened his

mouth as if he wanted to say something but closed it quickly. "I should probably head to work. Do you two need anything?"

"We're good." Chris plugged in the dryer. "We took care of ourselves before you started dating my sister. We'll manage again without you."

He shook his head. "You two make it hard to be a gentleman. For the record, I tried."

Caroline looked at her sister, then back at Ben. Would he leave without a real goodbye? Or worse—embarrass them both in front of her sister? He looked at Chris, then motioned toward the door.

Chris rolled her eyes. "Why don't I step out into the living room for a minute so my friend and sister can kiss without feeling weird about me knowing about it?"

As soon as she cleared the doorway, Ben was in the bedroom kneeling on the floor in front of Caroline. "Will you call me if you need anything?"

"Chris can take care of me."

"But you'll call me if the two of you need anything?"

"I promise."

"I'll come over right after work."

Caroline shook her head. "You need to go home and tell your family what's going on."

"Fine. I'll pick up some things, then come right over." He cupped her cheek. "I'll see you tonight."

Caroline tugged on Ben's shirt, pulling him close enough to kiss. She let her lips linger on his, savoring the light scratch of his stubble and the earthy musk of his skin. No soap or cologne, just the natural scent of Ben.

He sighed, his warm breath caressing her skin. "I should probably go."

"Yes. Don't make me feel guilty about making you late."

One more quick kiss and he was out the door. As soon as he left, Caroline's sense returned, as did the pain.

"Ready to dry your hair?" Chris stepped into the bedroom, but Caroline was already pushing herself off the bed. "What do you need? I can get it for you."

"I need to see the doctor. Let's find out what's really going on."

Chapter 27

The doctor hung the x-rays on the light case and pointed to different points along the neck and shoulder, not that Caroline understood any of it. "You're very lucky you didn't break anything, but you can see the slight—"

The rest of the words didn't make sense, but she didn't need them to. She just needed to know one thing. "When can I start dancing again?"

The doctor shook his head. "I can't tell you that for certain, but I would say don't dance for the rest of this week, at least. It will take several weeks to heal. With what I'm seeing in your shoulder here, I think you'll need to be in that sling for, at least, seven days. I'd like you to come back next week."

"Until then, what should I do?"

"Ice and ibuprofen. Take the muscle relaxers if you need them. Keep your arm in that sling. If you don't give your shoulder enough time to heal, recovery will take longer. How does your neck feel? If it's sore, we can order you a brace."

Chris snorted. "Can you imagine what you'd look like with the sling *and* a neck brace? You should see if any ambulance chasers want a picture to use for their billboards. You could make some good money."

"Why don't I get you that extra-large ice pack I was talking about?" the doctor asked as he stepped out of the exam room.

"Did you hear what he said?" Caroline asked, slouching in her seat. "I can't dance all week. What if I can't finish the dance-off?" She hadn't called Susan yet. Caroline and Ben had gotten the board's hopes up, but how much more money would they raise if they couldn't participate? Could they keep the donations if they withdrew?

"Don't worry about that. Is there anything you can do while you heal?"

"I can choreograph the dance, but even if I do that, I always adjust things once Ben and I start practicing."

"Don't worry about the changes. Do whatever you can now."

Which wasn't enough. "What if it's too hard and he can't do the dance when we finally start practicing. What if—"

Chris raised her eyebrows. "Don't. Worry."

Caroline grimaced. "I sound like Mom, don't I?"

"Yes. There will be plenty to worry about later."

Dr. Ron stepped back into the office. "Here's the ice pack. It should cover your entire shoulder." He repeated his icing instructions and reminded Caroline not to drive until the sling came off.

They left the office, and Caroline was easing herself into Chris's car when her phone rang. Tears filled her eyes when she saw the caller ID. "Hi, Susan."

"Caroline, are you all right? The news said something about a car accident at Morrison Insurance yesterday. They didn't give anyone's name, but it looked like your car."

"It was my car, but I'm okay."

Susan gasped. "Are you sure? The accident looked terrible."

"Big truck, small car. I haven't seen any pictures, but I think it might have looked worse than it was. I went to the emergency room last night and they released me, but"—Caroline braced her nerves—"I'm not going to be able to dance for the rest of the week."

"Of course not," Susan said. "I wouldn't want you to. You take off as much time as possible. I'll call Judy, and—"

"No!"

"Caroline."

"What if she makes us withdraw from the competition?" Images of the broken fan and hole in the ceiling flashed through her mind. And the cost estimates. "Give me a day or two first. Let me try to figure something out. Then, when we call Judy, we can present some options or alternatives. We can't just *not* dance."

Susan blew out a long breath. "We truly need that money now, but I won't let you risk your health, and I know the board wouldn't want that, either."

Caroline's tension eased. "Thank you for that, but I promise I won't do anything to hurt myself anymore. Just give me some time to figure something out."

"I'll give you three days. Then we really should let Judy know what's going on."

She couldn't argue with that. "Three days. One way or another, someone will dance for Pathways. I promise."

"You concentrate on getting better. I'll talk to the board."

By the time Caroline ended the call, Chris had driven them halfway home. Caroline reclined her seat enough to be comfortable, then closed her eyes.

"Do you want to stop anywhere while we're out?"

"I think I'm ready to go home and sleep." For the rest of the day, if she could. With so much uncertainty and so little control, some ibuprofen and muscle relaxers might help her survive the day.

Ben checked and double-checked traffic before he pulled out of the Morrison parking lot and started the drive home. He'd texted his mom about the accident and his offer to take care of Caroline, then promised to discuss it with her when he stopped at home.

He was leaving the city limits when his phone rang. The SUV's screen showed a downstate number. He had ten minutes before he reached his parents' house, so he answered. "This is Ben."

"Ben, this is Bill White with the Detroit Lions organization. I hope you don't mind me calling. I spoke with Coach Peters at Western, and he gave me your number."

The Detroit Lions? Ben's SUV rumbled as he drove off the shoulder of the road. He swerved back into his lane. "No, that's fine. Uh, how are you today?"

"It's a beautiful summer day in Michigan, so it's hard to complain. I'm sure you're wondering why I'm calling, and you're probably wondering who I am."

"Yes, sir."

"I work in the corporate office for the Lions organization. Specifically, I work in community outreach. Are you familiar with the work we do?"

"Some of it, yes. You've been working with victims of domestic violence, military veterans, hosting food drives—"

"I'm impressed. Not many players take the time to learn all about an organization. They only care about the coaching staff and players."

"I'm not a player anymore." His throat thickened.

"I was sorry to hear about that. You were one of the best."

Resentment boiled in Ben's veins as he white-knuckled the steering wheel. "Thanks."

"From what I've seen and heard, you're still one of the best."

"Excuse me?" What had this man heard?

"You're making quite a mark on the dance floor."

"I had the chance to help a friend and do some good in the community. I didn't see how I could turn it down."

"That's what I was hoping to hear. Involvement in and a heart for the community are things we value. As much as we want to win a Super Bowl, a championship season doesn't mean much if we aren't giving back to and playing an active role in our community. They support us, and we want to make sure we support them in turn."

"I can appreciate that." Now more than ever.

"After seeing what you've been doing in your northern Michigan community, I'd like to talk with you about how you might become part of the Detroit Lions community and family."

A meeting with the Detroit Lions office. The offer stung, but the pain didn't linger. It couldn't be any worse than life at an insurance company, and if it hadn't been for Morrison, he wouldn't know that. Maybe any role with a professional team would be better than no role. "I'd like that, but I'm driving right now. Could we schedule a time to talk next week?"

"That's what I was going to ask you. I'd like to invite you down here to see exactly who we are and what it is we do."

"Of course. It would have to be over the weekend. I'm working and dancing during the week."

"I understand. We're hosting a community health and wellness event next Saturday. I'd like to fly you down Friday night after work. We'll go to dinner so you can meet the staff, then go with us to the event on Saturday. Get to meet some of the players and the kids we support. See how things work. We'll fly you home Sunday."

He didn't know what to say. He didn't know what to think. The Detroit Lions? Hope, despair, confusion—which one would win?

"What do you think, Ben?"

"Honestly, I don't know."

"Then why not come down? See what's going on. There's no commitment beyond a weekend of your time."

And if it didn't feel right, he could come home. "I think that sounds like a great offer."

"Excellent. I'll have my assistant email you the itinerary and plane tickets. If you have any questions, don't hesitate to give me a call. This is my direct number, so call me here."

"I will."

"I'm looking forward to meeting you. Good luck with your dancing, and I'll see you next weekend."

Ben disconnected the call, disbelief steering him home. He hadn't seen that coming. An all-expenses-paid trip to Detroit? What would it look like if they offered him a job? What would his parents say? Or Caroline? Or worse—what if he told them, and the Lions *didn't* offer him a job? He was already famous for being one of the most recruited collegiate players not to make the NFL. He didn't want to go down as not making the pros twice. Maybe he'd just wait to tell anyone until after the visit.

Turning onto his parents' driveway, he was almost at the garage when the front door opened and Annie ran out. He hadn't even stopped before she opened his door, her eyes red and puffy. "Is Caroline okay? You have to take me to her. She needs her sister after something like this."

"She *has* a sister, remember? Two, actually." He tried to nudge Annie out of the way, but she leaned into him.

"Yes, but one of her sisters is in Europe. I should be there. I can help." Ben wrapped his arm around Annie's waist and picked her up so he could get out of the car. Instead of fighting him, she wrapped her arms and legs around him. "Please. Let me help. Besides, you and Caroline shouldn't be left alone. I can chaperone."

"Who says we need a chaperone? I'm taking care of her. That's all." He carried her to the front porch before tickling her side. She squirmed, giggling as she released him.

"But you're dating her. Do you want people to think that you're acting married before getting married?"

Ben's lunch curdled in his stomach. "I'm not talking with you about this."

He let himself into the house. Annie followed him through the living room, down the hallway, and right up to the bathroom. He stepped inside and closed the door in her face. "I'll wait right here until you're done," she said.

"I'm not feeling well. I could be in here for a few hours."

Something thumped against the door. "I can wait."

When he opened the door, she fell back into the bathroom. "Hey!"

He laughed. "Serves you right."

"Honey, is that you?"

"Hi, Mom." He followed her voice into the kitchen. The full force of her garlicy pot roast hit him, and his mouth watered. "That smells amazing."

"It should. It's been cooking for hours." She wiped her hands on a towel before facing both of her kids. "How's Caroline?"

"I haven't seen her since this morning, but Chris texted me and said she's hanging in there. I told them I'd grab some clothes and head over, but I might wait until after dinner."

Annie stepped in front of him, her arms crossed over her chest. "And I told him he should take me with him. What if Chris leaves and Caroline needs help with girl things? Ben can't help her with that. And he's dating her. What kind of example is he setting for me if he spends the night at his girlfriend's house?"

He looked at his mom and raised his eyebrows. "Why is she even talking this way?"

"I told you. My friends have sisters and brothers in high school. I hear things."

Even though he wasn't ready for her to hear those things, Ben couldn't argue with her logic. What would he have done if Chris hadn't been there to help Caroline out of the shower? Just thinking about it sent his pulse racing. He didn't want to admit it, but ... "Annie probably has a point."

She clapped her hands. "I do?"

"But I'm not taking you over without talking to Caroline first. It might be a better idea for Chris to stay the night if she can."

Annie ran for the phone. "Let's call and find out."

His mom leaned against the counter beside him. "How bad are Caroline's injuries?"

"Nothing's broken, but it's not good. I wouldn't be surprised if the whole left side of her body is a giant bruise. The good thing is the truck hit her arm, not her head."

"What are you going to do about the dance-off?"

Ben shook his head. "I haven't had time to talk with her about that yet. I can't imagine she'll be able to dance anytime soon, but that doesn't necessarily mean she won't try." He would, and he suspected she was every bit as competitive as he was.

"You could refuse to dance with her if she tries."

"I could." If he could muster the willpower to refuse her anything. If it meant preserving her health, though, he might be able to.

"Caroline said I can come over." Annie thrust the phone at Ben. "She wants to talk to you."

Ben took the phone. "Hello?"

"Your sister's a trip."

"You didn't have to say yes to her. She doesn't have to come over."

"Are you kidding? She promised me brownies."

He looked at his sister. "You didn't tell me you could make brownies."

"You don't need brownies the way Caroline does."

Caroline chuckled. "Yes, brownies will definitely help me feel better, although I think the muscle relaxers are probably doing more."

"Feeling better are you?"

"I'd call it tolerable, but that's better than how I was this morning."

"Is Chris still there? Do you need me to pick up anything?"

"Um ..." Caroline sucked in a loud breath, then giggled. "I'm not sure. You should talk to Chris."

Something crashed on the other end of the line as voices talked over top of each other. More giggling. "Ben?"

"Hey, Chris. Is Caroline okay?"

"Yeah. She didn't read the directions on her pills and took two muscle relaxers instead of one. She's pretty loopy right now."

Ben laughed. "Annie wants to come over. Are you planning to stay the night, or should she pack clothes?"

"I can stay this weekend, but I have some work to finish at home. I just ripped out my bathroom floor. If you can stay, I'll finish it tonight, then spend the day here tomorrow."

"I can do that. Do you need dinner?"

"My mom brought four casseroles. We have food for two weeks."

"Keep an eye on your sister for me. We'll be there soon."

Chapter 28

Ben knocked but didn't wait for an answer. He and Annie walked into Caroline's apartment and into the warm aromas of tomatoes, cheese, and oregano. "Oh, man. What are you cooking?"

Chris pulled plates out of the cupboard. "Lasagna, and I'm not cooking. Just warming it up."

"I'm glad we didn't eat at home."

"Me too. This pan is big enough for a family."

Annie tiptoed into the living room. Caroline slept on the couch, slightly tilted to the right and off her left side. Ben's guess had been right—dark bruises covered her left arm and part of her neck. The bone beneath her left eye had darkened while the area near her hairline glared red. Annie's eyes widened.

He wrapped his arm around her. "It could have been a lot worse."

"It looks like it hurts," she whispered.

"It does hurt." Caroline yawned but didn't open her eyes. "Sorry I fell asleep. I finally got comfortable and couldn't help myself."

Ben gave Annie a gentle shove toward the kitchen. "Why don't you see if Chris needs help?" He sat on the edge of the couch by Caroline. "Rough day?"

When she opened her eyes, he noticed the red edges. "I can't dance."

"I didn't think you'd be able to for a while."

"But I can't all week. The doctor told me to come back next week, but he doesn't know when I'll be able to dance."

"Take the time off. I don't think you have any career-ending injuries."

"I know." She sat up, grabbing his arm to pull herself all the way up. "But we only have three and a half weeks before the next competition. I want to start dancing next week, but I know my limits. I've never hurt like this before." Her lip trembled.

Ben's heart ached. "I know. Trust me, I know."

"Dinner's ready," Chris said.

"Come on." He slipped one hand under her good arm and helped her to the table. "We'll figure something out."

Annie pulled a chair out for Caroline. "Do you want me to cut up your lasagna for you?"

"That would be nice, thank you. It's too bad you can't dance for me."

Ben's sister paused. "Could I?"

He chuckled. "I don't think it would work if neither of us knows how to dance."

Annie cut up Caroline's dinner while Ben and Chris dug in. Caroline tapped her fingernails on the table. She looked at him, then at Chris. Then at him. Then at Chris. Her eyes narrowed. Chris didn't seem to notice as she stuffed another bite of lasagna into her mouth, but something uncomfortable settled on Ben's shoulders. He tried to ignore the feeling as he bit into his dinner, but it tasted like warm mush in his mouth.

After several bites, he put down his fork and crossed his arms. "Why do you keep looking at us like that?"

"Because I think Annabelle's brilliant."

"I am?" His sister managed to sit about four inches taller in her chair.

Caroline nodded. "We don't have to forfeit. Chris can dance for me."

Chris froze with her fork in her mouth. Annie's smile faded. Ben wasn't sure how to respond.

Caroline frowned at him. "Don't look at me like that."

"Like what?"

"Like you just bit into a lemon."

"I didn't realize I was. I'm just trying to figure out if you're serious."

"Absolutely."

Chris stabbed her food so hard the fork clinked against the plate. "I am not dancing."

"We might as well let Annie dance," Ben said. "At least she wants to."

"Can I?" His sister jumped up.

Caroline shook her head. "Chris can dance. She just doesn't want to."

"What?" Ben looked at his T-shirt-clad friend. "No way. I've seen you dance. You're terrible."

Chris pointed her fork at him. "I am not terrible. I just don't care what I look like."

"And she can, too, dance," Caroline said. "She started dancing when she was five and danced for seven years. She only quit to play sports, which was just before you guys met."

A strange, new light shone around Chris. "Why didn't I know this?" Ben asked.

"Why would I tell anyone? Do you tell people what you used to do as a kid?" She shrugged. "I danced. I quit. It's no big deal."

Maybe not, but Ben caught on to Caroline's plan. "You already know the basics, so Caroline just needs to teach you the steps."

"It's not that simple. I took tap and jazz. There wasn't a ballroom involved."

"But you know how to hold your hands and point your toes, right?" Ben asked, excited and hopeful. "And you watched your sister for years, so you know what it should look like."

Chris slouched in her chair. "Just because I know how it should look doesn't mean I can do it. I'm not exactly graceful."

"Because you don't try to be," Caroline said. "You are the most naturally talented athlete I know. You can pick up any stick, racquet, or ball and play. This isn't any different."

"Don't you think you should wait to recruit me until after you talk to the doctor? You're probably getting worked up over nothing." Chris practically whined.

Caroline sighed. "Do you remember the last time Tony and I competed? Three months before the competition, I fell down the stairs and hurt my back."

"Yes, and you were sure you wouldn't be able to compete, but you took a full week off. Two weeks later and it was like nothing had happened."

"And the pain level was about a third of what I'm in now. *If* the doctor says I can start dancing before the next competition, that doesn't mean I'll be able to move the way I need to, and Ben needs to start practicing *now*." Caroline covered his hand with hers. "He's an amazing student, but we've been practicing ten hours a week. It's going to take longer to teach two non-dancers the steps. I don't want to wait and hope that I'll be able to do it then find out I can't. I'd rather have Ben dance with someone else this month and hope that I can compete again next month."

Finally Forever

The idea had merit. Ben felt awkward enough holding Caroline the way she told him to. He couldn't imagine trying to be that intimate with a stranger. Dancing with Chris that way would be weird, but at least he knew her. "If I have to dance with someone else, I'd rather it be you."

"Aw, come on." She grimaced.

"Why don't you want to dance?" Annie slid her chair closer to Chris. "I would dance if they would let me, even if I had to dance with Ben. I can help you get ready if you want. My mom's teaching me how to use makeup."

He could almost see the arguments dissolve in Chris's head. "It should be you," he said. "It was your idea for me to dance with your sister in the first place. You can help us win this."

"I haven't talked to the dance-off committee yet because I don't want to give them an excuse to disqualify us, and Pathways needs the money." Caroline glanced at Ben before focusing on her sister. "There was an accident at the house. It's going to cost tens of thousands of dollars to fix it. That will take every cent of the money we've earned so far, but if we can finish *and* win ..." She smiled. "This will be life changing for them."

Chris groaned. "You don't have any other options?"

"Of course we have options, but I don't know how long it will take to find someone else who can do it. We could lose a week or two of rehearsals."

Ben understood Chris's hesitation—he'd had similar fears—but he also knew his friend's heart. He just needed to remind her of it. "I get why you never told me you danced, but I've never known you to back down from a challenge." If he hadn't been studying her so carefully, he might have missed the subtle pink in her ears.

She dropped her fork onto the table. "I'm no good at it."

"So?" Annie shrugged. "My dad says no one's good at anything unless they practice."

Caroline laughed. "Which is why you weren't any good at it. You never practiced at home. You were too busy playing basketball."

"I didn't practice because I wasn't any good."

Ben couldn't believe it. "You're scared."

"Of course, I'm scared! You want me to dance in front of hundreds of people and potentially make a fool of myself."

He leaned forward. "Like I'm doing?"

Chris growled as she skewered more food onto her fork. "Fine, I'll do it because I know how important this is to both of you, but it's not my fault if I'm terrible."

"She's terrible." Ben helped Caroline out of his truck after two practices with Chris. His friend had officially proven him wrong—she couldn't do everything.

Caroline swatted his arm as they walked up to her apartment. "She is not. You're just used to dancing with me."

"And all the other teams will have someone like you dancing with them. Is there anyone else you can call?"

"No. You saw how nervous Chris was. If I call someone else, it'll crush her confidence. You're her partner. It's up to you to lead her."

"And you think I can do it?"

"You have to."

"Maybe if you call—"

"I can't call anyone." Caroline sighed. "I already called around, but it's not like there are dozens of ballroom dancers in Traverse City. Plus, it's almost July. People are out of town or have family visiting. This late in the season, the only person I could find who's available all month is Chris."

Ben's confidence wavered. "So, it's up to me to figure out how to lead her?"

"Fake it till you make it."

He wanted to leave Caroline on the landing, but she smiled, so he kissed her. "You make it sound so easy."

"It's not going to be easy, but we'll figure out how to build her confidence. First, we have to make sure your confidence is up." She pulled out her keys, but Ben took them and unlocked the apartment. "I'm not a complete invalid, you know."

"I know, but you're a competitor, so you're going to push every limit everyone puts on you. I'm going to make sure you rest as thoroughly as possible for as long as possible." He gave her what he hoped was his best smile. "Even if that means opening your door."

"It's about time you got here. Dinner's almost ready."

Ben stepped in front of Caroline, blocking her from the home invader. The short, blonde invader. "Annie?"

She grinned at him from the kitchen. "I made dinner."

Caroline stepped around Ben. "Um, hi. How did you get in here?"

"Don't you check your messages?"

"Not recently." Caroline pressed her hand against his lower back, pushing him out of her way. "What are you making?"

"Hoagies and potato chips."

Caroline moved faster than Ben had seen her move since the accident. "Perfect. You didn't answer my question, though. How did you get in here?"

Annie rolled her eyes. "I left you a message. Mom and Dad had to go out, and they won't be home until midnight.

Since we couldn't get ahold of Ben, I convinced Mom to drop me off here. She told me to keep the door locked until you got here."

Ben took his sandwich. "But *how* did you get in?"

"The spare key. I texted Chris. She told me Caroline keeps one under the neighbor's mat."

What in the world? "How did you get her phone number?"

Annie sighed as she sat at the table. "I'm growing up. You have to accept it. How was practice?"

Ben sat next to her. "Chris is a great softball player, but I'm not so sure she has a future in dance."

"I wish I could help." Annie slouched in her seat.

"Maybe you can." Caroline pointed at Ben. "Your brother needs to help Chris be more comfortable on the dance floor. To do that, he needs to be absolutely confident, and I think the best way to do that will be to help him with his frame."

"That's his arms, right?"

"Yep."

His sister perked up. "How can I help?"

"You remember my friend Tony?" Annie's face turned cherry red. Obviously, she remembered him. "I'd like to call him again to help Ben."

"Do you want me to dance with him?" she whispered.

Caroline smiled. "He'll show you what a good frame feels like. Then you and Ben can practice, and you'll be able to tell Ben how to change his frame so it's like Tony's."

Ben frowned. It was bad enough that Tony got to put his arms around Caroline. He didn't need to put his hands all over Annie too. "Why can't you show us?"

"I'm not even supposed to take the sling off until the end of next week. I won't be able to demonstrate a good frame."

Annie leaned across the table. "When's Tony coming to help?"

"Friday."

"I'll talk to my mom!"

"Do you think it will work?" Ben could barely to remember his steps. He wasn't sure how much his frame would help.

Caroline shrugged her good shoulder. "It depends on you. For someone who's never danced before, you're good. I need you to believe that you can do it so Chris can lean on you. If you can learn from Tony, I know you can do it. Hopefully, it's just this month, then I'll take you through the last dance."

Ben could do that. Even if it was a disaster, he'd try his hardest to make it happen for Caroline. Especially when she looked at him with those eyes. When his phone rang, he didn't want to look away, but the sooner he answered, the sooner he could get back to Caroline. "Hello?"

"I suck, don't I?"

The defeated tone of Chris's voice poured guilt over Ben's conscience. "It's the second day of practice, and I don't know how to lead you yet. You'll be fine."

"I don't want to let you or Caro down."

"You're not going to."

"Then how are we going to make this work?"

"We were just talking about that. Hold on." He set the phone on the table and turned on the speaker. "Caroline has a plan."

"I told you I was terrible."

Maybe stroking her ego would help. "You're not terrible, you're just going to have to work hard for this one, and I know you know how to work hard."

"So, what's my sister's plan?"

"I called Tony this morning," Caroline said.

"Hairless Tony, your old dance partner?"

Ben choked on his sandwich. "Hairless Tony?"

Caroline rolled her eyes. "He waxes his chest before performing Latin dances. Go ahead and laugh. See if I don't make you wax before our final rhumba."

"Would you?" His hand instinctively went to his chest.

"Worry about your chest later," Chris said. "When's Tony going to help us?"

"Friday. He's going to show Ben how to hold the frame and show you how to stand in it."

"Can he still dance? Isn't he like fifty years old now?"

Annie gasped. "Is he really that old?"

Caroline huffed. "Tony's only two years older than me, but his age and chest hair are not important. You're losing focus."

"Fine, Tony's coming to Friday's practice. Regardless of who's teaching us, we need to look at our schedule. I got a call during practice, and I'm going to have to help with the softball league on Tuesday and Thursday nights, so we'll have to skip practice or limit it to an hour. I know you two weren't practicing on the weekends, but maybe we could add a Saturday practice."

"I can't this weekend, but maybe next week." Ben shoved chips into his mouth and hoped no one would ask any other questions.

"Why can't we practice this weekend?"

So much for that. He hadn't told anyone but his family about the trip yet, and he didn't want to lie to Chris or Caroline. How much should he tell them?

"It's his Detroit trip." Annie bit into her sandwich.

Ben winced. Caroline's eyebrows pinched together, and she sat a little straighter. "What's in Detroit?"

"The Lions," Annie said. "They invited him to fly down to meet with them."

Ben closed his eyes.

"I think this is a good time for me to go," Chris said. The call ended, but Ben didn't open his eyes. He couldn't.

"Why didn't you tell me about your trip?"

He sighed before finally looking at Caroline. Hurt etched around her eyes and mouth. "I was going to tell you after I got back."

Annie's lip wobbled. "I didn't know you didn't tell her."

He pointed over his shoulder at the deck. "Why don't you take your sandwich outside so we can have some privacy for a few minutes?"

"I didn't mean to tell. I'm so sorry, Ben. I promise I—"

He pulled his sister off her chair and into a hug. "I'm not mad at you, kid. I'll even take you out for some ice cream to prove it, but first I need to talk to Caroline."

Annie didn't say anything as she carried her food outside. Caroline didn't say anything, either, and that worried him.

Chapter 29

Caroline tried to calm her mind as Annabelle left the room. Why wouldn't Ben tell her about a trip to meet with the Detroit Lions? It was his chance at the NFL. What was he hiding? He was a good guy—the best guy she knew—but he was behaving like the others. How could she have fallen for someone like that again?

As soon as the sliding glass door closed, she leaned back. "Did they offer you a job?"

"What? No, of course not."

"Why are you going if not for a job?"

"It's hard to explain."

Doubtful. "Try."

Ben slouched. "Someone from the Lions contacted me about their nonprofit work. They've seen the stories about the dance-off, and they wanted to talk with me about their community outreach programs. They invited me down to see what it's about and to see if I might be interested. There's been no discussion of a job offer."

"Then why wouldn't you tell me?"

He scrubbed his face.

"Ben?" Her fears mounted. "What's so secret that you can't tell me?"

"I don't want to fail again!"

She flinched.

He sighed. "I don't know what's going to happen, and I didn't want people to get excited if nothing comes of it. *I* didn't want to get excited in case nothing comes of it."

Caroline's anger wavered. "You're scared?"

"Of course I'm scared! I don't want to disappoint everyone ... again."

Her heart broke. "You're not a disappointment."

"Really? Because I'm not playing in the NFL, am I? An entire lifetime of training wasted." He stood up, the chair rattling against the ceramic tile. "I didn't want to tell you about it and then have to explain later that I'm still not good enough."

"Ben." Her heart split into a thousand pieces as she hopped out of her chair, ignoring the lingering aches. Her bare feet carried her across the cool tile until she stood directly in front of him, looking up into sad, blue eyes that stared down at the floor.

She cupped her good hand around his firm jaw, loving the familiar angle of his face. "You have always been good enough. Better than good enough. And you didn't waste anything. If you hadn't learned discipline and your crazy work ethic, we wouldn't be doing so well in the competition, and you wouldn't have gotten that phone call from the Lions."

His eyes shifted back and forth studying her face, but the muscle beneath Caroline's hand tightened. She traced the edge of his lips with her thumb, hoping to coax out a smile. "I'm sorry I got upset," she said. "I wasn't thinking about how hard it might be for you. You deserve this opportunity, and I'm glad you're going to take it."

"Even if it means a job offer in Detroit?" His tone held a note of challenge.

The thought of Ben leaving made her knees wobble. Realizing how important he'd become in only a few short weeks made her head spin. It was bound to happen with them spending so much time together, but she hadn't been prepared for it to happen so intensely. Instead of admitting that to Ben, she leaned into him, enjoying the warmth and solidness of his chest.

As she rested her head against his shoulder, he wrapped his arms around her. "I wasn't trying to keep secrets from you. I didn't tell anyone outside my family."

She nodded, rubbing her cheek against the soft, worn cotton of his T-shirt. "I believe you." And she believed he'd impress everyone he met. "Are you prepared for your trip?"

"What's to do? I'll throw some clothes in a bag and get on a plane."

Caroline chuckled. "Of course you will."

The familiar swish of the sliding glass door whispered across the room. "Can I come back inside yet? It's hot out here."

Caroline nodded.

"Give me a few minutes, kid." Ben loosened his hold enough to wink at Caroline. As soon as the door closed again, he brushed his lips across hers once, twice. The third time his arms tightened, pressing her against him and capturing her mouth completely. Every nibble and taste pulled her closer to him. It had been so long since anyone had made her feel that way. She would miss it.

"Ben?" Annabelle's whine doused their heat.

His lips softened before breaking their connection. "Yes?"

"It's been five minutes."

Caroline bit back a smile as a blush warmed her cheeks. "Come back in, Annabelle. You and your brother should probably get ready to head home anyway. I need to take a shower, and it takes twice as long with my arm. Maybe you can help Ben pack."

Ben pressed his lips together. "You're kicking us out?"

"I'll see you tomorrow at practice."

"But that's twenty-four hours away."

"I think you'll survive. Besides, you can't stay too late. You need to stop for ice cream."

"And I'm hot now, so I'll need something big." Annabelle stopped beside Caroline and hugged her. "I hope you're not too mad at Ben."

"I'm not mad at all."

"Good, because I like being your friend."

"I like being yours too." Caroline hugged the girl until two strong hands circled her waist.

"All right already." He held out his keys. "Go start my truck. I'll be down in a minute."

Annabelle rolled her eyes as she took them. "Or five."

Chapter 30

Ben crossed his arms as Tony led Chris around the dance floor. He couldn't deny it—Tony was a genius. Whatever he'd said to Chris when he arrived had not only made her blush, it stiffened her spine and pushed back her shoulders so that she looked more like Caroline and less like a pitcher trying to dance. And Tony hadn't touched Caroline once since he'd arrived, so maybe having him around wasn't such a bad idea.

When the song ended, Annie clapped while Caroline cheered. Tony spun Chris out for a bow. "You've got it," he said. "It needs to be cleaned up, but all the parts are there. Caroline can help you with the minutia."

Chris nodded. "I feel better about it now."

"You should. You're going to do great"—Tony pointed at Ben—"as soon as I teach this guy how to hold you."

Ben pushed away from the wall. "This is going to be weird, isn't it?"

"No weirder than last time. Let's see your frame."

Ben shuffled to the middle of the room, keeping his eyes on Chris. "I hope you all appreciate what I'm doing here." He raised his arms in a way that he hoped reflected Tony's frame. A shorter, solid body pressed against his back before two hands wrapped around his arms. Obviously, he wasn't there yet.

For the next thirty minutes, Ben danced between Chris and Tony. He nearly took down Chris twice during their first few laps around the room, but by the time they'd finished their third full routine, they'd settled into a comfortable, weird system that had somehow boosted his confidence. So far Tony was two for two.

"That looks so good." Caroline beamed at them from the side of the room. For the first time since the accident her eyes sparkled. Ben would dance with Tony himself if it kept her that happy.

Ben let go of Chris's hand to join Caroline and tried to ignore the ridiculous look on his sister's face as she walked out to take her turn with Tony. As Ben approached Caroline, he slipped an arm around her waist. "I don't know how Tony does it, but you two are turning us into dancers." When Caroline leaned into him, he pulled her closer.

"I've never doubted you or Chris, but I wasn't sure how to teach you without being able to show you. I know you're not a fan of dancing with Tony, so I really appreciate this."

He pressed a kiss to her temple. "You're hard to say no to."

Annie giggled. Ben tightened his hold on Caroline.

She chuckled. "Thanks for letting Annabelle help out. I know this isn't comfortable for you."

"You said it would help. Will it? Because if this is just some excuse to let Annie hang around, it isn't really necessary. I could take her home and lock her in her room."

"I always wondered what it would be like to have a big brother. I wouldn't have needed parents with someone like you watching out for me."

"I'd rather be too protective than find out something terrible happened when I could have prevented it. Besides, she takes care of me too. She packed a week's worth of clothes for me to take downstate this weekend."

Her back stiffened. "When do you leave?"

"In two hours."

"I hope it goes well." The tension in her voice didn't match the sentiment of her words though.

"Are you sure?"

"Of course." She leaned away to look at him. "I want you to get everything you want."

"You don't sound like it."

She tucked her head into his chest. "I do ... even if it means you don't come back."

Was she really worried about that? "I'll come back."

"Even if they offer you a job?"

Chris, Annie, and Tony laughed behind them, but Ben turned to look only at Caroline. "I'm coming back. I don't know what's going to happen with the job or with us, but I'm not going to disappear."

"Good, because I'm getting used to having you around."

Her confession, coupled with the pink tinge of her cheeks, filled a part of Ben's heart that he hadn't realized was empty. He didn't think he'd be able to take any job offer that took him away from her.

"Ben!" Annie stomped across the dance floor and plowed into him. "Tony said we could go get ice cream."

Panic seized his throat. "You and Tony?"

She looked at him like he'd grown a third eye. "No. He's older than you. He said we could all go."

"That was nice of him, but I can't take you. I need to get to the airport."

Chris wrapped an arm around Annie's neck. "I've got you, Squirt. I'll make sure you get home."

Ben crossed his arms. "Did you call Mom?"

"Can you call her for me?" She pressed her hands together as if in prayer. "If you call her, maybe she'll let me stay out."

"I'm not sure *I* want you staying out with people twice your age." He pointed to his phone. "If you want permission, you call Mom." Then he turned to Chris. "I'm trusting you with my sister."

Caroline leaned into him. "I've taught Chris well. Annabelle's in good hands."

"I know." Ben ignored his audience and kissed her. "I'm a little bit jealous of her right now."

"Don't be jealous. Enjoy your trip to Detroit, and when you get back, maybe I'll take you out for ice cream too."

Chapter 31

Caroline checked her watch again. The PA system announced another TSA warning regarding luggage and strangers. A horn sounded an instant before the luggage carousel started moving.

Where was Ben? His plane had landed twenty minutes ago. She'd wanted to surprise him and pick him up at the airport, but what if he'd taken a different flight? He didn't know she was meeting him—he might have changed plans. The automatic doors whooshed open behind her, letting in a blast of summer air before the chill of uncertainty crawled across her skin.

Maybe she should meet him near security instead. As she walked the short distance through the small airport, the chatter grew louder. A few giggles, some hand-slapping, and the familiar click of digital cameras met her ears. When she rounded the corner, her heart fluttered.

A small group of people surrounded Ben, posing for pictures and getting autographs. Standing nearly a head taller than the next tallest person and decked out in Hawaii-blue-and-gray Detroit Lions gear, he was hard to miss. Ben spoke with each person, shaking hands and giving hugs. He smiled easily, seemingly comfortable and at ease as he greeted each stranger. She'd never seen him so relaxed. He looked completely natural as he talked with everyone. How could he give that up?

Several minutes later, Ben finally saw her. The instant he spotted her, his smile widened. Her fluttering heart quickened. She expected him to rush over, but he finished signing autographs and took two more pictures before heading toward her. With each step, his already imposing presence grew more impressive. He seemed taller. Broader. More confident than she'd ever seen him.

"What are you doing here?" He didn't wait for a response as he wrapped his arms around her. "Should you be driving with your arm?"

"I didn't drive. Chris and your mom dropped me off with your car." Not the welcome she'd hoped for, but at least he was home, and she was back in his arms. "You'll have to take me to my place before you go home. Are you mad?"

"Are you kidding me?" He stepped back but didn't let go of her, leaning close to her ear so his breath tickled her neck. "If I didn't have a crowd of people behind me, I'd show you just how happy I am to see you."

She shivered, relieved. "Oh."

He brushed a feathery kiss behind her ear. "I can't wait to take you home."

Caroline's knees wobbled. Did he have any idea how he affected her? She tried to respond, but no words came out.

Ben laughed, his chest rumbling against hers. "Come on. I have my bag. Let's get out of here." He wrapped his hand around hers before pulling her toward the door. She could tell by the nodding and whispering that a few more people had recognized him, but they kept their distance and let him head out of the airport.

Once they'd pulled out of the parking lot, Caroline finally found the courage to ask. "How was your trip?"

"I didn't know what to expect, but I didn't expect that. It would have been enough to be flown down and back, but they flew me down first-class and sent a car to pick me up at the airport. That wasn't even close to the best part of the weekend. On Saturday, I went to the stadium and met some of the office staff, then the players came, and we met with these kids who come from some of the worst situations, and one little girl found a video online of me dancing, and she asked if I'd dance with her, which started this whole miniature dance lesson."

Ben talked all the way back to Caroline's house, up the stairs, into the apartment, and onto the couch where she sat next to him, expecting to cuddle, but settling for looking at picture after picture after picture on his phone. The more he talked, the more energy he exuded. Not a hyper, crazy energy, but a quiet sizzle that stirred an excitement in her spirit.

"It looks like you had an amazing time." She stared at his phone's screen, captivated by the sincerity and joy on his face in each photo.

"I didn't think I could be that close to the football field without being on it, but just being there ... I don't know how to explain it. It wasn't just football, you know?"

Like dancing for Pathways, even though she wasn't officially part of the board or staff. "I think I get it."

Ben sighed but he smiled, wrapping an arm around her and pulling her close. Finally. When the warmth of his lips pressed against her forehead, she closed her eyes and relaxed against him. "I'm sorry. I've been talking since we left the airport. How was your weekend?"

"Nothing I can say could compete with yours."

"That doesn't mean I don't want to hear about it."

"Why don't you tell me more about Detroit?"

"I don't know what else to say."

The words threatened to clog her throat, but Caroline worked up the courage to push them out. "What's next?"

He tugged on her ponytail holder, releasing her hair and running his fingers through it. "Next for what?"

"For the Detroit Lions."

His hand paused in her hair. "They want me to come back."

Her heart cracked. "For a job?"

"Not officially."

"Unofficially?"

He caressed the side of her neck and whispered, "It's on the table."

Her head spun.

Ben brushed his lips against her ear, leaving only a breath's distance between them. "Detroit's nice, but there's a lot to love about Traverse City."

Everything inside of her fluttered. Did he really care for her enough—*love* her enough—to give up the NFL? Again? Could she let him?

From the moment she'd spotted him in the airport, his smile was bigger and his voice lighter. His whole being radiated happiness. How could he give that up?

How could she ask him to? She couldn't. She wouldn't. But instead of worrying about it, she'd snuggle close for as long as she could have him.

Chapter 32

Caroline pinned another piece of Chris's hair into place. The muted chatter of the audience pulsed through the theater's walls. One more dance before Chris and Ben took the stage. Caroline was afraid she might vomit.

"Ouch!" Chris pushed Caroline's hand away. "I think my hair is fine. I'll probably set off the metal detectors, there are so many pins in there. It's not going to move."

"Sorry." Caroline crossed her arms as she examined her sister's reflection. Chris hadn't fought the hairstyle, but she'd been pretty vocal about the stage make-up, not that it stopped Caroline from applying it. She'd never seen her sister with smoky eyes or ruby lips. It took her a few minutes to get used to it, but Caroline couldn't deny that the splash of color brightened her sister's face.

Chris stood, straightening the long, purple skirt of Caroline's favorite dancing dress. "I look so ... weird."

"You look amazing."

"At least it's comfortable." Chris let her head drop forward before rolling it from side to side, then she shrugged her shoulders back one at a time. "How much longer?"

"Maybe ten minutes?"

"What do we do until then?"

"Let's go find Ben and Tony." Caroline opened the dressing room door. Chris checked her reflection one more time before strutting out the door. Caroline shook her head. At least Chris would look the part on the dance floor because she wasn't fooling anyone in the hallway.

In the lobby, Ben and Tony laughed about something but stopped when they saw Chris and Caroline. Caroline didn't look much different than she did on a daily basis, so she was pretty sure they were staring at Chris.

Ben winked at her. "That's a new look for you."

"Don't get used to it. I could stand for a little less hair spray." She twirled, fluttering the purple skirt around her waist. "This dress is pretty cool, though."

Tony whistled. "You're gorgeous, Christine."

"I'll be me again in about thirty minutes. Let's practice that last turn again." She grabbed Ben's hand and pulled him to the middle of the lobby.

Tony's eyes never left Chris as he followed her and Ben at a distance. When he stepped behind Ben to correct a frame slip, Chris avoided eye contact.

Interesting.

Susan rushed out of the auditorium wearing a fire engine-red Pathway's T-shirt. Her eyes brightened when she spotted Caroline. "We're next. They're introducing the Pathway's video now. Where are Chris and Ben?"

"Right here." Ben led Chris across the lobby. "We'll head backstage now."

Susan pulled the dancers toward her as she stretched onto her tiptoes to kiss each of their cheeks. "We really lucked out with you."

Ben swooped down and kissed Caroline's cheek as he walked past. When he and her sister walked away, Tony tucked her hand under his arm. "You look terrified."

"I don't know how our coaches did it, sending us into competitions week after week without throwing up."

"Yeah, well, they weren't in love with us."

Caroline's hand clenched around his arm. "I don't know if I'd call it love."

"Call it whatever you want. You're nuts about the guy."

"I won't deny that." She followed him to the auditorium doors, but he stopped a foot short. "Don't you want to go in?"

"Not for a second. I'm scared witless about what's going to happen in there."

Caroline laughed as she leaned against him. "Look at us. Championship dancers, but scaredy-pants teachers." Pushing Tony a few inches further to the left, she stretched to look through the porthole-like window in the door.

Judy stood in the middle of the dance floor, her floor-length, silver gown twinkling in the stage lights. She swept her arm into the air as she backed off the floor. A spotlight illuminated the far corner. People applauded. Caroline recognized Erica's high-pitched whistle as Ben led Chris onto the dance floor. Caroline didn't know what had happened between the lobby and the dance floor, but the awkward tension and uncertainty of the past month had somehow disappeared, and best friends—nearly unrecognizable in their dance clothes—smiled at each other with an ease Caroline hadn't seen in a long time.

Maybe they could pull it off.

The music started. Caroline couldn't watch—she didn't want to watch—but she couldn't look away. She couldn't move. Every muscle in her body tensed as she stood frozen at an uncomfortable angle watching her sister hold her right arm up and out, her head turned to the left. Ben's back straightened as he guided her across the floor. Their feet glided effortlessly, but they rushed through the second turn, and Caroline was sure Ben moved his hips. Through the entire set, they never stopped smiling and never stopped dancing.

An eternity later, the music stopped. Ben and Chris bowed. Gratitude, joy, and pride swelled in Caroline's chest. Filling her heart. Breaking it. Unsure how to quench the emotions, she turned to Tony's chest and cried.

"Whoa, what's wrong?" He patted her back and moved her away from the door. "What happened?"

She shook her head. She couldn't find the words. Couldn't talk without sobbing. Couldn't believe how much everyone had done for Pathways. What had she done to deserve such amazing people in her life?

"Come on. They're going to give the scores soon."

Caroline stepped back, wiping away the tears. As her vision cleared, she noticed the matching black smears on Tony's shirt. She sucked in a gasp and tried to rub out the mascara marks.

His chest vibrated under her hand. "Forget about my shirt. Look at your face."

"Oh, no. Do you have a handkerchief I can use?"

"Do I look like my grandpa?"

Caroline rubbed her cheeks, pulling at the delicate skin under her eyes as she rubbed mascara smears off her face and onto her hands. Tony nudged her toward the theater doors. She willed her feet to keep moving as her heart thundered in her chest. It didn't matter how well Chris and Ben did. By simply dancing, they'd kept Pathways in the race for the grand prize, but Caroline wanted the best for them. She wanted Ben to stay positive, and she wanted Chris to be empowered, not embarrassed.

Tony looked through the window, but Caroline couldn't make herself take the final steps. People clapped, but she couldn't tell if they were more or less excited than they'd been for the previous couple. Not that the audience's excitement level mattered. They didn't know the difference between good dancing and entertaining dancing.

The double doors flew open as Ben and Chris burst into the lobby.

Chris walked straight to Caroline. "Did you watch? How was it?"

"What do you mean? Didn't you get your scores?"

"I don't care what they think. I want to know what you think."

The tears started again. "You were ..." Wonderful. Beautiful. More than Caroline could have expected. But none of those words made it out. Instead, her lips twisted into her ugly-cry face. Someone pressed a tissue against her hand, so she took advantage and covered her face.

She didn't have to look up to know whose arms wrapped around her. The solid strength of Ben's arms and the familiar scent of his skin tickled her nostrils.

"You were great," said Tony. "I'm so proud of you guys."

"I know we weren't perfect, but I didn't think we were so bad you'd cry about it," Chris said. Someone bumped into Caroline's shoulder. Probably her sister. It pushed her closer to Ben, so she took advantage and wrapped her arms around his waist.

He kissed her above her ear. "Are you okay?" he whispered.

She nodded, not ready to talk. She wanted to soak in the amazingness of the people around her.

"Come on, crybaby. Help me get out of this costume so we can go celebrate."

Caroline knew she needed to go with Chris, but she didn't want to let go of Ben. She didn't want to lose that feeling ... to think about him leaving.

"Caro?" Chris's voice softened.

No, she wouldn't ruin their night with her runaway emotions. Stepping away from Ben, Caroline winked at him before grabbing Chris's arm. "Let's go. We'll have you looking like a tomboy again in no time."

Chapter 33

Caroline pulled the last weed out of the flower bed and tossed it into the wheelbarrow. Even in the shade of the Pathways house, sweat clung to her. Not that she minded. After a month of caution and limited movement, she savored the opportunity to use both arms, even if she still had a limited range of motion. The doctor said she wouldn't need physical therapy if she took her time, kept it easy. Caroline had no plans to risk prolonging her injury.

Looking along the side of the house, she admired the evidence of her hard work. Who knew weeding could be so fulfilling?

The back door opened, and Mary stepped onto the deck. She carried a tall glass of water toward Caroline. "I brought you some water like you asked."

"Thanks." Caroline brushed her hands on her shorts, effectively transferring the dirt before taking the offered glass. "Did you enjoy the dance-off Friday night?"

Mary nodded as she passed off the glass. "They danced pretty, but they didn't win."

"They finished third out of six. That's not bad. Why don't you sit with me for a while?" She motioned to the patio furniture.

Mary offered a hint of a smile, which Caroline had come to realize was Mary's happy face. Pulling a chair into the still-humid though slightly cooler shade, Caroline sighed as she pressed her back against the thick seat cushion, stretching her arms overhead to pull at her tight back muscles.

Mary's chair bounced and squeaked as she dragged it across the wood. "Does your arm hurt?"

"Not much anymore. It's a little weak, though, so I'll have to take care of it."

"Why did it get weak?"

"Because I didn't use it for a month. Maybe I should lift weights, but only with that arm."

"That would be funny. Are you sad about Ben?"

Caroline choked on her water. "Why would I be sad about Ben?"

"Because he danced with another girl instead of you."

Caroline sagged against the chair at Mary's innocence. "I'm not sad. He danced with my sister, and I like both of them. Besides, Ben's going to dance with me again this month."

"Because he likes you more?"

"No, because we're dance partners."

"Did he kiss your sister too?"

Heat overwhelmed Caroline. "No, Ben and Chris didn't kiss. Why ... why would you think that?"

Mary shrugged. "Erica said you and Ben were boyfriend and girlfriend. Boyfriends and girlfriends kiss. It's hot out here. I think I want to go inside."

Caroline didn't try to stop Mary because she wasn't sure if she was ready for any more of her questions. Apparently, Caroline and Ben needed to be more careful about how they behaved in front of the ladies, and probably everyone else. She couldn't actually think of a single instance when she and Ben had so much as held hands in front of any of them, let alone kissed.

"There you are!" Susan walked around the corner of the house, a light breeze teasing the bottom of her skirt. Dressed in a flowy pink skirt, a blouse, and sandals, it looked like Susan had come from church. "Lucy said you were back here. How's the weeding?"

"I just finished. Do you have time to sit for a while?"

"I wish. Todd's waiting for me in the car. I was hoping you might have a few extra minutes this afternoon." She hustled across the yard and onto the deck. "Will you be around for a while?"

"I can be. What do you need?"

Susan sat in Mary's vacant chair. "I need help filing some things."

Caroline mentally pictured Susan's office. They'd repaired the hole in the ceiling, but that meant moving the desk and filing cabinets. Everything had been moved back to their original spots, but papers and files filled most of the surfaces as they'd emptied the filing cabinets to make things easier to move. Caroline had been itching to help reorganize. She smiled. "Of course. Do you need it done today?"

"Unfortunately, yes. A contractor called the board president yesterday to donate some of the repairs for the house. He freed up time tomorrow morning, so I need to get everything put away by then. Todd's niece is having a baby shower this afternoon. I can skip it if I need to, but—"

"Don't you dare skip it. I can put everything away. Most of it should be in order anyway."

Susan clasped both of her hands around Caroline's. "Thank you so much. You have been such a help to me the past few months. I'm not sure what I would have done without you."

"It's my pleasure." Getting all those files safely tucked away would give Caroline more pleasure than she wanted to admit. No one wanted to be that nerdy.

"I'll unlock the office on my way through the house, but please don't wait too long before you go in. I don't trust Lucy not to let herself in to reorganize. It took me weeks to find everything the last time she got in there."

"I don't want to risk anything like that happening again." Caroline chugged her water before pushing her achy body out of the chair. "I'll dump the weeds on the compost pile, then go right in."

"You truly are wonderful. Someday I'll find a way to repay you for all of this."

Caroline knew exactly how they could repay her, but she wouldn't bring it up until the board officially announced an open position. Until then, she managed to keep the wheelbarrow steady across the bumpy yard before emptying it in the back. After putting it away and giving her hands and arms a thorough scrubbing in the kitchen sink, she let herself into Susan's office.

The piles on the chairs didn't look as big as she remembered. Maybe it wouldn't take too long. Double-checking to make sure the files were still alphabetized, she scooped up her first arm full and hauled it to the filing cabinet. She opened the empty drawer, except it wasn't empty. At least two dozen files had been stacked on top of each other inside. She put those files on top of the cabinet so she could hang the files in her arms appropriately.

Once she'd finished the first drawer, Caroline checked the next three to make sure they were empty. Not a single one. Each one contained stacks of random files. Okay, so it would take a bit longer than she'd expected.

Finally Forever

An hour later, Caroline shut the last cabinet drawer, having combined duplicate files and reorganizing the misfiled. Between the outdoor and indoor work, her lower back and shoulders begged for relief. A warm shower had never been so appealing. She'd just leave a quick note for Susan, then head home.

Plopping into the desk chair, Caroline scanned the area for a clean sheet of paper, but she'd done her job well and cleared off the desk. She opened the top drawer and pulled out a few documents while she searched for paper. After finally finding a small notepad, she scribbled a quick explanation of her work, then ripped off the page and taped it to the computer monitor.

As she returned things to the drawer, she couldn't stop herself from scanning them. Donation letters. State paperwork. A résumé with a bright green note stuck to it. Her gut told her to put it in the drawer and walk away, but her eyes kept reading while her hope fizzled.

> I think he's perfect for the job. Let's start the process. He can relocate at the end of the year. RM

RM. Richard Merchant, the Pathways board president. Caroline pulled off the sticky note and scanned the résumé. Lane Plamondon from Cedar Rapids, Iowa. Executive Director for At Home, a residential nonprofit for special needs adults. Former executive director for two other nonprofit organizations, both working with special needs adults.

Her chest constricted.

How could she have been so stupid?

Pathways wasn't going to hire a volunteer as their house manager. They needed an experienced executive director to lead the entire organization, and they'd found one. With thirty years of experience. Glowing recommendation letters attached.

Her hand shook as she reapplied the sticky note and tucked the traitorous paper back in the desk. She should have known. She should have asked. She should have done more than just volunteer to dance for money.

There wasn't going to be a job at Pathways. As a volunteer, sure. Maybe someday as a grossly overqualified executive assistant, but not like she'd hoped or planned. Not like she'd dreamed. She should have talked to Susan.

That realization blocked her breath, but her next thought nearly strangled her—Ben was going to sacrifice his dream for her. She couldn't let him, not when she knew how much it hurt.

Without so much as a goodbye, she pushed in the chair, shut the office door, and slipped out of the house. It wasn't until she was back in her apartment complex parking lot that the reality of her situation overwhelmed her. Caroline dropped her head against the steering wheel and cried.

Tuesday evening, Ben pulled into the dance studio's parking lot not sure what to expect. After spending the weekend helping his dad retile two bathrooms, he'd been looking forward to Monday night's dance practice. When Caroline canceled, he had about five seconds to think of a way to spend their free time together before she told him she wouldn't be available the rest of the night. He'd called once, texted twice. She finally responded at ten o'clock with Thursday's dress rehearsal schedule, but nothing else. And now he sat in the parking lot looking at a vehicle he didn't recognize. Maybe it was Caroline's loaner car.

It wasn't. He didn't know how he knew it, but somehow, he knew Caroline wasn't inside. Something was going on, and she was shutting him out. Grabbing his dance shoes off the passenger seat, he headed inside. His heartbeat pulsed through his ears as his eyes honed in on the double metal doors. Stepping into the studio, he froze.

Tony stood on the other side of the room tapping away on his phone.

Ben's frustration simmered. "What are you doing here?"

"Dance practice."

"Where's Caroline?"

"Didn't she text you?"

"Just the time. She didn't tell me she wasn't coming." What was going on?

"Man, I'm sorry. I don't want to get in the middle of this."

"Don't worry, you won't. Sorry you came all this way for nothing." Ben stomped out of the studio. He wasn't sure if he should be afraid or upset or angry, but he was going to find Caroline so he could figure it out.

Peeling out of the parking lot, he ignored the speed limit signs as he wove through traffic and out to Caroline's. His hope deflated as he pulled around to her building and spotted her vacant parking spot. Taking the empty space beside where she usually parked, he left his truck running as he ran inside and up the stairs. He reined in every ounce of emotion to knock as gently as he could.

No answer.

He knocked again. Then he pounded. The door shook with each hit, but no one answered. He ran out to his truck, his mind listing and checking off possibilities.

He'd start at Chris's house. He wanted to call ahead to make sure Caroline was there and safe, but he didn't want to give either of the sisters a chance to talk him out of coming over. He certainly didn't want to give them enough time to run away.

Ben drove back into town as fast as he could without hitting anyone and desperately tried not to lose his temper with the idiot drivers on the road. Fine if they didn't want to speed, but could they at least drive the speed limit? He pulled into Chris's neighborhood, then onto her street, then in front of her house. The small, yellow-and-brown bungalow sat on a long, narrow lot like the rest of the homes in town. Instead of parking in the back alley, Ben saved three seconds and parked out front.

Before he reached the front door, Chris swung it open. "What are you doing here?"

"Is Caroline here?" He stood toe-to-toe with Chris as he tried to look past her into the house.

She didn't move.

Caroline was definitely there.

"Have you called her?"

Ben crossed his arms to prevent himself from moving his friend out of the way. "Can I please see her?"

"Call her."

"She won't answer. She won't text me. She's canceled two dance practices." As he listed the unusual behaviors, his panic level increased until his arms shook with the effort not to plow into the house. "At least, tell me if she's okay. Is she sick? Did something happen? I'm imagining the worst of everything here, so please tell me that she's alive and whole."

Chris laid a hand on Ben's chest and tried to push him back. He didn't budge. She sighed, then lowered her voice, "Step back so I can close the door and talk to you outside."

Ben didn't know if that was good or bad, but he didn't care. At least he'd have some answers. Giving Chris barely enough room to close the door, he stepped back and waited for her. Instead of standing with him, she nodded toward the sidewalk and walked past him. He had to follow. "What's wrong? She wasn't at work yesterday or today, was she?"

Chris shook her head as she led him away from the house and through the neighborhood. "I'm breaking about a dozen of my personal rules here, so I hope you appreciate this. I don't want to get involved—at all—but I also don't want to see my sister this upset again."

"Upset?" Had he already done something wrong? Was it her arm? "Stop stalling and tell me what's wrong."

Chris groaned. "You had to date my sister."

Ben grabbed her arm, stopping her beside him. "Christine!"

"She's not going to get the job at Pathways."

"How does she know that?"

"She was working in the office at the house when she found the information."

Ben's mind whirled. He knew exactly how she felt, but how did that explain her disappearance? "Why wouldn't she tell me?"

Chris shifted from foot to foot as she avoided making eye contact. "Because she wants you to go to Detroit, but she doesn't know how to break up with you."

The news nearly tackled him. He needed to see Caroline. He needed to tell her he wouldn't leave, he knew how she felt, and he'd help her through it. Two hands grabbed his arm, holding him back. "Let me go. I need to talk to her."

"She doesn't want to talk to you."

"Well, she's going to!" Ben wrenched his arm free as he stormed toward the house.

As he reached the stairs, Chris jumped in front of him.

"She doesn't want to talk to you."

He stepped forward, but she braced her hands on his chest and her feet against the door. "I need to help her!"

"She doesn't want it!"

"I need to try!"

"Give her some space!"

The door opened. Ben fell into Chris who fell through the doorway. They crashed to the floor.

"What are you doing?" Caroline glared down at them, her arms crossed against her chest. "Get up before someone calls the police."

He scrambled to his feet, his back twisting uncomfortably as he tried not to crush Chris. He should have helped, but he couldn't pull his gaze from Caroline. In running shorts, a wrinkled T-shirt, and an uneven ponytail, she reminded him of Chris, but he'd never seen Chris with such swollen, red eyes. The breath stopped in his throat. "Please talk to me. Tell me what's going on."

She pulled him further into the house then slammed the door behind him. "Fine, but not out there."

"You don't have to do this." Chris scrambled to her feet, her hair messed up and fists clenched. "He can leave."

"It's fine. I'll just rip off the band-aid and get this over with."

"I'm not going to Detroit." Ben couldn't stop himself from blurting it out. She had to know that he wasn't going anywhere, that he didn't want to. He'd do whatever he had to do to convince her.

Instead of looking relieved, Caroline's eyes watered. Chris glared at Ben, but Caroline shook her head. "It's okay, Chris. Give us a minute."

Chapter 34

Caroline waited until her sister shut her bedroom door, then she sat in the lone armchair, securing space between herself and Ben. She'd expected him to come looking for her—she'd imagined what the encounter might be like—but she hadn't prepared herself for a redneck brawl on the front lawn. Now he sat in her sister's living room, disheveled and wild looking. And as handsome as ever. Caroline prayed for strength to resist his charms.

Ben sat on the end of the couch, as close to her as possible. "Chris told me about Pathways. I'm so sorry."

She didn't doubt it. She also didn't doubt that he would comfort her if she asked him to, but she couldn't continue to rely on him, not if she was going to do what needed to be done. "It'll be fine. It was never a guaranteed thing anyway."

"But it was your dream. I know how hard it is to lose that."

"That's why I didn't want to tell you. I didn't want to bring up any bad memories or whine about my silly little job."

"It's not silly or little if it's important to you."

Caroline gave half a smile. "Sounds like you've heard that before."

"I could give you positive affirmations and encouragements for days. I will if you need me to. Whatever you need, just tell me."

He reached for her hand, but Caroline pressed it to her chest. She couldn't let her guard down, even for a second.

Confusion clouded Ben's face. "Why are you doing this? Chris said you want me to move to Detroit."

"You need to go."

"There hasn't been an official job offer."

"There will be, and when they make it, you have to take it. Whatever it is, whatever they offer, you have to go."

"Why are you so adamant about this?"

Caroline's eyes watered again. She didn't try to fight it this time. Instead, she grabbed the box of tissues. "Because I wasn't prepared for how much it would suck to watch my dream disappear. I can't imagine how hard it was for you. You spent *years* preparing. You have a second chance at being part of the NFL. You need to take it."

"My dream was to *play* in the NFL, not just be part of it."

"But you were so happy when you came back from that trip. You're a natural with the fans." She smiled at the memory despite the heartache. "You should have seen yourself at the airport. If there's any chance that you could do that full time, then you need to take it."

"*If* I do, that doesn't mean we need to end anything."

But her past said otherwise. "I couldn't make two relationships work with both fiancés in town. I don't know if I have the strength to try it again long distance." She closed her eyes to force out the next part. "And I don't want you to feel tied down in case you meet someone amazing."

"I've already met someone amazing!" Ben dropped his head into his hands, raking his fingers through his hair. "What do I have to say to convince you this isn't a phase or a fling?"

"You don't know that yet because this is the first relationship you've been in. You deserve a chance to see what else is out there."

"I don't care what else is out there!" Ben jumped off the couch, his hands clenched at his sides. "Why are you so convinced this won't work between us?"

"What chance will we have if I'm here and you're in Detroit?"

"I'm not in Detroit!"

"But you should be!" Caroline stood on the chair so she could look down at Ben, desperate for any advantage to help him understand. "You will be. You deserve better than some twice-engaged cast-off and a boring insurance job. Don't settle for the first job and the first woman that comes along. You don't want to end up like …"

She tried to say it, but she couldn't admit what a failure her life had become. Ben must have sensed it because his hands relaxed. He reached for her. She stepped back, but she didn't have anywhere to go. As she fell backward, Ben caught her, securing his arm around her like a vice and pulling her against his chest. She wedged her arms between herself and his shoulder, but he only held her tighter.

"Let go of me."

He wrapped his arms around hers. "I could only hope to turn out like you."

"Don't." She shook her head as she thrashed in his arms, needing to get away from him. "You need to let me go." Ben pressed a kiss to her forehead, but he loosened his hold. Caroline allowed herself a moment to relax against him, listening to the strong rhythm of his heart, before stepping out of his arms.

Putting the chair between them so she could hide her shaking legs, she straightened her spine and faked a confidence she didn't feel. "I mean it. You need to let me go because I'm letting you go. Your training period at Morrison is over, so we don't need to see each other there. We're both adults. We can dance together for the rest of this month, raise as much money as possible for Pathways, then you'll be free to leave."

Ben's face turned red as he opened his mouth, then quickly clamped it shut. He muttered something, but she couldn't make it out. He walked toward her, stopping on the other side of the chair. "You are the most ridiculous person I have ever met."

"That should make it easier for you to leave then."

The anger melted off his face, replaced by a dark sadness. "Yeah, but I love you too."

Her knees failed her then, but Ben didn't stick around to catch her that time. Instead, he finally listened to her and walked out the front door.

He loved her? Two other men had loved her, but Ben wasn't like them. Nothing about their relationship was. Those words coming from Ben's mouth rattled every bone in her body.

"You're making a mistake."

Caroline crashed into the chair as Chris shuffled into the room. "I don't need this right now," Caroline said.

"I know, but you need to know that you're making a mistake. Ben's crazy about you, and he's the best guy I've ever known. He wouldn't lead you on if he wasn't serious."

"And I won't do the same to him." But even as she said it, Caroline knew it was a lie, because, with Pathways out of the picture, she wanted Ben's strength and comfort even if she only had it for a little while. Still, she pushed her desires down. "I want him to have the best."

Chris wrapped her arm around Caroline's shoulder and guided her to the couch. After they'd settled in, Chris revealed a long blue tube of chocolate chip deliciousness. "I hope you two figure this out someday. Until then, we have cookie dough."

Ben propped a pillow behind his head as he tried to get comfortable. It was hard being at home when he wanted to be at Caroline's. With Caroline. Talking to Caroline. It had been a week since their conversation at Chris's house, and she hadn't caved an inch.

She had deemed him "talented enough" to forgo long rehearsals, so she cut lessons back to an hour. Somehow, she'd talked Tony into attending almost every session and handling the majority of Ben's questions. Afterward, she'd rush out ahead of him. She wouldn't take his calls or answer his texts.

He struggled to concentrate at work, but that was nothing compared to nights at home. He tried not to remember the softness of Caroline's skin. The music of her voice. The joy that she found in life, for herself and others. Man, was he glad he'd never gotten involved with a woman when he was in school. He'd never have graduated.

Someone knocked on his bedroom door. "Can I come in?"

"Yeah."

The door inched open. Annie peeked through the crack. "Are you sure?"

"I'm sure." He patted the mattress beside him. "What's up?" She sat on the bed instead of jumping on it and lay next to her brother. He put his arm around her, letting her snuggle against him.

"Is Caroline okay?"

"She's fine. Why would you ask that?"

"Because you don't go over there anymore, and you never talk to each other." Annie tilted her head so she could look at him. "Did you break up?"

He'd been avoiding that conversation, but the time had come. "We did." His sister's eyes watered. He tried not to groan out loud. What did she have to cry about?

"Are you sad?"

"Of course, but why are *you* sad?"

"I miss her."

His chest ached. "Me too."

"Are you going to get her back?"

"I don't know how."

"Did you tell her that you love her?"

"What makes you think I love her?"

"Why wouldn't you love her? She's the best big sister ever." Annie sighed as she rolled onto her back, staring at the ceiling.

There was the sister he remembered. "She was good for you, wasn't she?"

"What am I going to do without her?"

"You survived your first twelve years without her. I think you'll make it."

Annie flopped onto her stomach, propping her head in her hands so she could look at him. "But that was before Caroline was in my life. Now that I know how awesome she is, I know how empty my life will be without her."

He couldn't have said it better himself. "I know, kid."

"So, what are we going to do?"

Good question. "I don't know. What do you think we should do?"

"Text her."

"Tried it."

"Call her."

"Did it."

She pushed herself up. "Go see her."

He shrugged. "I did."

Annie pressed her lips together. "How many times?"

"I'm not going to stalk her. What else have you got?"

"I don't know. I'm just a kid. Talk to Mom and Dad. Talk to her mom and dad." She slapped a hand on his leg, her eyes wide. "Call Chris."

"I would if it could help, but none of them can make Caroline change her mind."

Annie's shoulders sagged. "That's it? She's just ... gone?"

The finality of her statement threatened to strangle him. "I'm afraid so." His sister teared up again. Great. On top of his heartache, he had to worry about hers. "Don't cry. We'll get through this."

She shook her head. "I don't want to get through it. I want to fix it." Her nose scrunched up in a way that Ben recognized—Annie's planning face.

Grabbing her wrist, he pulled her to his chest and draped an arm around her neck. "I want to fix this too, but there's nothing we can do. It's Caroline's decision, and we need to respect that, okay?"

"But I don't—"

"I don't either, but there's nothing we can do. I don't want you to get involved, do you understand?"

"What if I called—"

He flexed his arm, tightening his hold, but not too much. "Do not call Caroline."

"But Ben—"

"Promise me you won't call her."

Annie went limp. "Fine. I won't call Caroline." Then she poked him in the ribs, wiggling her fingers across the tender skin.

Ben jumped as he laughed. "Hey! None of that."

"Then let me out of the headlock." She reached around and tickled some more. Ben released her but had his hands around her ankles before she knew it. Jumping off the bed, he pulled her with him, hanging her upside down facing away from him. "No fair!" She swung her arms around, but she couldn't reach him.

"Benefit of being the big brother."

"Someday I'll be too big for you to drag around."

"Until then, I'm in charge."

She snorted. "You wish."

Another knock on the door. "Ben, don't hurt your sister."

"Ha!"

He rolled his eyes, but he carefully lowered Annie to the floor. When he could see her face, she was smiling. For now. "Why don't we take Mom and Dad out for ice cream?"

"Yes!" She bolted from the room, yelling for her parents along the way.

Now if he could find a way to distract himself as easily as he had distracted Annie.

Chapter 35

Caroline sat on her back deck alone. Friday night at seven o'clock and the sun was still high in the sky. Hours away from sunset, the descending rays warmed her exposed skin, relaxing her achy muscles. Though she and Ben weren't practicing as long as they used to, her out-of-shape muscles were still adjusting to the once-familiar movements.

It didn't help that she couldn't relax while they danced. Not with Ben's hands on her, reminding her of how nice it was to let his large hand wrap around hers, almost completely surrounding it. Every night, she rushed home to take a shower, desperate to wash away his scent. It didn't always work. Like tonight. When the breeze stirred up, it brought with it Ben's scent that had somehow transferred itself to her skin and hair.

She needed a hobby or new friends. Anything that didn't remind her of Ben.

Her phone vibrated. She recognized Ben's parents' phone number. He might be desperate enough to call her from a different phone, but her gut told her it wasn't him. "Hello?"

"Hello, is this Caroline?"

Her back tightened. She didn't recognize the voice. "This is she."

"This is Jennifer Allen, Annabelle's mom. I'm sorry to bother you, but she's been begging me to call you for her. She said she'd explain it if you'll talk to her."

"Of course, I'll talk to her."

"You can hang up, Mom. Thanks."

Caroline smiled. "Hi, Annabelle."

"Oh, Caroline, I've missed you so much. Thank you for talking to me."

"Anytime. I told you that you could call me. You don't need your mom to call."

"I sort of do. I promised Ben I wouldn't call you. He's afraid I'm going to stalk you."

"What? Why would he think that?"

Annabelle sighed. "I shouldn't talk about it. I promised Ben I wouldn't."

Caroline could guess what the girl was talking about, and she appreciated Ben's interference. She didn't want to talk about their breakup with anyone either, much less his little sister. "What did you want to talk about then?"

"Can I still be your friend?"

The fact that Annabelle even had to ask hurt Caroline's heart. "Of course, you can."

"Can I ask you sister questions?"

"Absolutely."

"Good, because I'm confused."

"About what?"

"Why did you break up with Ben?"

"Annabelle ..." Caroline didn't know what to say.

"I won't try to get you back together, I promise. I just don't understand why you broke up with him."

Caroline slumped in her chair. "What part don't you understand?"

"My friend's sister said that all she wants is a good guy, because there are no good guys out there, but isn't Ben a good guy? Was he mean? He wasn't kissing other girls, was he?"

Caroline's eyes watered. "Yes, he's a good guy. No, he wasn't mean or kissing other girls."

"Then what happened? Didn't he make you happy?"

"He makes me very happy." Her voice tightened. "But relationships can't be about one person. There are two people involved, so you have to consider both people."

"I don't understand that."

Her mind whirled for an example that Annabelle might understand. "Look at your parents. Is there anything your mom likes to do that your dad doesn't like?"

"She likes her stand-up paddleboard, but my dad doesn't like to be in the water."

"Imagine what would happen if she planned all your vacations based on where she could paddleboard. She might have a great time, but your dad probably wouldn't. Something like that happened between Ben and me. If we stay together, Ben will have to give up a lot. I can't only think of myself. I have to think of him too."

"I don't think my friend's sister does that."

"How old is your friend's sister?"

"She's in high school."

Caroline smiled and took full advantage of the teaching moment. "That's a pretty common reaction for a high schooler, and it probably should be. You don't want to be too serious with boys when you're that young, but Ben and I are older. I have to think about him as much as I think about myself."

She sighed. "That's really nice of you."

"Thanks. I hope I'm always able to be that nice." She didn't know if she had the strength to do it again, so she hoped this would be the last time she had to do it. "Is that all you wanted to talk about?"

"No, I wanted to know if you would go to the Harbor Parade with me tomorrow."

"Isn't Ben taking you?" Annabelle had been talking about it for weeks, about how excited she was to see the parade of boats floating through the harbor.

"He's in Detroit. He won't be back until Sunday night, but he said I could have his tickets. My dad has to work, and my mom said she'd go, but I'd rather go with you."

And Caroline wanted to go, but ... "I don't think I can."

The little girl sighed again. "That's okay. Mom said you might not want to because I would remind you of Ben. Do you think someday you might be able to look at me without thinking about him?"

Doubtful, but that wasn't Annabelle's fault. And if Caroline was considering Ben's needs above her own, why couldn't she do the same for his sister? Besides, Caroline had never seen the Harbor Parade before. She could make a new memory with Annabelle, completely Ben free. "One condition. We can't talk about Ben or our relationship."

"Really?" The squealing nearly pierced Caroline's eardrum.

"Ask your mom first, then—"

"Mom!"

While Annabelle chattered in the background, Caroline finally started to relax. Annabelle wasn't the perfect distraction, but she might be just what Caroline needed.

Chapter 36

Ben walked into the office Monday morning with a smile on his face. Another amazing weekend in Detroit, and he couldn't wait to tell Caroline about it. She wouldn't want to talk about it, but he wasn't going to let her ignore him this time. And maybe he could convince her to listen to a few other things once he had her attention.

Saving himself the frustration of waiting for the elevator, he took the stairs two at a time up to the third floor. One more flight and he could visit Caroline in her office, but he didn't want to rush her. Didn't want to start a conversation he couldn't finish. And, oddly enough, he couldn't wait to get to the marketing office. No one there cared who he was. All they cared about was his ability to compile, analyze, and interpret numbers and information. Without the pressure of having to live up to his football reputation, he'd found a way to connect with his coworkers.

When he stepped into the office, a soft chorus of hellos greeted him. He made his way to his desk and logged onto his computer. Several work emails and one from Caroline. He opened that one first.

Can you practice right after work today?

Not nearly as personal as he'd like, but pretty much what he'd expected. He typed a quick *yes*, then got to work.

He checked analytics, typed up reports, and jumped out of his seat when a hand landed on his shoulder.

Cole the intern laughed. "It's almost lunchtime. They're sending me on a sandwich run to Swiches. Do you want anything?"

"Just order me my sandwich. Thanks."

Cole's face contorted. "Okay, but what do you want?"

"The Ben Allen. It's a turkey club with apple and pear slices."

"You've got your own sandwich? Sick." Cole smiled and offered Ben a knuckle bump.

Ben touched fists before pulling some money out of his wallet. As soon as the intern disappeared, Ben popped his head into his boss's office. "I'm heading upstairs. Do you need anything?"

"How's the report?"

"Coming along. I'll be done in a day or two."

"Perfect. As long as you have that ready by Thursday, I'm good."

"Thanks. I'll be back in a few." Ben tried to control his excitement as he headed up to Caroline's office. When he stepped onto her floor, he buried his hands in his pants pockets. If he didn't get them out of the way, he'd be tempted to reach for her. Dance practices were hard enough. No need to torture himself further. As he neared her office, however, his excitement fizzled.

Empty.

How did she always manage to avoid him? Did she have security cameras following him?

Stepping into her space, he closed his eyes and inhaled the flowery sweet scent of Caroline. He didn't know what it was, but it reminded him of the beach and flowers and her. He could wait for her, but who knew how long that would be. Not wanting to leave without letting her know that he'd stopped by, Ben circled the desk and searched the drawers for paper.

As he pulled out the top center drawer, it vibrated. Her phone lit up in the middle of the drawer. He hadn't planned to snoop, but his gaze went straight to the bright screen.

U-Haul Rental Confirmation, Caroline Novak.

A U-Haul? She was moving?

Ben's mind spun as he tried to imagine where she could be going. And she hadn't told him, not even as a friend. Not as her dance partner. Caroline was leaving, and she wasn't going to tell him. The hole in his chest widened.

"Ben." Her soft voice started him. She stood in the doorway staring at him, her eyes wide and her hair wrapped tight in a bun on the back of her head. "Did you need something?"

"I, uh …" Didn't know what to say. Needed time to process. Missed her so much it hurt. Somehow, he managed to clear his throat. "Sorry, I was looking for some paper to leave you a note."

"Now you can tell me." She straightened her back as she stepped forward. "What do you need?"

"I don't remember."

"Are you okay?"

"No, I'm not. I'm not sure if I can make practice tonight."

She sucked in a loud breath. "We have one week left. We need every minute of practice to make sure we're perfect."

"Perfection is a myth, Caroline. We can do our best, that's all anyone can ever do."

"Perfection on the dance floor is completely possible if we work hard enough."

She walked around the desk, probably expecting him to move, but he waited for her, his mind charging with a thousand questions while he struggled to keep his temper and emotions in check. "You're willing to work hard with me on the dance floor, but not off of it?" He hadn't meant to say it, but he didn't regret it. He almost smiled when she crossed her arms and looked at him like a teacher ready to lecture her student.

"This is not the time or place to talk about this, not that there's anything to talk about."

"There's plenty to talk about." Ben stepped toward her. Caroline gasped before rolling her chair between them. The black leather squeaked as she squeezed the back. Accepting the challenge, Ben slid his knee onto the seat so he could close the gap between them. Caroline didn't move, but her knuckles turned white. "I don't know where you're going, but I figure I've got a week left to make you see reason."

"Where I'm going? What are you talking about?"

"When I was looking for some paper, you got a text. Your U-haul rental is confirmed."

All the color drained out of her face and neck. "That's none of your business."

"I know it's not, but I thought you'd at least tell me." She swallowed. He leaned closer. "I'll tell you this again. I'm not moving to Detroit. I don't know where you're going, but I promise you, I'm going to pursue you, Caroline. Once you stop being afraid of me and afraid of relationships, I'm going to be there, and I'm going to win you back."

"Who says I want you back?" Her voice wavered.

He smiled, not able to stay angry while she looked so vulnerable. "If you would stop looking at my lips, you might be able to convince me."

She shrugged. "You're a good kisser. Big deal."

"You're not that shallow. If you don't want to tell me where you're going, that's fine. I'll find you."

"That's kind of stalker-ish."

"Only if I'm sneaking around and you don't want me there. I'll keep my distance as long as you want me to, but I promise you I'll be around as soon as you stop torturing both of us. And you know what? I changed my mind. Practice tonight after work. As long as you think we need it."

She nodded.

"I'll see you soon."

Before she could say anything—and before he could talk himself out of it—Ben leaned forward and brushed his lips across her cheek. As he stepped through the doorway, she let out a shaky breath.

Now to figure out where she was going, why she was moving, and how to change her mind.

Sweat rolled down Caroline's back as she tried to catch her breath. Ever since she'd found Ben in her office, he'd strutted into the dance studio with all the confidence and attitude she expected from a professional athlete. Whatever happened in Detroit had sparked something in him. Aside from their awkward conversation on Monday, he'd been the perfect dance partner. His work ethic would put Tony to shame.

And in one week, it would be over. She'd never felt so equally relieved and heartbroken.

"One more time?" Ben grabbed a towel out of his bag and wiped down his face and arms. Not that he'd sweat much. He walked around the studio like he had enough energy to practice all night.

As much as she wanted to make sure they perfected their routine, Caroline shook her head. "It's been almost two hours. You're doing great. Let's call it a night."

"Are you sure? I can go another round."

"I'm sure." Caroline grabbed her water bottle from where it sat on the other side of the studio. "I take it you're not going back to Detroit this weekend?"

Ben paused. "How did you know I went to Detroit?"

Busted. "Annabelle told me."

"She promised not to call."

"Technically, she didn't. Your mother did."

He growled.

"Was the trip to Detroit a secret?"

He shook his head as he walked toward her. "I'm still keeping things to myself until the details are finalized."

"Then something *is* going on?" Relief and heartbreak. Her constant companions.

He gave a slow smile. "There is. I wanted to talk to you about it. I hoped you'd talk to me about it."

To twist the knife in her heart? No thank you. "I'm happy for you, I am, but I don't think I can do this right now." Caroline grabbed her bag. As she walked past him, he grabbed her wrist. Every muscle in her body tensed.

"Please don't run out."

She didn't want to, but she couldn't listen to his future plans without her. She knew she needed to keep moving, but her brain and feet had stopped communicating. With him still holding her arm behind her, and without turning around, she said, "Then let's talk about something else."

"Anything you want."

Caroline turned slowly, pulling her arm out of his grasp. "How's Annabelle?"

"She misses coming to dance practice."

"I miss having her around."

What else were they supposed to talk about? The fan turned on, humming quietly above them. There was so much to say and so much she couldn't say that she stood there silently. Unwilling to keep them both in such an uncomfortable standoff, she adjusted her bag. "I really should get going. I have some things to finish at home." She headed out the door with Ben right behind her.

"Packing?"

All the heat drained out of Caroline's skin as a chill washed over her. "I have a few things to box up."

He stepped up beside her but kept several feet between them. "When are you moving?"

"Next weekend."

"As soon as we finish the competition? You're not even going to stick around to celebrate?"

"You're that confident?"

"Not really, but I figure anything we earn will be worth celebrating."

"Good point." She couldn't believe she hadn't thought of it. Man, she'd gotten more self-centered than she'd realized.

"I guess we'll have to celebrate the night of the competition then," he said.

"I guess." She unlocked her car and opened the driver's door. "Will you let Annabelle know that she's welcome to call me without using your mom?"

He sighed. "Fine."

"Good luck with the Lions."

Ben stepped closer. "If you'd just let me explain, then—"

She smacked her hand against his shirt, not minding the sweaty cotton because the warm heartbeat beneath it calmed her soul. Pulling her hand away, she tossed her bag into her car. "Whatever it is, you'll do great."

"I'm meeting with Roger Fink tomorrow."

"Fink? How do I know that name?"

"He's the football coach at Northern Lower Michigan College."

The little, division three college in town? Caroline's insides rolled. "You can't be serious."

"They're looking for a new coach."

"Since when?"

"Since I contacted them and told them I was in town."

"No!" Caroline slammed her door. "You can*not* give up a chance with the Detroit Lions—a chance to be part of the NFL—to coach at NLMC. You're throwing your talent away!"

"No, I'll be using my talent, *and* I'll get to stay in the area."

Bile stirred in her gut. "You can't give up on your dream just to stay here."

He stepped closer, forcing her to tip her head back to look at him. "My dream was to play football. That's not going to happen, so I'm calling an audible."

"Don't lie to me, and don't lie to yourself." Caroline crossed her arms. He obviously wasn't going to take the hint. If she didn't want him to repeat her mistakes, it was time for the whole truth. "Do you know why I took the job at Morrison Insurance? It was my 'starter' job. I wanted to make some money while I prepared for my real job. I was going to start a nonprofit or work for a nonprofit or move out of state to get involved with a larger nonprofit. I didn't have an exact plan, but I knew that I was going to make a difference and touch people's lives."

She swallowed. "Instead, I've spent eight years planning corporate retreats, training college graduates, and writing employee handbooks. Instead of working full time with the people and programs that I love, I tried to volunteer my way into a job, and I lost my shot. Now I'm thirty years old with no real nonprofit work experience because instead of going after the right job—instead of chasing my dream—I waited around to see if it would suddenly materialize out of nothing. And guess what? It didn't."

The humidity pressed against her, rolling off her skin and melting away the façade of her controlled, contented life. Failure soaked her shirt. She sucked in a deep breath, trying to calm her racing pulse.

Ben's face softened. "I'm sorry you didn't get your dream."

"That's not the point of the story."

"It's the only part that matters to me. I wish there was something I could do to change it for you."

He reached for her, but Caroline jumped back. How dense was he? "You can't change anything, and that's the point. You don't want to turn out like me. Don't settle. Don't wait. Do whatever you need to do to make it happen." Her frustration with him welled up, trembling through her arms. With a low growl, she shoved him away. "You deserve better than this."

"You mean better than you?"

Her chest ached, but she couldn't deny it. "Yes."

Chapter 37

Caroline shoved one last box into her car, leaning all her weight against the back door. On the second push, it finally closed.

"Do you have room for one more?" Chris hauled another large box out of the apartment complex and onto the curb. "Or maybe I should put it in my car."

"Would you mind?"

"You should have paid for the bigger U-Haul. I wasn't planning on spending my Sunday afternoon moving your stuff. I took next weekend off for that." Chris picked up the box she'd set down.

Caroline opened the front passenger door of Chris's car so her sister could add the box. "Thanks for helping me."

"Why the hurry to move?"

Caroline shrugged, not trusting her voice. She would have preferred to start moving yesterday, but she hadn't been able to call her sister without blubbering. After six tries, she'd finally managed to talk. It was better that she not try to explain herself until she could control her emotions.

"Fine, don't tell me. I'll meet you at the storage facility. Dad texted me. He's waiting for us there."

After unloading Christmas decorations, kitchen essentials, linens, and pillows, their dad returned the U-Haul, and Caroline followed Chris across town and into her driveway. It took thirty minutes to move Caroline's clothes and toiletries into her sister's guest room. She unpacked for a while, but voices in the living room piqued her curiosity. Picking up the empty boxes, she stepped into the short hallway, walking past Chris's room and the bathroom before stepping into the living room.

Tony and Ben stood side by side talking with Chris. All three of them turned to look at Caroline, but she kept her focus on Ben. His eyes widened, looking her up and down.

When his gaze landed on the boxes, he smiled. "You're moving in with Chris?"

"For now."

"Why?"

"Because." She wasn't ready to explain herself. "What are you doing here?"

Ben nodded at Tony. "Turns out Tony's not bad when he's not making me dance with him. Rumor has it there might be a Tigers game on this afternoon."

Which Chris would have known about yet hadn't mentioned to Caroline. She glared at her sister. Chris grabbed Tony's hand and dragged him through the living room. "Help me get the grill going."

Because that wasn't at all obvious. Caroline ignored Ben as she dropped her boxes by the front door. She expected him to try to stop her, but she walked back to her new bedroom without incident. Good. And disappointing. Not ready to face him again, she fell face-first onto the bed.

"Why are you moving in with Chris?"

Caroline jumped off the bed and spun around, her heart racing.

He stood in the doorway, leaning against the door frame with his arms crossed.

"You about gave me a heart attack!"

"And that's twice that you haven't answered my question."

"Get out of my room."

"Answer my question."

"Then will you leave?"

"If you want me to."

She rolled her eyes. "Yes, I want you to leave." But even as she said it, a smile tugged at her lips. She'd missed him so much.

"So?"

"So"—she pushed back her pride—"I listened to all that advice I was giving to you. I want you to make better decisions than I did, but I want to make better decisions too."

"Like what?"

"Like leaving Morrison Insurance."

"What?" Ben's arms dropped. "How is being unemployed going to help?"

"I'm not unemployed. I got a job waitressing at the Breakfast Nook."

His jaw dropped next, then Ben took a step toward Caroline.

She held up a hand, stopping his movement and whatever argument he'd been formulating. "I also talked to Susan at Pathways. I told her that I'm interested in more than simply volunteering, which I should have told her a long time ago. It's too late for the executive director position, but at least she knows that I'm interested.

"She was excited to know about my interest and education. She's either involved with or has connections at several nonprofits in the area, so she's going to work with me, kind of mentor me, as I get more involved and learn about some of the other organizations. The Breakfast Nook closes at two each day, so I'll have all of my afternoons and evenings free to work with her."

Ben's posture relaxed as Caroline watched him process the information. He nodded. "If you're not working forty hours—"

"Or fifty."

"Or fifty hours a week at Morrison, then you'll have more time to make the connections you need to pursue your dream."

"And since I won't be making as much money as I did at Morrison, Chris is going to let me stay here." Caroline could practically hear the cogs turning as Ben worked through the information, his facial expressions morphing from confusion to processing to—unexpectedly—delight as he flashed her his most brilliant smile.

"You're not leaving Traverse City."

She shook her head, not sure why it pleased him so much. Annabelle had let it slip that Ben signed some sort of Detroit Lions paperwork. Caroline assumed it was a job offer.

Somehow his smile widened. "I need to go."

"I thought you were here to watch the game."

"I have something much more important to take care of." Ben literally ran out of her room.

Not sure what to think about that, Caroline followed him into the living room. The front door slammed as Tony and Chris walked in from the kitchen.

"What did you say to him?" Chris asked.

"Nothing. He wanted to know why I moved, so I told him."

Finally Forever

"And he stormed out?"

Caroline shook her head. "He didn't storm. He was smiling like an idiot. Said he had to do something, then ran out. I don't think he was mad."

Tony chuckled. "Life's never boring around you two." He kissed Chris's cheek. "I'll man the grill."

Caroline tried not to smile as her sister blushed a fire-engine red. As soon as the back door closed, she wiggled her eyebrows. "Not boring at all. What's going on with Tony?"

Chris cocked her head to the side. "I don't know. What's going on with Ben?"

"Touché."

"How about we watch the game and not talk about guys for a while?"

"I'll unpack until dinner's ready." Caroline returned to her bedroom and her piles of clothes, but her mind wouldn't focus. Where had Ben run off to, and why was he so excited about it?

Chapter 38

Caroline flinched when Chris picked up the can of hair spray. "Whoa! I need this hair to move. You've sprayed it enough."

Chris tossed the can on the dressing table. "I don't know why you wanted my help with this. You look fine."

Caroline sighed. "I don't want to look fine. I *need* to look perfect. We're only two points ahead of second place. Pathways needs the money. Everything needs to be perfect."

She checked her reflection one more time to see if there was anything else she needed to do before she and Ben danced their final dance. The black lace of her one-sleeved, asymmetric gown clung to her body in all the right places, perfect for highlighting her legs and hips during the rumba. The rhinestones in her ears twinkled. Her hair fell in large waves around her shoulders. The look was perfect. Now to nail the dance.

"Are you sure you're okay?" Chris crossed her arms. "You're not usually this quiet before a competition."

"I'm always quiet before competitions."

"Maybe, but your lips are always moving as you talk your way through each step. And you're usually either dancing by yourself or making your partner walk through everything with you."

"I'm not that bad."

"Mom and Dad dragged me to all your competitions for years. Trust me. I've seen your pre-game ritual a thousand times." Chris nudged her sister's shoulder. "What's going on? You didn't ask me here to help with your hair."

Caroline studied her sister's reflection. Tall, trim, and naturally beautiful in a sleek navy sheath dress with minimal make-up, her blonde hair hung straight down her back. They couldn't look more different, but they had one thing in common. "Have you talked to Ben this week?"

"Not since he ran out Sunday. Why?"

"Because he's up to something, but I don't know what."

"Did you ask?"

Caroline rolled her eyes. "Of course I did. He keeps saying it's nothing."

"Maybe it is. How do you know something's up?"

"He's been smiling and happy all week."

"So?"

"For two weeks before that, he was focused and intense. All week, he's been acting like it's almost Christmas instead of our last competition. I don't get it."

"Maybe you're paranoid."

Muted laughter reverberated through the wall, followed by a round of applause. Next up would be the second-place couple. Ben and Caroline were scheduled to perform last, to increase the event's tension. It was having the same effect on her insides.

"Come on." Chris tapped Caroline on the shoulder. "Let's go find Ben and Tony. You need to calm down, and they're better at it than I am."

Not entirely true anymore, since everything about Ben put Caroline on edge, but it couldn't hurt. Being one of the last two people in the women's dressing room certainly wasn't helping. Caroline followed her sister to the green room. Inside, Ben and Tony sat next to each other on the overstuffed couch as they stared at Tony's phone.

Chris popped her fists onto her hips. "Are you two watching the game?"

"Maybe." Tony winked at Chris.

Ben looked at Caroline and froze. After several awkward seconds, the familiar, unexplainable smile consumed his face. "Wow."

Caroline turned to her sister. "Do you see what I mean? Look at him."

Chris shrugged. "He's smiling."

"He's been smiling like that all week."

"He paid you a compliment," Tony said without looking up from the game. "Don't overanalyze it."

Caroline pushed down her frustration. Was she the only person who could tell something was going on? Maybe they were in cahoots. She didn't need the extra stress right now. Closing her eyes, she drew in a slow breath and rolled her shoulders as she mentally danced through their routine. Her last night in Ben's arms. Pain swelled in her chest. Another thing she didn't need to worry about.

Something creaked as Caroline swayed in the dark. A moment later, Ben stood next to her. He didn't have to say or do anything—she recognized the earthy masculine scent of him. She opened her eyes to find him standing in front of her, the silly smile still on his face, but something in his eyes had changed.

He wasn't simply looking at her. He was studying her. His gaze traveled across her face, pausing at her lips before returning to her eyes. "I hope you can wait a little while longer before we dance."

Panic threatened to topple her. "Why? What did you do?"

"I haven't done anything yet."

"Why are you being so obtuse? Just tell me what's happening."

He took a tiny step forward, closing the already small gap between them. "I've been trying to talk to you about it for weeks, but you wouldn't listen to me. You brought this on yourself."

"I don't know what you're talking about."

Ben looked at the closed-feed monitor on the wall. She followed his gaze to the screen where the second-place couple was taking their bow. He wrapped an arm around her waist. "Looks like you're going to find out." He pressed a kiss to her cheek. "I'm going to go make sure everything's set. I'll meet you in the wings."

He walked out of the green room with the confidence Caroline had come to associate with him. Once he closed the door, she turned her attention to the couch. Instead of watching the game, Tony sat with his arm around Chris, both of them watching Caroline.

She pressed a hand against her rolling stomach. "Do you know what's going on?" They both shook their heads. She sighed. "How could he do this to me before we dance? I think I'm going to be sick."

Tony shook his head. "Don't worry about it. That man's crazy about you. He wouldn't do anything to jeopardize the event, and he certainly wouldn't do anything to hurt you."

"I know." Sort of. Maybe. Forget butterflies—a flock of ostriches stampeded through her stomach.

Someone knocked on the door. "Ms. Novak, you're up."

Tony helped Chris off the couch. "Come on," he said. "It's showtime."

She let him usher her and her sister out of the green room and into the wings. Ben was talking with Judy. She said something, and he laughed. When he spotted Caroline, his eyes darkened. His smile softened. He offered his hand to her.

As Tony and Chris walked toward their seats, Ben stepped beside Caroline and brushed his lips against her ear. "Thank you for letting me dance with you. This whole experience has opened doors that I didn't even know were there." He pressed a kiss to her temple. She closed her eyes and savored the feeling. "You've changed my life forever. Thank you."

The emcee said something, and the audience clapped as the spotlight moved across the stage toward their hiding spot. Ben tugged Caroline's arm, pulling her out of the darkness and into the warm, yellow stage lights. Despite her nerves, her face smiled without having to think about it. Time to perform.

Ben led her to the center of the floor, lifting an arm to twirl her into place beside the emcee. As her eyes adjusted, she noticed the extra-large crowd with people standing along the wall, many of them holding cameras. In the back corner, the women from Pathways, the Novaks, the Allens, and Tony clapped and cheered.

"Our last couple to compete tonight is our current leader, Ben Allen and Caroline Novak. Before they perform their version of the rumba, however, I'm excited to hand over the microphone to Mr. Allen who has a very special announcement to make. And, judging by the number of reporters here, it looks like he may have invited a few friends. Mr. Allen."

The crowd applauded as Ben took the microphone. He squeezed Caroline's hand before releasing it and taking a step forward. "Thank you so much for being here tonight and for supporting all these amazing charities. I can admit I wasn't familiar with most of them before the competition, and this has been a great way to learn about the people and organizations. It's also been a great way to stay in shape."

Caroline chuckled with the crowd, though her curiosity made her want to shake the truth out of him. Instead, she clenched her hands together behind her back.

"I don't have time tonight to tell you all of the positive ways the dance-off has impacted me, but Bill White is here to tell you about one of them."

Caroline's throat constricted. Was Ben going to announce his new job here, before their last dance? A middle-aged man in khaki pants and a Detroit Lions golf shirt appeared from the wings on the other side of the dance floor. He waved and smiled as he accepted the microphone.

"Thanks, Ben. I'm Bill White with the Detroit Lions organization. I can't tell you what an honor it is to be here tonight. The Lions have been following Ben's career for a while now, and his involvement in this dance-off caught the attention of many people in our organization, including me. I'm the head of our community outreach programs, and when I saw the kind of man Ben is off the field, I knew he was someone I wanted to work with.

"For the past two months, Ben and I have been working together to expand the Detroit Lions' programs throughout the state, and this evening I'm thrilled to announce that he has accepted the position—and challenge—of expanding our youth outreach programs to northern Michigan."

The crowd murmured as Caroline held her breath.

"Next year we will host our inaugural Detroit Lions' youth outreach summer camp programs at Northern Lower

Michigan College, which will be run by Ben Allen, NLMC's new defensive coordinator."

The room erupted. Caroline struggled to stay upright. Bill started talking again, but she couldn't pay attention. A strong arm anchored itself around her waist, holding her up. As Bill and Judy talked to the crowd, Caroline looked into the eyes of the man beside her.

Ben was already watching her, his smile smaller and less confident. "Surprise."

"You took a job with the Lions."

"And I don't have to leave Traverse City to do it."

She closed her eyes against the shock. Breath escaped her.

He was staying. The man she loved had figured out how to follow his dream without moving away from her.

Ben rested his head against hers. "I'm glad I can still be part of the NFL, and I still can't believe I'm going to be a Lion, sort of, but none of that would matter without you."

It was too much. Caroline couldn't believe it. As Bill and Judy walked off the dance floor, she realized she didn't have time to worry about it. "We have to dance now."

"This won't be our last dance together, I promise." As the music started, Ben led Caroline to their starting spot and wrapped his arms around her, settling them into their starting pose. "I love you, Caroline."

His confession blended with the music, seeping into her heart and soul. She took her first step, letting her hips sway with the emotions that coursed through her. In and out of Ben's arms, stepping slowly, moving intimately, accepting his confession as she poured her own love into each touch and turn.

As the music ended, Caroline twirled into Ben's arms, her gaze locked with his. Their breath mingled as they panted, exhausted yet exhilarated. They needed to get their scores. Needed to find out how much money they raised for Pathways, but Caroline didn't care.

Her hands slid up his arms, wrapping around his neck and locking him close against her. "You're staying."

"If you would have let me tell you about my trips to Detroit, I could have told you sooner."

"I'm so sorry."

"Don't apologize. Just tell me I can take you out tonight. And tomorrow night. And every night next week."

Relief bubbled up in Caroline's chest, spilling out as she laughed, burying her face in Ben's chest.

Cameras flashed and dozens of people mingled as Caroline stood on one side of the auditorium watching Ben smile for photos. He talked to the Detroit-area reporters about his new job while Susan talked with the local reporters about Pathways' new funds. Not sure who else she should talk to, Caroline sat at the closest table.

"Caroline Novak. Just the person I'm looking for." Judy Jones sat beside her. "I have to tell you, this year's dance-off was our most successful event yet."

"A lot of that is thanks to Ben."

"And you. If you hadn't turned him into such an amazing dancer, we might have received some very different attention." Judy handed her a business card. "Thanks to all that attention, we've already received dozens of inquiries from potential organizations and sponsors for next year's event. I could barely handle everything myself this year. Susan Miller mentioned you might be interested in working with us. It's part-time to start, but I don't think it'll be too long before the dance-off coordinator could become a full-time job."

Caroline accepted the card—not sure how to respond. She'd never considered working with Judy, but it made sense. "I'd love to learn more about it."

"Give me a call, and we'll set something up."

Caroline was still in shock and staring at the card when Chris took Judy's empty chair. "Another win for Novak. How does it feel?"

Caroline couldn't stop smiling as she sighed. "I'm exhausted, but I'm so happy."

"Happy because you won the dance-off or happy because Ben's staying?"

Caroline didn't answer. She couldn't. She didn't know how to put into words the joy that filled every part of her being.

Chris smiled as she squeezed her sister's shoulder. "No more excuses, Caro. Ben's not Brett or Chad. And Tony's right. He's crazy about you."

"Are you crazy about Tony?"

Chris stood. "It looks like Ben's on his way over. I'll leave you two alone."

As Chris rushed away, Ben took Caroline's hand and pulled her to her feet. "I missed you," he said.

"We were only apart for thirty minutes."

"Thirty horrible minutes."

Caroline couldn't wipe the smile off her face. "You were amazing tonight. I can't believe we won by six points."

He wrapped his arms around her, holding her close. "What about the rest of the night?"

She swallowed. "That was pretty amazing too." A light flashed. "You know there are still people here with cameras, right?"

Without a word, Ben ran toward the wings, pulling her behind him. He didn't stop until they were in the green room with nothing but the muted sounds of the crowd to accompany them. When they were finally alone, his smile disappeared. "Be honest," he said. "What are you thinking?"

So many things. She settled on, "I'm overwhelmed."

"I won't pressure you into anything, and I'm not staying in Traverse City just for you. I want to spend more time with my family, and I'm excited about bringing inner-city kids up north for football camp. I almost didn't believe it when Bill told me what he'd been thinking about doing. They'd been working on it for years. My being here—available and passionate about football and now experienced with service organizations—was perfect timing."

"For the job?"

"For everything. I love football, but that was all I knew until this summer—before dancing and Pathways and you. I used to panic when I thought of life without football." He inched her closer. "I don't anymore. Not when I'm with you."

Uncertainty clouded Ben's face. Caroline didn't trust herself to say what needed to be said, so she threw her arms around his neck and kissed him. As he locked his arms around her, she melted against him, letting him claim her as she surrendered to him. Finally, slowly, she softened the kisses, separating their lips without stepping out of his embrace.

When Ben's eyes finally opened, she cupped his face in her hands, savoring the warmth and scruffiness of his cheeks. "I love you." He smiled beneath her hands, bending down for another kiss, but she leaned away. "Let me finish."

His gaze flickered to her lips. "Talk fast."

She brushed her lips across his before retreating again. "I love you. I think I've loved you for a while. And even though I was forcing you away, I wasn't completely honest with you at Chris's house."

"About what?"

"About leaving Morrison." Relaxing her arms, she rested her head on his shoulder. "I did leave to pursue nonprofit work, but I wasn't planning on staying in Traverse City. I was getting ready to move down to Detroit ... to be closer to you."

Ben sucked in a breath as he squeezed his arms around her. For long moments, he crushed her against him, stroking her hair and pressing kisses to her forehead, ear, and temple. When he finally pulled back, something deep and powerful shone in his eyes. "You were going to follow me."

She nodded.

"Because you love me."

She nodded again.

He laughed as he picked her up and spun her around. Caroline smiled as her feet dangled in the air. "You can set me down now."

"Not a chance." He swept an arm under her knees and cradled her to him before claiming her lips again. Caroline didn't doubt for a second that he would hold on to her forever, and she didn't mind at all.

About the Author

A writer and reader of hopeful fiction with a healthy dose of romance, Karin Beery can find the hope (and humor) in most any situation, including her marriage, her career, and her menagerie of fur babies, who all insist on sleeping on her side of the bed. She's a multi-published author and editor with experience in traditional and self-publishing, freelance editing, and editing for publishers. When she's not writing, Karin runs Write Now Editing, helping authors turn good manuscripts into great books.

In the office, Karin stays active as a member of Advanced Writers and Speakers Association, Christian Authors Network, the Christian Proofreaders and Editors Network, and the National Association of Independent Writers and Editors. Out of the office, she enjoys kayaking, spending time with family and friends, and living in a Hallmark-ready small town.

KARIN BEERY

Made in United States
Troutdale, OR
02/28/2024

18053160R00176